KELLY ORAM

BLUEFIELDS

First Edition, 2010

Cover/book design by Joshua Oram

ISBN 978-0-615-37754-4

*For Joshua,
the original Ryan Miller*

Acknowledgments

My deepest gratitude goes to everyone at Bluefields for taking a chance on me. Thank you for all of your faith, hard work, and especially for the amazing book trailer!

Thank you always to my best friend/biggest fan/muse, Christy Ann. For way too many reasons to mention them all.

And finally, thank you to Zak, Julia, Sarah, Mare, Dee, Rose, Meg and all of my many other "absolutely chaotic" writing buddies. For so many years of advice, encouragement, inspiration, and criticism. I never could have made it this far without you.

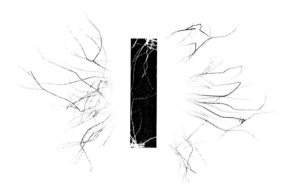

Most superhero stories start with a meteor shower or a nasty insect bite, but mine actually starts with a kiss. Whether it was a kiss of life or a kiss of death I still haven't decided, but it was, surprisingly, a really good kiss. Not that I'd ever tell *him* that.

The kiss didn't actually give me my powers. Those came earlier, in a freak accident involving toxic waste and something like 40,000 volts of electricity. But it was that kiss that forced me out of hiding and changed my life, eventually making me who I am today, and blah, blah, blah… You know the drill.

Mike Driscoll actually started it, three weeks before our senior homecoming, when he got in an argument with Ryan Miller over who to ask to the dance. Mike and Ryan were basically the two most popular guys in school, and Becky

Eastman held that title by a landslide among the female population.

"I think I'm gonna take Becky to homecoming," Mike said casually one day over his cold chicken patty on a bun and coleslaw.

"Dude, you took her to junior prom," Ryan immediately protested.

"Yeah, so?"

"So it's my turn. I'm taking her to homecoming."

"Over my dead body. She's the hottest girl in school. As captain of the football team it's my right to have first pick."

"Says who?" Ryan laughed. "I'm the quarterback. Everyone knows I'm the real star. Besides, I'm better looking than you. I bet if we asked her at the same time, she'd pick me."

"Would not."

"Would too."

"So would not."

I'm not sure exactly how long they fought about that, but it was long enough for me to want to rip my hair out.

Superhearing can come in handy every now and then, but most of the time it royally sucks. Especially when you're stuck in a crowded school cafeteria, surrounded by a bunch of spoiled suburban teenagers, most of whom are having conversations every bit as ridiculous as the one Ryan and Mike were engrossed in. I try to drown out the noise, and it works to an extent, but the annoying chatter is the reason I always sit in the far corner, all by myself. Well, it's one of the reasons.

I'd managed to block most of the nonsense from my mind by focusing on the sound of my own chewing, but I'm kind of like one of those government computer programs that you see in spy movies, where they pick up key words and then home in on the conversation. Translation: I'm sensitive to my own name, and when it escaped Ryan Miller's mouth, I was immediately paying close attention.

"Technically," he said, "Jamie Baker is hotter than Becky. If you want to take the hottest girl in school, then you have to take her."

Mike burst into obnoxious laughter. "Yeah, she's hot all right, for an ice queen. Becky is the hottest *normal* girl in school. Jamie would never go to the dance with anyone."

"Not even the great Mike Driscoll?" Ryan laughed. "You always say you could get *any* girl in this school."

"Jamie doesn't count. The chick's a total loner."

"Maybe she's just misunderstood," Ryan teased.

"Maybe she's just a cold-hearted freak."

I smirked, quite happy with Mike's opinion of me. When I first arrived here at Rocklin High, Mike Driscoll hit on me before I got to the front steps. He and his buddies were all hanging out at the back of his truck like they were having some sort of tailgate party before school. I knew exactly what was coming when he straightened his letter jacket and smiled at me with that classic crooked smile that every major womanizer has perfected. Maybe laughing in his face in front of the entire varsity football team was a bit harsh, but it did the trick. He hasn't bothered me since. None of them has.

Anyway, I'm glad he hates me. Having him spread all those rumors makes it a lot easier for me to keep my preferred "loner" status.

"I bet I could get her to go with me," Ryan mused, breaking both Mike and me from our thoughts—which I'd bet were the same right then, though I can't be sure. Mind reading is not checked off on my list of superhuman abilities.

This time I nearly joined Mike in his wild laughter. I don't know why Ryan thought he was so special, and apparently, neither did Mike. "*Jamie Baker*? I'll bet you couldn't even get her to talk to you."

"Yeah, I could," Ryan said. "I bet I could go over there, strike up a conversation, and get her number by the end of lunch."

"You think you could get Jamie's phone number?"

"I just said I could, didn't I?"

"No way," Mike said.

"Okay, how about this. If I can get Jamie's number by the end of lunch, then I get to take Becky to homecoming. If not, then you get to take her instead."

"Make it a kiss, and you're on."

"I kiss Jamie Baker, and I get to take Becky to homecoming?"

"Not exactly—anybody can just kiss someone," Mike said. "You have to get her to kiss you, or the deal's off."

I could feel Ryan looking at me again, probably trying to figure out if he could really do it, and then after a moment he said, "Before lunch is over?"

"Yup." Mike slapped his hand loudly on Ryan's back. "You've only got ten minutes, Casanova. Better go make your move."

I heard Ryan scoot his chair out from the table and smiled to myself. The guy didn't stand a chance, but I had to admit, the bet was highly amusing, and I almost couldn't wait for him to try. When he approached me, I waited for him to quote something I'm sure you could find in any book of cheesy pickup lines, but much to my disappointment all I got was a "Hey, Jamie. Mind if I sit for a minute?"

I had no comeback. It's hard to insult Ryan if he's not making an idiot of himself. So, since I couldn't make a scene worth any gossip, I decided not to make a scene at all. I didn't even acknowledge his presence. It didn't stop him from sitting down, though.

Ryan pulled out the chair to my right and turned it so that he was facing me. I'm not sure if he sat like that, thinking it would make me look at him, or if he just wanted to have his back to the other genius behind this master plan, so that he couldn't see Mike laughing.

He sat there for a minute, no doubt still trying to figure out his strategy, and when I smiled at the way he was bouncing his knee nervously, he immediately leaned forward, resting his elbows on his legs. "Here's the thing," Ryan finally began. "If I can't kiss you by the end of lunch, then I have to let Mike take Becky Eastman to homecoming, and I already made dinner reservations at her favorite restaurant."

Of all the things in the world, I never for one second expected him to tell me the truth. I was honestly amazed.

No, I was impressed. This guy was on a whole different playing field than like 99.99 percent of all humans cursed with Y chromosomes. What he said was ridiculous, but surely it deserved, at the very least, a response. "That's one I've never heard before," I said dryly, still not bothering to look his direction.

"A girl as hot as you can't be a stranger to the game, so I figured honesty might be my only shot."

"I'll admit, it was probably the closest thing you had to a shot."

"Okay, what about bribery?"

"Sorry."

"Aw, come on, Jamie. It won't mean anything. I won't even use tongue. You don't really want Mike to win, do you?"

It was true—Ryan was definitely the lesser of two evils. I sighed, obviously softened by the surprise truth tactic, and finally looked at him.

"I'll owe you," he said hopefully.

I studied him for a minute. He definitely wasn't bad-looking. Honey-blond hair, blue eyes and a tall, lean build. Okay, fine, he was hot. If you like the All-American-boy-next-door type.

Which, unfortunately, I do.

Plus, the pout Ryan was giving me was kind of charming, in a pathetic sort of way, so I considered my options. After realizing that all giving in to his request would do was make people think I'm a freak—which they already think anyway—and give them something to talk about for a few days, I figured, why not? At least this way I could take a little pleasure in Mike's disappointment and save Becky from a night of drunken groping. "Fine," I said with a sigh. "Knock yourself out."

I sat back and waited for Ryan's shocked look to fade. I smiled when it finally turned to a frown.

"Actually," he said, cringing, "you have to kiss me or it doesn't count."

I already knew that, but I still raised an eyebrow at him. May as well make him sweat a little.

"You don't have to pretend to like it," he said, sounding a little desperate for the first time. "Please?"

I didn't say anything. Just glanced over Ryan's head at Mike, who was analyzing my every move, then leaned over and pressed my lips to Ryan's.

It was just over a year since my accident, the one that made me join the comic book persuasion, and I hated to admit it, but I hadn't kissed a guy since I'd changed. And I know I have a little extra electricity running through me now—I can jump-start a car with my hands if I want to— but I never imagined it would affect something like kissing a guy.

There weren't actual physical sparks, but something pulsed through me and pulled me to Ryan. I'd meant to just touch my lips lightly against his, but the instant we connected I lost all self-control. I threw my mouth on his so forcefully that he nearly fell out of his chair—not that he seemed to mind any. Energy passed right through me, and I could feel the warmth of my electricity coming from his hands as they found their way to my face. The next thing I knew, I was straddling his lap with my arms wrapped tightly around his neck.

Everyone in the cafeteria went silent, or at least to me the sound faded away, and that's when I realized what was happening. I knew it was not a normal kiss by any means, and if I acted as freaked out as I felt, I risked Ryan realizing that there was something different about me. I just kept kissing him until I had my emotions in check, and when I finally pulled away we were both pretty breathless.

"You can keep the gum," I said, trying to keep up my nonchalant reputation, and slowly climbed off him. "Have fun at the dance."

When I left, Ryan was still sitting in his chair, kind of speechless. I wondered if maybe I'd electrocuted him or paralyzed him or something, but by the time I turned around he was stumbling back to Mike. He was in a bit of a daze, but he appeared to be okay, so I kept walking. I headed straight for the girls' bathroom, where I could have a minute to completely freak out in private before I had to get to my next class.

I was pretty useless the rest of the day since the only thing I could think about was that kiss. Of course I liked it, and I'm pretty sure he did too, but it was weird. It wasn't a normal kiss, a human kiss. It was some kind of superkiss. Kind of freakish, like me.

It was just one more thing to remind me that I would never be able to live a fully normal life now, and aside from depressing me it scared me. What if I'd hurt him? What if something bad had happened? What if this meant I could never have a physical relationship ever again? What if some-one finds out the truth about me? Or, what if, because of the superkissing abilities I apparently possess, Ryan already knows?

It was that last question that scared me the most, and the one that had my mind so preoccupied during last period that I didn't hear the bell ring. Nor did I realize that Ryan was there until he plopped down at the desk right in front of mine and spun around. He actually startled me, and that annoyed me very much, but not as much as the fact that he laughed at me for it. I gave him an evil glare, but he just asked, "Do you want to go to the dance with me?" as if we were best friends and the answer was a given.

I couldn't stop the confusion in my mind from spread-ing to my face, and he laughed at me again. I glanced across the room, since English was the one class that Ryan, Becky, and I all had in common, and frowned at the girl who'd been the reason for our strange encounter in the first place. "All that effort and she turned you down? Sucks to be you."

Ryan shrugged. "I didn't ask her."

"Hey, I did my part in this idiotic little scheme. You'd better go do yours now. I'd hate to think I made myself the star of the school's gossip column for nothing."

"It doesn't have to be nothing." Ryan shrugged again. "You want to go?"

I didn't get this guy at all. Not that I'm like this big scary monster or anything, but talking to Jamie Baker is kind of taboo around my school. People usually avoid eye contact with me, not ask me out.

"Sorry," I said. "That kiss was a one-time deal, and it wasn't an invitation for anything else. Trust me, you've got a much better chance of getting some action if you go with Becky."

I wouldn't say I sounded hostile just then, but I definitely wasn't being friendly, and when Ryan just laughed at my comment my annoyance turned into real anger.

"It's not like that," he said.

"Right."

"No, really. I just think it could be interesting."

I gave him the dirtiest look I could, but he shrugged it off like it was nothing. He looked over at Becky just as she left the room, and then looked back at me as casual as ever. "I think it'd be more fun to go with you."

Okay, now I was curious. I mean Becky and Ryan are basically attached at the hip. Best friends since kindergarten or something ridiculous like that. Ryan worships her as much as every other boy in this school, if not more, so I couldn't for the life of me understand why he'd ask me when he could take her.

"I know Becky," Ryan explained when he saw my frown. "But you're a mystery to me. I like mysteries."

"Well then, Sherlock, it's in your best interest to stick with the original plan. If we went to the dance and you accidentally got to know me or something, then I wouldn't be a mystery anymore." I grabbed my bag and stood up. "I'm not going. With you or anyone."

I walked out of the room without looking back, but I heard him sigh as I left. It was the strangest day I'd had since

I moved here and the most social interaction I'd had with any one classmate. It hadn't been bad, but I prayed it was over now and that when I went back to school the next day things would be back to their normal, uneventful selves.

I wondered if Ryan would keep bothering me, but he didn't. Aside from Paul Warren, Rocklin High's resident Eminem wannabe, giving me what he thought passed for "the nod" every time he saw me, everything was back to normal within a couple of days. At least it was until the following Thursday, when I ran into Ryan at the movies and he actually had the nerve to talk to my parents.

Ryan works at the theater, and I knew there was a chance he would be there, but I never imagined he would do anything with my mom and dad standing there. I also couldn't not go because Thursdays are too big a deal. See, my accident happened on a Wednesday, and the next day, when my parents should have been planning my funeral, I was released from the hospital, and we all went out to celebrate the fact that I was alive. Every Thursday since then has kind of become our day. Like a family day. Sure, my parents are completely corny and like to get all mushy on me sometimes, but I still love Thursdays.

Maybe it's lame to hang with your parents, but I wouldn't give up Thursdays for the world. My parents are all I've got. They're the only two people in the world that I can completely be myself around. So despite their quirks, when we go out and have a good time together, it's the only time I ever feel like a normal kid. That's why my parents would have known something was up if I'd suddenly opted to stay home in order to avoid seeing Ryan.

I've seen Ryan at the movie theater lots of times, and he always looks at me weird and then takes our tickets without showing any other hint that he actually knows who I am, so I figured it would be okay. But I knew I was in trouble this time because his face lit up as we walked through the door. I guess making out with him changed the rules somehow and made it acceptable for him to say hi to me, because he gave me such a cheerful "Hey, Jamie!" that it actually startled my parents.

He flashed me that stupid, charming, boyish grin of his, and I glared back, but my mother practically swooned. Before she could ask, Ryan held out his hand and said, "Hi, Mr. and Mrs. Baker. I'm Jamie's friend Ryan. It's really nice to meet you."

So we're friends now? One random kiss and a rejected date make us friends? I wanted to argue the point, but he didn't appear to be sarcastic at all, and the sad fact is, I don't have any friends. The fact that he even talked to me made him the closest thing to it, so I guess there was no harm in letting my parents believe it. At least then they might get off my case a little.

Ryan shook my parents' hands, and my mother all but pulled him in for a big, tight hug. I know she's a little desperate for me to make friends and have a normal life, but if I had been trying to do that, she definitely wouldn't have been helping any.

You have to understand my mom, though. She and my dad are a normal teenager's worst nightmare. Seriously, they're straight out of one of those after-school specials about teenage pregnancy or anorexia or whatever. You know, always trying to help me be strong by telling me how proud of me they are and how much they love me and stuff.

In today's world of divorce and family dysfunction, my parents are basically freaks. They've always been cheesy and way overprotective—I suppose that's just what happens when you're raised in a little farming town in Illinois—but it's gotten much worse since my accident. Sometimes I think they act like that because they're afraid I'm tiptoeing on the edge of sanity, and if my home life isn't perfect I'll crack. But the truth is, my accident has affected them as much as me, and with everything we've been through in the last year, we're all probably borderline lunatics. I'm sure they need the image of perfection as much as I do.

While I should have been mortified when my mom greeted Ryan with a hug, I couldn't really blame her. Instead, I just wanted to kill him. Buttering up my parents and getting their hopes up like that was a pretty low blow. But the boy really knows how to play the game, I'll give him that much.

"I'm surprised Jamie's never mentioned such a good-looking boy to us before," my mother gushed. "You're just the type she usually blabs my ear off about."

Ryan smiled proudly for my mom's sake, but the glance he shot me seemed to say, "So I'm your type, huh? Good to know."

I could be mistaken, but he seemed a little disappointed when I was unfazed by his taunting. He turned his attention back to my mom and asked, "She's *never* mentioned me? Not even after what happened last week?"

I groaned at Ryan's pout, and especially at his feigned surprise, but my mother ate it up. My father, on the other hand, was now watching both Ryan and me meticulously, and very cautiously asked, "Why? What happened last week?"

"Nothing," I grumbled.

"It definitely wasn't nothing!" Ryan argued.

I felt the chunks rise in my stomach at the thought of Ryan telling my parents that I'd kissed him. As I vowed inwardly to murder him if he gave up the secret, the jerk winked at me, happy to see he'd finally gotten to me. Thankfully, he divulged only a tiny piece of the story. "I finally got up the courage to ask her out," he explained.

As much as I wanted to believe that I'm not the only superpowered freak in the world, and that Ryan didn't mention our kiss because he had some kind of mind-reading ability, I knew that wasn't the case. I was being pretty obvious that I was contemplating murder, and I know Ryan picked up on it. My father saw it too, and even though I could tell he found Ryan's harassing me funny, he tried his best to hide his amusement.

My mother, however, didn't notice me at all. She was too busy glaring at a group of girls flirting with Ryan as he tore their tickets. She raised her voice above their giggling to say, "Ryan, Jamie didn't tell me you two have a date!"

"That's because we don't," I said quickly.

You should have seen the look my mother gave me right then. She was so utterly disappointed in me. But Ryan laughed and muttered, "I'm still working on it, Mrs. Baker," making her frown vanish instantly.

The two of them being all chummy together was making me ill. "Isn't there a movie we're supposed to be watching right now or something?"

Ryan is the last person to need any help with the dating game, but my mother wasn't about to miss out on an opportunity to play matchmaker. "There's at least ten minutes of previews before the show starts. If you want to talk for a few minutes, we'll get out of your hair and call you when the movie starts."

Yeah, like that was going to happen. "And miss out on ten minutes of Thursday time to talk to *him*? I wouldn't dream of it."

My mother started to protest, and my dad went to stop her before she could start a fight with me, but Ryan beat him to the punch. "It's all right, Mrs. Baker. My boss would be on my case for socializing anyway, and I'd hate to interrupt you guys. I think it's cool that you spend so much time together. I wouldn't want to impose on that."

Surprisingly enough, I couldn't tell if Ryan was just kissing up to my parents or if he was actually serious. It's that stupid grin of his. It's too natural. My mother was a goner for it, that was obvious, but my dad was a little skeptical, like me. "And do you spend lots of time with your parents?" he asked.

My dad was definitely trying to use his I-have-a-gun-and-I-doubt-anyone-would-miss-you voice, but Ryan didn't seem to mind. "Well, my stepdad is away on business quite a bit, but he's an all right guy, and I actually spend a lot of time with my mom when he's away so she won't get lonely." Ryan shrugged and I couldn't believe it, but there was a hint of redness in his cheeks, so he quickly added, "She makes me." Not that it helped any.

I think it was the blushing that finally convinced my dad that Ryan was being sincere. He nodded slowly and said, "Good kid."

"Thank you, sir. I just hope you remember you said that when Jamie finally agrees to go on a date with me."

My dad laughed, finally succumbing to the charm of Ryan Miller, and I'd had just about as much of this as I could take. "The movie's probably starting now," I snapped, and then stalked off to the theater.

I heard my mother sigh, and after she apologized for her rude daughter, both she and my dad said good-bye, but Ryan stopped them before they could follow me. "Is there a trick to getting on her good side?" he asked.

My dad just laughed, but my mother took pity on him and said, "Don't push her too hard. That only makes it worse."

"I'll remember that. Thank you, Mrs. Baker."

I tried to figure out if there was any discouragement in Ryan's voice, but without seeing his face I couldn't tell. I wish my mom had used the words "don't bother" or "never going to happen," but still, at least she didn't just tell him to go for it and give him some spiel about me needing friends, like she does at home all the time.

Getting my parents to stop bothering me about going out with Ryan was easy, but getting Ryan to stop bothering me about going out with Ryan was a different story. I was so nervous to go to school the next day because if Ryan had the guts to approach me when I was with my parents, then he would have absolutely no problem continuing the harassment at school.

Friday actually came and went without any real trouble, though. I was kind of surprised but really relieved at the same time. I figured Ryan's reservations had something to do with my mom telling him not to push me, because every time he saw me he smiled like he was buckets of friendly, but he didn't actually talk to me.

After that, I figured the crisis was averted and hoped that Ryan just thought I was some loner who happened to be a really good kisser, but then things changed drastically the week of homecoming. It was Monday, and English started off the same as any other day—with me sitting in the far back corner, and Becky and Ryan somewhere up front with the majority of the rest of the class gathered around them like a flock of sheep. Ryan glanced my direction every now and then, just as he'd done ever since our kiss, but it still took me by surprise when he decided to end our silent streak.

Ten minutes before the bell rang, setting us free for the day, Mr. Edwards told us to pick a partner, since for our next assignment we would be writing biographies of a classmate. Usually, picking partners meant I sat there doodling in my notebook until everyone else picked a partner. Then, when Mr. Edwards tried to group me with two other people, I'd tell him I could do the project by myself.

With most teachers, I'd never get away with that, but this is Mr. E's first year of teaching, so he hasn't figured out yet that you shouldn't let your students push you around, and he always gives in. Today, however, it didn't go down that way, and I was totally caught off guard.

"Take the last ten minutes," Mr. Edwards said, "to pick a partner, exchange numbers, plan a date, or do whatever you have to do, because these papers are due in two weeks."

Becky, of course, automatically turned to Ryan with a big smile. "This will be easy," she said. "I already know everything about you."

But then, much to everyone's surprise, and not just mine, Ryan replied, "Why don't you partner with Paige on this one? I think I'm going to do my paper with Jamie."

I didn't have any time to protest because I think Becky was actually angrier about it than I was. "What?" she yelled, and then glared my direction. "Did I miss something? The freak jumps you like a dog in heat and suddenly you're best friends?"

"Is there a problem, Ms. Eastman?" Mr. Edwards asked.

Ryan was quick to step in. "We're fine, Mr. E. It's just that this is one assignment Jamie can't do by herself, and I know no one else is going to be her partner."

"Got that right," Becky scoffed with an Oscar-worthy pout. I think she would have gouged my eyes out right then, if she could.

Mr. Edwards glanced from me to Ryan, trying to cover his look of shock, and then whispered to Ryan as if the whole class couldn't hear him anyway, "Are you sure?"

"I'm not scared of her," Ryan said, flashing me a big grin.

Mr. Edwards shook off his surprise and started to write down our names.

"Uh, Mr. E.?" I snapped. "I'm not working with him."

I glared at Mr. Edwards and waited for him to back down as usual, but this time when he sighed, he didn't say "fine," the way he normally did. Instead he said, "I'm afraid Ryan's right, Jamie. This is an assignment you can't do by yourself."

"Mr. E., I'm not telling some stranger all the intimate details of my life so he can spread it around the whole school!"

The entire class was now watching the confrontation with great intrigue, still trying to get over the shock of Ryan offering to be my partner. You'd think we were on *American Idol* and Simon Cowell had just complimented someone.

Mr. Edwards studied me for a moment, deliberating, and when he smiled, I thought I'd won him over, but he shook his head. "If you're that uncomfortable with your classmates, I suppose you can interview me."

"You?" My jaw dropped to the floor, and I heard gasps and giggles all around the room. "You want me to partner with *you*?"

"I'm not so bad," Mr. E. said lightly.

It's true, for a teacher he's not that bad. He's funny, plays the bass guitar in a band, and lets us eat in class. He's even kind of cute. You know, for a teacher.

But still!

I couldn't believe Mr. Edwards didn't grasp the horror behind that idea. I may be a complete social outcast, but even I have my limits. "Can't I just write an autobiography?"

"It's not the same thing. You're going to be graded on how well you can extract information during the interview process. You can't do that with yourself."

I just sat there gaping at Mr. Edwards. He's always given me my way. Where was this coming from? It's just a stupid paper. And it's not even about anything important!

The silence was broken by Ryan's cheerful voice. "Come on, Jamie. You have to admit that I'm a better alternative than partnering with your *teacher*. No offense, Mr. E."

What other choice did I have? Mr. Edwards is one of those teachers who still cares about his students. He's actually kept a close eye on me since his first week here, when he pegged me as one of those "troubled" teens they have seminars about in college. He's always trying to give me pep talks and stuff. I did *not* need to give him extra opportunities to ask me if I'm okay and try to get me to see a school counselor.

Knowing about my powers or not, Ryan really was the better option. I glowered at him, but he seemed to already know that he'd gotten his way. He winked at me, and then Mr. Edwards sighed again as he scribbled down our names. "Okay, Ryan and Jamie are partners," he said, and then muttered, "Good luck," to Ryan under his breath.

The smile Ryan gave me as he plopped down in the desk in front of mine was almost a victorious one. "Well, this is convenient," he said cheerfully. "I can finally ask you for your number."

"You won't get it."

"Even better, just give me your address, and I'll come over this week."

"Nice try."

"We're going to have to get together sometime."

"Just make something up. No one will know it's not true."

"Won't work." Ryan laughed. "Even if I did, everyone knows me. They would know if you made up yours."

"I just won't turn one in."

Ryan sighed, but I could tell by the look on his face that he wasn't discouraged at all. It's kind of annoying how peppy and cool under pressure he seems all the time. "Would it really kill you to go out with me?"

"Oh, so we're talking about a date now and not just a paper?"

"It could be just about the paper, if you'd rather."

I can be a patient person if I have to be, but the truth is, his little puppy-dog act was almost cute, so I had to get rid of him before I ended up giving in like last time. Getting to know people can be hazardous to my health, especially when it involves telling him about my past. "I'd *rather* it be neither," I quipped, and then promptly headed out of the room.

He didn't follow me, which I was happy about, but then Tuesday at lunch he was back, as diligent as ever and being really cute in a way that annoyed me no end. "Hey, Jamie!" Ryan greeted me as he plopped his lunch down next to mine.

"What will it take to get you to go away?"

"An interview."

I rolled my eyes, but Ryan pulled out a notepad and pen as if he knew I would give in. "Right here, in the middle of the cafeteria so it's not a date in any way," he said. "No funny business, just the basics, and then I'll leave you alone. I promise."

That was almost worth it. I glared up at him, but he smiled, somehow knowing he'd just gotten his way. "Fine, what do you want to know?"

"Everything."

"Okay, I like rainbows, puppies, and long walks on the beach. My dislikes include rap music, sauerkraut, and people. Mostly you."

"Perfect." Ryan scribbled my words down on his notepad, knowing full well I was feeding him crap. "What else?"

"There is nothing else."

"This isn't helping, Jamie. I'm supposed to be writing a biography, not a *Playboy* article."

"What else do you want to know?"

"I want to know a lot. I have lots of questions about you."

"Like?" I asked sarcastically.

"Like, the other day I was wondering why you dye your hair."

Okay, I expected him to ask where I was born or what my birthday was, but why do I dye my hair? Where did that come from? "What?" I asked, trying not to laugh because I didn't want him to think he was winning me over.

He smiled as though he enjoyed my confusion. "Well, you're not Asian, and you're not really trying for the Goth look. Not that your hair doesn't look great with those bright green eyes, but it's clearly not your natural color, so why the jet black?"

I thought about it for a moment. Dodging the question would have raised more suspicions than answering it, but I couldn't think of anything to say, so I figured if he could tell the truth, then so could I. "Well, it's naturally green," I admitted dryly, "and the black works better than bleach."

He frowned for a second, almost daring to believe me, but then laughed. "Green?"

"And the eyes aren't natural either, they're blue contacts."

"But if you're wearing blue contacts, to get your eyes that shade of green they'd have to be—"

"Yellow."

"So your hair is green, and your eyes are yellow?"

"Yup. Are we done yet?"

I hoped that my answers, while true, would give Ryan the hint that he wasn't going to get a real interview out of me and he would stop. He was quiet for a second, staring at me with pure curiosity, and I could tell he was debating asking me something else.

I glared at him, breaking his stare, and when he shook himself from his daze, he smiled. "Just one more," he said, and didn't pause quite long enough for me to say no. "Where'd you learn to kiss like that?"

Again, Ryan was full of surprises. I was not expecting that. At the mere mention of our kiss, my heart nearly stopped. I tried to hide my reaction, but he noticed me flinch and leaned a little closer to me with a cocky grin. "Did I hit a nerve?"

"Interview's over," I snapped.

I probably should have tried to stumble through some kind of fake explanation because it was obvious that I was upset, but I panicked. Being in my position's not easy, though. I mean how many times has Clark Kent been caught and had to fumble through some stupid explanation? And he's been dealing with it his whole life. I've only been different for a year. And actually, since we moved here, I haven't had to try to cover anything up yet.

When I grabbed my bag and walked out of the cafeteria, I prayed that Ryan wouldn't follow me, just like all the other times I'd walked out on him, but no such luck today. He wasn't exactly inconspicuous about it either.

"Jamie, wait!"

I quickened my pace, hoping I could at least get out of earshot of the curious spectators of the cafeteria, but Ryan grabbed my arm just as I got out the door. "Will you stop?" he pleaded. "I've been going crazy since you kissed me."

"It was just a kiss, Ryan, that's it! It didn't mean anything. I might have gotten a little carried away, but it had to look good if it was going to be in front of the whole school."

I glanced around nervously, and he finally realized that I didn't want anyone to hear this conversation because he lowered his voice and began walking me away from any people. "Just a kiss?" he asked incredulously. "I've never felt anything like it."

I tried to compose myself and smirked as best I could. "Are you trying to say you thought there were sparks?"

"Oh, there were definitely sparks! That kiss was hot. But that's not what I'm talking about. It's like I was charged up like a battery or something. I went home, ran five miles on the treadmill, and still couldn't sleep until four in the morning."

"So you got a little excited."

"You had to have felt it too. Maybe that's what they mean by chemistry."

"We don't have chemistry, Ryan."

"Well, I say we do."

"Well, I say you're wrong."

I tried to walk away again but he stopped me. "Then prove it. Kiss me again and tell me you feel nothing."

"No."

"Aren't you even a little curious?"

Man, that must have been quite the superkiss for him too because the poor guy was trying so hard. I actually really wanted to do it. I was probably more curious than he was, but I simply couldn't get involved with someone. Ever.

I'd thought about that every day since I realized I was different, and the superpowered life is a lonely one indeed. I totally understand now why the heroes in the comics are always so grumpy and depressed. They can't live their lives. I can't get involved with Ryan no matter how much I might want to. I have too big a secret, which he can't find out.

Even back when the accident first happened, before I realized I had powers, the doctors ran all these tests trying to figure out how I had survived, and within hours there were reporters and scientists knocking on my door. There was even this one tabloid journalist that became obsessed and started stalking me. He didn't even know about my powers, and I had to move clear across the country to get away from him. Imagine if someone found out that I could run the round trip from Sacramento to New York in ten minutes. The stalkerazzi would be the least of my worries. The government would be here with machine guns and giant plastic bubbles. I don't exactly want to be experimented on like I'm from Mars.

"You see?" Ryan accused, breaking me from my obsessive thoughts when I didn't answer him. "You are curious!"

Ryan reached his hand out to my cheek like he was going to kiss me again, and I immediately jumped back. I should have been cold to him, the way I was to Mike, but Mike made it easy, and I was finding Ryan extremely hard to resist. "I can't," I gasped, and then realized that I would never convince him to stop trying if I couldn't sound like I meant it. "I won't!"

He gave me this look, and it was so sad that for the first time since this whole Ryan thing started, I wished he still had that annoying happy-go-lucky attitude. "Why do you do this to yourself?" he asked.

His tone was genuinely one of utter confusion, but it wasn't his voice that upset me, or the sad expression on his face clearly showing that he pitied me, it was the question itself. It meant that I was doing something to myself, and whatever it was, was a bad thing. And he said it like I have some kind of *choice*. That was the worst part. I didn't ask for this to happen to me. It's not like I want to do this to myself.

His question made me so bitter that my body started trembling with anger. I could barely choke out a reply. "That's not your problem."

"Okay, I'm sorry." He backed off, startled by my sudden mood swing. "But this paper is my problem, and I don't feel comfortable cheating, so will you at least help me out and give me a little to work with?"

I felt terrible. I mean, deep down, he actually wasn't a bad guy. He deserved a little more respect than I was giving him, and mostly I just hated to think that I'd in some way crushed those impossibly happy spirits of his. I was already depressed, confused, scared, and angry at the world. I didn't need to feel guilty on top of it. "Fine," I said, and then took a minute to compose myself as I scribbled my address on a piece of paper and placed it in his hand. "If you really want to get to know me, be there Friday night, right around nine."

"Friday night? But that's the homecoming dance."

"Exactly."

"But—but," he stammered, "it's our senior homecoming, and I'm supposed to be there. I'm nominated for king. If you're not busy, why don't you just go to the dance with me? You should be there as much as I should."

"I know it's a big night for you, but that's why it has to be then." I was finally able to force a small smile. "If you haven't noticed, I don't exactly let people in. It's kind of a trust issue. If you expect me to break the rules for you, then I have to know how bad you want it."

Ryan examined the paper in his hand with my address on it. I wasn't sure if I had just made a really stupid decision or not, but as much as I hoped he wouldn't show, a part of me really wanted him to come. "I don't expect you to be there," I said, "but I'm not likely to give second chances either, so think about it and I'll see you Friday. Maybe."

It was an impulsive decision, and one that I couldn't take back. I'm not sure how Ryan got me to invite him over, but when he was standing right there, talking about chemistry and wanting to kiss me again, it's like he was the one with superpowers and he Jedi mind-tricked me into handing over my address.

I even started to believe it was a good idea until I caught him staring at me at lunch the next day and realized that he might actually take me up on my offer. He was sort of smiling, but he mostly just looked like he was trying to figure me out. I felt like I was going to be sick, and I must have looked it too, because he stopped staring and actually patted the table as if he was offering me the empty seat next to him.

I looked at him like he was out of his mind and not just for show. It was honestly a crazy suggestion, and I wasn't the only one who thought so. Becky was the first to glance my way, and when she gasped, she caught Paige Shultz's attention. When Paige realized what Ryan had done, she accidentally sprayed the soda in her mouth all over Tamika Larson.

Paige and Tamika are sort of Becky's ladies-in-waiting. They're best friends and constantly talk about Becky behind her back, but they put up with her because of how close she is with Ryan. (No one is more in love with Ryan than Paige. The way she rattles on about him to anyone that will listen is nauseating.)

"What the freak?" Tamika grumbled as she tried to wipe the sticky beverage off her arms. "It's a good thing this is your shirt, Paige."

"Jamie Baker—are you crazy?" Paige hissed at Ryan, instead of apologizing to, or even answering Tamika. "What if she comes over here?"

Ha! Even with the pout Ryan was giving me there was no way I was ever going to join them.

"Well, considering that's kind of the point of the invitation," Ryan said, "I hope she does."

I suddenly had all of the most popular kids in school staring at me. It was the only time in my life I was glad I am the only freak with deathly powers, because I'm sure any one of those girls would have loved to go supervillain on me just then, especially when Mike laughed and told them all to take pity on his poor horny friend. "Aw, cut the man some slack. Did you see what Baker did to him? I'm jonesin' for her myself after that kiss."

All the guys at the table roared with laughter, and Ryan draped his arm around Mike. "Amen, Mikey," he said. "Who knew the Ice Queen could be so incredibly hot?"

I guess I'm not the only person with superpowers after all. Mike apparently has the ability to lower Ryan's IQ. Morons.

Anyway, I knew Paige, being scary in love with Ryan, wouldn't like that answer, and I was sure Tamika was going to have to catch her when the poor thing passed out from heartbreak. But Paige had a little more attitude than I gave her credit for. Instead of going into shock when Ryan waved at me again to come over, she actually gave me a look three times more evil than the glare Becky was burning into me.

That's when I turned my attention back to my lunch. Or at least I turned my eyes away. I couldn't really tune them out completely, and even if I could, it was kind of hard to ignore Paige's next comment.

"You can't possibly want to hook up with that slut?"

I found it ironic that Paige was calling me the promiscuous one, when everyone knew she'd been with pretty much the entire football team at one point or another. I didn't have time to get mad, though, because just as soon as the word escaped her lips Ryan defended me. "Jamie's not a slut. It was just one kiss, and she only did it because I asked her to."

"Was mounting you in front of the whole school part of the plan?" Paige asked. "The freak practically ripped your clothes off!"

Okay, I knew that was going to haunt me. And when Paul Warren said, "I'd let her mount me any day," making all jocks present laugh and high-five one another, I cringed inwardly. I didn't really care if every girl in the school thought I was easy, but the last thing I needed was more guys trying to hook up with me.

Again, though, I didn't have any time to worry about it, thanks to Ryan. "Hey, that wasn't really her fault," he said. "She didn't know how irresistible I was when she agreed to kiss me."

I couldn't believe he'd said that, but I think he only did it to bug Paige because he smirked at her and said, "Besides, if one little kiss makes her a slut, I'd hate to know what that makes you."

I guess I wasn't the only one who thought the pot was calling the kettle black. Ryan's comment shut Paige right up, and I'd have kissed him again for that one had I been standing there, but Becky and Tamika didn't appreciate it the way I did. They pulled Paige to her feet and called Ryan a not-so-nice name before making a very dramatic exit from the cafeteria.

When I finally glanced over at Ryan, my heart just about stopped because he was staring right at me. He was confused but intrigued, and I realized that I was laughing along with Ryan's dumb jock buddies. He'd just caught me following a conversation I technically shouldn't have been able to hear.

I instantly wiped the smile from my face and went back to eating my lunch, cursing myself for being such an idiot. I was so upset that I didn't notice when Ryan got up and made his way across the cafeteria to me. I actually wasn't pulled from my panic attack until his voice was right behind me.

"Jamie, if you heard that back there, I'm really sorry. Why don't you come over and eat lunch with me? I'll introduce you to everybody and give them a chance to redeem themselves. The guys are all just as curious about you as I am, you know."

He didn't seem to wonder how I heard him, he just felt bad that I did, so I started to calm down a little. "Of course they're curious. They all think they can get into my pants now." The look on Ryan's face made me feel bad for saying that, so I added, "I really don't care if everyone thinks I'm a slut."

"Well, I do. I asked you to kiss me. It's my fault Paige said that about you, and I don't want the whole school thinking it."

That surprised me, and it was kind of sweet, so I couldn't stop my face from softening a little, no matter how much I wanted to stay mad.

Oddly enough, the cocky smile Ryan gave me when he realized that he was getting to me made it a lot easier to keep focused when he tried to get charming on me again. He was standing there with this cute little hopeful pout and said, "Whether you're upset or not, I feel bad, so how can I make it up to you?"

"You really want to make it up to me?"

"Of course I do."

"Then stop talking to me before other people start to think it's okay. Please. I don't want to have to get mean."

I grabbed my things and walked out the door before he could argue with me. I didn't even wait to see him frown. I couldn't—I was too weak around him.

I didn't want to have to live up to my reputation this time because shockingly enough, Ryan actually seemed to be a pretty decent guy. He shouldn't really have to be punished for wanting to get to know me. And to be honest, had our kiss been a normal one, I might have considered letting him talk to me occasionally.

But the fact that he was charming and I was mildly attracted to him only made us a hopeless case. We couldn't have a relationship, and I couldn't have him asking why that was, so I didn't see how any kind of friendship was going to work.

Ryan didn't speak to me the rest of the week. We made eye contact quite a bit, but I'm not sure if I caught him looking at me, or if maybe it was the other way around this time. Either way, I was pretty sure he wasn't going to show up at my house, and I was surprised that I felt almost as much disappointment about that as I did relief. I think that's why, come the day of homecoming, I decided to go to my first school sporting event since I moved here.

I didn't actually go to the game. I watched from a hilltop just about a mile away, but that may as well be a seat on the sidelines for me. I don't have eyesight quite like Superman because I can't see through things, but it's definitely more than your average twenty-twenty vision. I think of it as having built-in binoculars with super zoom control. Even at a mile away I could see the cute little excited smile Ryan got on his face every time he threw a good pass.

Our team won the game, and even though I was happy for Ryan, it proved to be just as unexciting for me as I thought it would be. Pretty much the only good thing I got from going was hearing an interesting conversation between Becky, Ryan, and Mike. I was about to go home when Becky asked Ryan about the dance, and I couldn't help but listen.

"Are you riding in the limo with us tonight?" she asked.

"I'm not sure yet," Ryan replied.

"Who are you going with, anyway?"

"I'm actually dateless tonight."

"You're going stag? Why?"

"Well, I knew how much Mike wanted to go with you, so I took one for the team."

The flirty little "Aw" he got from Becky made me want to puke, but it was worth it to see the look on her face when Mike said, "Plus, he wanted to take Jamie, but she turned him down."

I couldn't tell if Becky looked disgusted or insulted, but she didn't try to hide her horror as she gasped, "You asked *Jamie Baker* to homecoming?"

I waited for Ryan to deny it or defend himself with some BS excuse about feeling bad for me or something, but he didn't. He just smiled as he slumped his shoulders in a guilty shrug and said, "Twice actually. But don't worry, she told me to get lost."

"Yeah, rejected him like he was a fat guy in a Speedo," Mike added, laughing hysterically as he elbowed Ryan.

Becky was far too concerned for her friend to share Mike's laughter. "You're not seriously trying to hook up with that girl, are you?"

"I don't know, maybe. I think I'm still trying to decide if she would be worth the hassle."

I answered "No" every bit as forcefully as Becky did, and, sadly, our depictions of me weren't that different. Basically, she said I was a freak with issues, but in not such nice words. She was right, though, and Mike seemed to agree, but Ryan defended me. Well, sort of. "I'm sure there's a decent human being buried under all that hostility somewhere," he said.

"Are you kidding?" Becky asked.

"Nope," he replied cheerfully. "I think she may have a bit of a soft spot for me too. Why else would she have kissed me like that? I bet I could break her down eventually."

That cocky little…

I thought about smacking him upside the head for that—I'm fast enough that he'd never know what hit him. But on second thought, the boy did get me to kiss him, invite him home, and go to my first football game in more than a year, without even breaking a sweat.

Apparently I had quite the little crush, and as I stood there asking myself what was with me and quarterbacks, Becky went all soap opera with a big cheesy sigh. "Oh, Ryan," she said, shaking her head as if she were so much older and wiser than him. "You want my advice? Stay far, far away. Not only would she kill your reputation, but you could do so much better."

"I don't know, man," Mike disagreed. "I say go for it. Jamie Baker's hot and basically impossible to crack. If you could get with her, you'd be a legend around this place."

That was the point in the conversation where I started to get mad. It wasn't the fact that Mike was telling Ryan he should nail me for bragging rights, but Ryan laughed with him about it, which meant he either liked the idea of nailing me, or the idea of being revered as some sort of high school god for it. Knowing him? Both.

Whatever the reason, I'd learned my lesson. Ryan Miller might be charming, but he certainly would not be "breaking me down" anytime soon.

I didn't stick around to hear the rest of that conversation. I was angry, so I went somewhere I could think in peace. There are a lot of spots in the country that work well for that, and this time I went with the Grand Canyon. I like it there because even though it gets a lot of foot traffic, it's big enough that I can still find a spot far enough off the beaten path that I don't have to hear tourists the whole time. Plus, the beauty of the Grand Canyon at sunset makes it hard for me to stay in a bad mood, and I was especially grumpy now.

I don't know what made me think Ryan was different. I should have known by the sheer fact that he was charming enough to break me. He was just like any other hormonal high school boy on the planet, only he was better at playing the game, which made him dangerous.

I shouldn't have gotten my hopes up in the first place. It's not like I could ever tell him the truth about myself, and I can't exactly be his girlfriend when I have to constantly lie to him about myself. Apparently, I can't even kiss him, so it's not like he would stick around long even if I could be honest.

I sat there thinking for a long time, long after the sun went down. When I finally decided to go home, I told myself there would be no more wasting any energy on Ryan Miller. Of course, it took me almost as long to tell myself I wouldn't think about him anymore as it did to get home, and the stupid boy was at my house when I got there, so I kept my promise to myself for only like half a second.

I heard his laugh from down the street and stopped dead in my tracks. It was just after nine thirty now, so theoretically he could have been there for half an hour already, and judging from the conversation he was having with my parents, he probably had been. The picture he was laughing at was the last one taken of me before my accident, and knowing my mother, she started with the baby pictures.

"She's a beauty queen too?" Ryan asked, full of surprise, and then giggled as he read the title. "Miss Sweet Corn?"

"You laugh, young man," I heard my mother say, "but that's a big deal in Illinois. People come from all over the Midwest to go to that festival, and Jamie worked very hard to win that crown."

"And she looked every bit as beautiful as her mother did when she won the crown in high school," my father added. I didn't need supersight to see the proud look on his face; he was always looking at my mom that way.

It got quiet for a second, and I thought about interrupting the party, but then Ryan said something that made me stop. "She looked so happy," he said in this really pensive voice. "What happened to her? How come she's not like this anymore?"

I wanted to run inside and put a stop to this invasion of privacy, but my mom answered his question before I could make myself open the door. "Jamie was in a car accident."

Car accident isn't exactly the right term for what happened, but it still cut through my heart. Painful memories flooded my mind as my mom continued her very watered-down explanation. "Her boyfriend was killed," she said hesitantly.

If Ryan reacted to the news at all, he didn't do it vocally. He didn't make a single sound. I wish I could have seen the look on his face or known what assumptions he was making as he tried to justify the way I act, but I could hardly breathe, much less keep myself composed.

"Jamie won't talk about it much," my father said. "The accident changed her, and she's had a really hard time dealing with it. She blames herself."

I couldn't believe what I was hearing. They may as well have told him I was now a superpowered freak. How could they be so cavalier about it? What if he started asking questions they didn't have answers for?

"We moved here, hoping that a fresh start might help," my mom explained, breaking the awful silence that was now in the house. "But she's just not the same girl anymore. She won't get close to anyone. In fact, I'm really surprised she invited you over. You must be pretty special."

As angry as I was, I was kind of relieved to hear the hint of a laugh in Ryan's response. "Not special, just stubborn," he said. "I think she only caved because she thought I wouldn't come. Tonight's the homecoming dance."

I cringed when I heard my mother gasp. I knew the former prom queen was not going to like that. I finally pulled myself together and pushed open the door. I tried my hardest not to glare at my parents too much because for all Ryan knew I had no clue what they were talking about. My parents knew I'd heard them, though, and when I walked into the room they both jumped to their feet, looking every bit as guilty as I knew they felt.

My father started the conversation with, "Where have you been? You've kept this poor boy waiting for nearly forty minutes."

"I wasn't really expecting him."

"And you made him miss the homecoming dance?" my mother whined. "Jamielynn Baker, how could you?"

"I didn't *make* him do anything."

"It's all right, Mrs. Baker." Ryan laughed as he shot me that same carefree smile that either makes me melt or boil—tonight the answer was boil. "I'm pretty sure Mike is going to be king anyway, and I can always take Jamie to the prom."

I gave Ryan an annoyed glance as my mother's eyes bulged from her head. "You're nominated to be the homecoming king?" she gasped, and then immediately gave me a desperate look. "For heaven's sake, Jamie, go put on a dress and take this poor boy to the dance."

When Ryan spouted nonsense about what an excellent idea that was, I couldn't take it anymore and ushered my parents into the kitchen. "What are you doing?" I hissed as soon as the door was safely shut behind us.

I was surprised when my father spoke up first and said exactly what I thought I was going to hear from my mother. "He seems like a nice kid."

"Cute too," my mother added excitedly.

I felt my head starting to hurt and barely tried to control my temper. "Yeah, Mom, he's really cute. He's also charming and sweet and funny. But that's what they say about the devil, and you don't want me hanging out with him."

My parents were both frowning their disapproval now, but I didn't care. "He's practically a stranger. How could you tell him about the accident? About Derek!"

"What were we supposed to say to him, honey?"

"Nothing! It's none of his business!"

When tears dropped from my eyes, I realized how worked up I was and stopped yelling. My mother started crying too, and when my dad held out his arms I practically collapsed into them. I know how much my parents worry about me, and when my father squeeze me, I couldn't stay mad.

"We didn't tell him anything the people in Illinois don't know," he whispered. "We had to tell him something, though. He's writing a paper. If we didn't answer any of his questions he would only get suspicious."

Sometimes I forget that my parents are struggling with this just as much as I am. They don't always know what to do either, but this time my dad was right. "I'm sorry, Daddy."

"I know, honey."

My mom pulled me from my father's arms for a hug of her own. She motioned with her eyes toward the door that separated us from Ryan. "I know this is hard for you, Jamie, but you didn't die that night and you can't keep living like you did. I think Ryan could be good for you. I'm not saying I think he should replace Derek, but—"

"There will never be another Derek! Ever!"

The lights in the house flickered, instantly putting me in check. I didn't mean to lose control, but I still have a hard time keeping my emotions in line when it comes to the late quarterback of Mendota High School. Derek is by far my most sensitive subject.

I watched my mom gulp and then force a smile through her fear. "I know you're scared," she said, and then in a whisper added, "we all are."

Seeing your parents afraid of you is probably the worst feeling a human is capable of experiencing, but at least it makes me feel a little better about being scared of myself. And I'm grateful that they try to be strong, even if they can't always manage it.

"You need to go out there and talk to that boy," my mother continued. "And if I were you, I would try to be nice. You could use a good friend, Jamie."

My mom said that in her I-love-you-but-I-mean-business voice, so I knew the discussion was over. Without saying anything else, I went back into the living room, secretly hoping Ryan had decided to go to the dance after all, but I had no such luck. He was still looking through our family photo album, but he stood up when I entered the room. He smiled at me, but it wasn't that classic innocent Ryan smile—it was much more serious. "She's right, you know," he said. "You should really think about letting me be your friend because I'd really like that, and I don't think there's anyone else at school brave enough for the job."

I swear, Ryan is the most confident person on the planet, and it is so annoying. I stood there glaring at him, so angry that he'd overheard us, and he just smiled back completely relaxed. Knowing him, he was probably waiting for me to tell him he was right, and give in to his request for friendship. Well, I wasn't going to give in anymore, remember? No more giving in to Ryan Miller!

I took the photo album from the coffee table, glancing at the picture of me winning the pageant as I put the book back in its place on the shelf. "You've got more than enough to write a full biography on the life of Jamie Baker already, so I guess the interview's over. You can go now."

"Oh, no!" Ryan said. "You're parents are pretty cool, but I didn't miss my homecoming for a chance to look at pictures all night. I came to see the real thing, and you had me under the impression that you would be here if I showed up, so I think it's only fair that you give me a little Jamie time before you kick me out."

I grunted because I was so frustrated just then. Ryan's serious smile had turned back into his cocky little you're-about-to-give-me-exactly-what-I-want smile, and it is just so hard to stay angry when he's looking at me like that. So much for not giving in to Ryan Miller. "Ugh, fine, but I don't promise to be nice!"

Ryan actually had the nerve to laugh at me as I stormed into my room and slammed the door in his face. I wasn't surprised when he let himself in behind me. Somehow I knew my overly dramatic tantrum wasn't going to work with him.

I flopped down on my bed with a book, preparing to ignore him as best as I could. I'd agreed to let him spend time with me, but I hadn't promised to entertain him. And I wasn't about to do anything that could give him the impression that I enjoyed his company, even if part of me did. The guy had a big enough ego as it was. He didn't need to add me to his list of victories.

He stayed quiet for a minute as he looked around my room, and then decided to just make himself right at home.

He climbed up next to me on my bed, leaving a whole three inches of space between us.

"Do you mind?" I snapped.

"Yeah, a little"—Ryan chuckled—"but I'm dealing with it, so you can too."

"Well, if it bothers you so much—"

"I didn't say it bothered me. I'd just rather be closer, is all."

"Closer? Can you even get closer than you already are?"

I knew I'd put my foot in my mouth the instant the words escaped it, and Ryan didn't miss a beat in putting his arm around me and pulling me tightly against him. "Never ask a guy if he can get closer," he said, refusing to let me go. "The answer is always yes."

The way he clamped his hands together so that I couldn't push him away was playful, but I didn't think he was teasing when he shuddered. That's probably because I haven't been held by anyone in a really, really long time, and I reacted the same way I did when I kissed him. I guess it's not so much a superkissing ability as it is a case of superhormones.

Ever since I got juiced up by some knocked-over power lines, I'm more amped than a power generator. The fact that there was friction when Ryan touched me meant that it doesn't just seep to the surface when I get angry. I guess it's every time I lose control of myself in any way.

Obviously, that's not good, so when he shivered, I panicked, elbowed him hard enough to leave a bruise, and made my way across the room to the much safer single-person chair that sat at my desk. "You should have stuck with the compromise," I grumbled. "I probably wouldn't have moved if you'd kept your hands to yourself."

"It was worth it." He was laughing at me again.

"Why are you so annoying?"

"Why are you so compelling?"

It was useless. I was never going to win. He was much better at the witty comebacks than I was and a lot less easy to get flustered, so I gave up the argument. I was pretty sure getting on my nerves was what he was aiming for at the moment, so I figured not fighting with him would be a better tactic. I dropped the attitude and probably sounded a little bit desperate as I asked, "Why are you doing this? What exactly do you want from me?"

"Is it really so bad to have to talk to someone other than your parents?" he asked in all seriousness. "I don't want anything from you. Okay, no, that's a lie. I would *love* to make out with you again, but that's not why I'm here tonight."

"Then why *are* you here?"

"I just wanted to understand you. I couldn't imagine why anybody would exile themselves the way you do."

"Yeah, well, now you know. I killed my boyfriend, and my friends hated me for it. The whole town did, actually. People can turn on you and hurt you, even the ones who say they love you. I don't want to go through that again. It's that simple."

Ryan didn't say anything after I stopped talking. He just watched me, and I haven't felt that insecure in a long time. The silence made my heart race like a million miles an hour, and if I couldn't calm myself down I was likely to trip a circuit breaker in the house.

It wasn't exactly mature, but I chose hostility to cover up how vulnerable I felt. "Mystery solved," I said coldly. "And I'd appreciate it if you didn't put any of that in your paper. Mr. Edwards likes to read things out loud, and I'd rather the student body kept calling me the ice queen instead of boyfriend killer."

"Of course not."

I was surprised by the amount of sincerity Ryan displayed, but then he smirked again. "I won't say anything," he teased. "But it wouldn't really matter even if I did, because everyone will be in so much shock over the beauty pageant thing that they won't even hear the end of my paper."

I couldn't stop myself from cracking a smile at that, and the way Ryan's face lit up when I did actually made me blush. "I don't suppose you'll consider leaving that part out too?"

"Not a chance." Ryan laughed. "I am going to have to figure out something to tell Mr. Edwards, though, because he's never going to believe I didn't just make it all up. I saw the pictures, and I can hardly believe it."

"Just tell him I wouldn't tell you what happened. He'll have no trouble believing that. It's the truth anyway. I didn't tell you. And I wouldn't have. My parents are the ones with the big fat mouths."

"Well, I'm really glad you stood me up then because it's a relief to have the real story."

"The real story?"

Ryan shrugged with a bit of a guilty smile. "I've been making my own up for weeks. I had myself convinced that you were in witness protection, and that you were hiding until you could testify against the inner workings of some vicious mob."

"The witness protection program?" I was smiling again. I couldn't help myself. "I guess that could explain the hair dye, but why was I connected to the mob?"

"A girl as hot as you? You were dating the boss's nephew, of course. You witnessed a violent crime, and when you got scared they threatened you. But you're tough, and your boyfriend was a big, murderous jerk, so you went to the cops anyway. And now here you are with your jet-black hair, hostile attitude, and distrust of basically the entire human race."

I didn't think he was kidding. On the bright side, I guess it was good to know that it wasn't just me that couldn't stop thinking about him these last few weeks. "Sounds to me like you've already written the end of your paper," I said, and then sighed. "I like your version better."

"Me too," Ryan admitted shyly. Well, shy for him. "It involves a lot less of you getting hurt. I really am sorry you had to go through all of that."

I tried to smile appreciatively, but I don't think I accomplished it, and things got really quiet. Awkwardly quiet this time. Thank goodness Ryan's unusually perky because he successfully changed the subject and managed to bring back the light mood as well. "So, tell me what it feels like to be crowned since now, thanks to you, I'll never know."

Two seconds ago I was wallowing in the memory of the single worst moment of my life, and here, with one little comment, Ryan had me smiling again. How does he do that?

I didn't exactly know how to answer his question, so I went to my closet, pulled the stupid tiara from the old shoebox I kept it in, and joined him on the bed again. "It feels kind of like this," I said, and placed the crown on his head.

Ryan feigned a look of surprise and wiped away fake tears as he spouted thank-yous to an imaginary audience. When he tried to wave, though, I absolutely had to step in. "No, no, no, no! A beauty queen is all about poise and grace." I sat up very straight as I proceeded to show him the trademark Miss America wave.

"All I need is the dress," Ryan said as he diligently tried to copy my perfect wave.

He looked so ridiculous that I actually burst out laughing. It was the first time I had laughed an honest-to-goodness laugh since the accident, and it felt surprisingly good. "That can be arranged," I said.

"You still have the dress?"

"It's a *gown*, and yes, it's hanging in the closet."

"Well, what are you waiting for? Go put it on. I want to see Miss Sweet Corn in all her glory."

It was the strangest thing, but I was actually having fun for the first time in I don't know how long, and when Ryan asked me to put my dress on, I didn't even think twice about it. I grabbed the dress, dashed into my bathroom, and came back a few minutes later in the baby blue silk that won me my crown over a year ago. I pulled the sash over my chest and took a spin. "What do you think?"

"I think I feel sorry for any girl that had to compete against you."

Ryan pulled the tiara off his head and gently placed it on mine. "It looks much better on you," he said, and then stepped back to get a good look at me.

I was surprised by all the butterflies I had in my stomach as Ryan looked me over. He was obviously a little enamored, and I blushed under his gaze. I think he was glad to see it because he grinned and then rather boldly pulled me into his arms. "What do you know?" he whispered in a tone that instantly turned the playful atmosphere to something much more intense. "It looks like I'm going to get my dance after all."

I may be the poster child for *Marvel Comics*, but at that moment as he began to dance with me, I was completely powerless to stop him. I wondered for a brief second if maybe my parents were right. What if Ryan really was good for me? Right then I felt normal. I felt better than normal. I felt accepted, wanted. It felt so right to be in his arms. I didn't say anything, just stood there feeling a little over-whelmed, and the next thing I knew, his lips were almost touching mine.

I'd be lying if I said I didn't want to kiss him again, and both of us knew it. I was scared out of my mind because I didn't think I'd be able to stop him if he tried. Especially not when my brain kept telling me that the first kiss didn't seem to hurt him any. But when he reached up to brush a loose strand of hair from my face he felt a shock. It was enough of a shock to make him flinch, and I watched, horrified, as he stuck his finger in his mouth as though it hurt.

Ryan just laughed and made some cheesy comment about the sparks between us, but I knew the truth, and my stomach literally did a few leaps up into my chest. I managed to jump back before he could kiss me and glanced his direction only long enough to see him roll his eyes. "How long are you going to play hard to get?" he whined, immediately attempting to get the moment back.

The poor guy had no idea that he would never have another moment like that. This time he only received a shock, but what if next time it felt more like sticking a metal fork in an electrical socket? I felt kind of bad because I couldn't explain all the mixed signals, but now that my worst fears were being confirmed, there wouldn't be any more mix-ups, and he wasn't going to like the outcome.

"Forever," I whispered as soon as I could find my voice.

I ripped the tiara off my head to put it away. My hands were shaking as I reached to put the old shoebox back on the closet shelf, and Ryan startled the life out of me when he walked up right behind me. "Forever doesn't really work for me," he said, and I jumped so high I dropped the box and spilled a mess of old pictures all over the floor.

"Somebody's tense," Ryan teased as he bent down to help me pick the pictures up. "I'm not making you nervous, am I? Because you know, if I am, it's probably because you like me and you don't want to admit it."

There were so many ways I could have answered that if I'd been paying attention to him even the least little bit, but I wasn't. I was now sitting on the floor staring at an old picture of Derek and me at a football game. I don't know how long I sat there, and I didn't notice when Ryan sat down next to me. I'd forgotten he was even there until he pointed at the picture. "Is that him?"

I shook myself from my daze and handed over the picture with a nod, glad for the change of subject, even if it was about my dead boyfriend. "This was at the beginning of sophomore year. Right after I met him," I explained. "We grew up in the same town, but he was older than me so we never really talked until then. I was the only sophomore to make the varsity cheerleading squad, and when the cutest boy in school—a senior, and the star quarterback—asked me out, I was kind of star struck. I think I was in love before the end of our first conversation."

Ryan's eyes sparkled, and I knew what he was thinking before he said it. "So you have a weakness for good-looking quarterbacks, huh?"

"It was just a phase," I grumbled, snatching the picture back and shoving it into the box. "I am so done with your kind."

"We'll see about that."

We'd officially come full circle now, and the almost sincere conversation was back to him annoying me. "You are so egocentric," I groaned as I got to my feet.

"And you are so in denial!" Ryan answered. "You may have everyone else in the school fooled, but you are not as mean as you think you are. Why don't you just admit that you're tired of all the self-exile crap? Stop trying to be the ice queen, and start being Jamie Baker again."

"Just start being Jamie Baker again? Because it's just that simple?"

I finally lost it, and not just a little. As tears filled my eyes, rage filled my heart, and the electricity in the house immediately responded. Ryan looked up at the light, confused, and that only made me all the more upset.

"Not everything's black and white, Ryan! Don't think spending the evening here means that you know me. I can't ever be that Jamie Baker again. You have no idea how bad I wish I could, but I can't. That Jamie Baker is dead! Okay? She doesn't exist anymore!"

The lights flickered again, and I tried to calm myself down. "I want you to leave now."

Ryan didn't have a witty comeback this time. He looked really upset, and I hate that I hurt him, but I'm only human. Well, when it comes to my emotions anyway. I was so angry that I couldn't think clearly anymore, and I just let the tears flow.

"Jamie, I'm sorry. I didn't mean to make it sound like I—"

"Just go!"

I was so upset that when I screamed, the lights got really bright, and then all the electricity in the house went out. My parents were knocking on my bedroom door within seconds. My mother sounded worried as she entered the room with a flashlight. "Jamie? Ryan? I think we're having a little trouble with the circuit breakers, is everything okay in here?"

Trouble with the circuit breakers? Right, because I just blew them up!

"Mrs. Baker, I'm so sorry," Ryan stammered. "I have no idea what happened. One second we were laughing, and then she just... I didn't mean to upset her."

"It's not your fault, honey," my mother insisted as she ushered Ryan out of my room.

It felt like his fault. It felt like it was all his stupid fault. I wanted to drown out the voices as soon as my bedroom door was shut, but no matter how hard I tried, I still had to listen to my mother try to explain my unstable behavior and assure Ryan that he did nothing wrong.

It was awful because I wanted to be angry. I wanted to hate him, but deep down I knew my mother was right. Ryan really didn't do anything wrong, and the only person I really hated was myself.

Some nights there's just no sleeping. After Ryan left I had one of those nights. I liked him, and I hated that I liked him. I went to bed wondering how I could make myself stop liking him, but the only flaw I'd found in him so far was an abundance of confidence that I wasn't sure wasn't completely justified. There was no way to hate him. I could only hate myself because I couldn't have him, and it was that wonderful thought that kept me tossing and turning all night.

I think I finally dozed off sometime after sunrise, and when my mother came creeping into my bedroom, it felt a lot earlier than the noon she claimed it was. "Rise and shine, Jamie, before there's not any shine left to rise to."

"Mom, I really don't feel good. I think I'm just going to stay in bed today."

"You're not sick, Jamie, you're wallowing. Moping around your room all weekend is not going to make you feel any better. Come on—up, up, up! I heard somewhere that Macy's is having a sale. Let's go pick out cute new outfits and get our nails done the way we used to."

I have to admit that even though I knew exactly what she was up to, the offer was still tempting. I missed those spontaneous day trips I used to take into Chicago with my mom whenever one of us had a really bad day. But the thought of a cute new outfit brought on a whole new wave of depression, and I pulled the covers over my head. "You go ahead, Mom. I don't have any need for a cute new outfit, anyway."

"We also need to hit the beauty supply store. You're running low on hair dye, and your roots need a touch-up."

"And you don't know what brand and color I use by now?"

"All right, fine," my mom said, refusing to let my face stay buried beneath my covers. "I'll get some new clothes, and you can go crazy in Borders."

That offer was even better. I love reading. I didn't always, but now I found it such a quiet, peaceful, relaxing hobby. It gave me the chance to read about people like me, even if they were just pretend. My mom, however, only saw it as an easy way to be antisocial and didn't like the fact that I did it so much. So her bribing me with books meant she was truly concerned this time.

It was clear that she was never going to let me lie in bed all day, so I grudgingly got up. The next thing I knew, I was sucking down an Orange Julius in an overcrowded food court, trying not to let my mother see how much the noise was making my head hurt. She already felt bad enough to spring for eight new books, so she didn't need to feel any worse.

I hadn't really touched my lunch. After last night I wasn't all that hungry. My mom noticed, but she hadn't jumped on my case for it. I could tell she was still trying to figure out a way to cheer me up, and I knew she was dying to ask me about what happened with Ryan, but so far it was all just conversation that could easily avoid the subject.

"What if you got a job?" she asked randomly when it got quiet.

I just looked at her skeptically.

"No, I'm serious, Jamie. You go to school, and that seems to work just fine. And eventually you're going to grow up and have to get a job anyway. What's wrong with you getting one now? It would give you something to do besides read."

"I like reading, Mom."

"Yeah, but you need to get out and be social more often. And besides, how else are we going to keep paying for all these books?"

"That's what the library is for."

"Come on, Jamie. Having a job is a normal teenage activity. You're always saying you wish you could be normal, but you won't do anything about it. You don't have to make friends at a job if you don't want to, but it might be a good structured activity for you."

"Yeah, because hours of school every day—plus all the homework—isn't enough."

"I know you're having a bad day, but don't you get an attitude with me," my mother said sternly, suddenly making me feel like a jerk. "You are not as handicapped as you think you are. If your life is miserable, it's because you let it be."

"Sorry," I muttered out of guilt even though I didn't actually believe what she'd said. My life was miserable and it was out of my control, no matter what she thought. I didn't want her to feel bad, though, so I tried to keep the conversation going.

"A job might not be so bad," I admitted. "It's just that after hours of being at school with all the noise, my head usually hurts like crazy, and I need some peace and quiet. It's hard to be around so many people all the time."

My mom's sour expression turned into concern as she looked around the crowded mall. "Are you feeling all right now? Do we need to go home?"

"No, Mom." I sighed even though I wanted nothing more than to be back home, lying in bed. "I'm fine right now. I'm just saying it might make it difficult to have a job while I'm in school."

She sighed and things got quiet again. I glanced at her before I reached up to rub my head, but she didn't notice my discomfort because she was too busy frowning at one of the books I'd just purchased. "Why always with the aliens or superheroes?" she complained.

"Freaks with powers, trying to conceal their true identities?" I laughed bitterly. "I wonder."

"And this?" My mom held up a biography of Stephen King with a disapproving look.

"Hey," I said defensively. "That's not fiction. It's nice to know that there're bigger freaks out there than me."

"Sweetheart, that's not going to make you feel more normal. And there's a whole lot more to you than just having powers, you know. Why don't you find a good drama? I'll bet you could relate to that really well."

I love my mom. She was being dead serious, and yet she still made me smile. "*You're* calling *me* the drama queen?" I laughed. There was no questioning where I get my theatrics. "No thanks. I have enough drama in my life already. And besides"—I took the biography from my mother's hands—"I have to read this one for class."

"This is an assignment?" My mom was a little more than skeptical.

I shrugged. "We're all about biographies in English right now."

"And you chose Stephen King?"

"Mr. E. never specified who, and you have to admit, Stephen King is way more interesting than President Obama or Taylor Swift or whoever."

My mother sighed dramatically and then frowned at another book. "All right, fine. But you could still try other books too. You never know, you might really enjoy a nice… *romance*."

And there it was. Clever but not quite sneaky enough to fool me.

"Didn't you say there was a sale around here some-where?" I asked, pulling myself from our table.

My mom sighed and followed me down the mall until I stopped in front of a store window with a really nice dress in it. "You should buy something like that, and then make Dad take you someplace nice."

My mom paused a minute, and I smirked because she was finally going to say it. Sure enough, she blurted, "I like Ryan," failing at her attempt to be subtle.

I wandered into the store pretending to be clueless. When she gave me an expectant look, I muttered, "Not gonna happen."

"Jamie, what on earth happened last night?"

"Nothing." I knew she would never buy it, but I still had to try.

Yup, I was right. The look she gave me was definitely a don't-make-me-angry look. "You had me worried sick, and you scared that poor boy half to death."

"Good. Maybe he'll leave me alone now," I grumbled. My mother shot me another death look so I shrugged. "I can't help it. I don't need him telling me how to live my life too. You and Dad do that enough already, and it's not as easy as everyone thinks it is!"

I noticed that my tone of voice was all of a sudden really harsh when my mom's eyes glossed over with moisture, and I felt like crap. "I tried, okay?" I said, calming myself. "I tried to talk to Ryan and it didn't work. I nearly blew up the house! Face it, Mom. As much as I wish I could be normal, I'm just not."

My mom looked upset, and I could tell she wanted to disagree, but she didn't know what to say. She couldn't argue that I fried the circuit breakers last night, and I was sure she knew it could have been a lot worse. I felt bad, but what could I do?

Sometimes there's just not anything to say, so to break the awkward silence I pulled a little black cocktail dress off the rack and handed it to my mom. "You should try this on."

It took her a second, but my mom eventually gave up and took the dress. When she disappeared into a changing room I started flipping through some of the nearby racks. Once she wasn't standing there distracting me, I started to notice all the chatter going on around me. Two voices stuck out right away. I couldn't see them, but it was definitely Paige and Tamika, and they were happily discussing their favorite topic. "She's still not answering her phone. I hope she's all right," Tamika said.

"It's Becky," Paige grumbled. "She blows us off all the time."

"Yeah, but she usually calls."

"I'll bet she's still with Mike. Did you see the way he was all over her last night? Why do you think they didn't come to the after party? I wonder what they were doing."

"I don't think so. Becky told me they were going to Ryan's house to figure out why he didn't come to the dance, but that's the last I heard from her. I'm telling you, Paige, I think something might be wrong. She always answers her phone, and she never misses a good sale."

I smirked when Tamika mentioned Ryan because I knew Paige had to be a little sore about him being a no-show at the dance. She'd actually turned down three different guys, thinking that Ryan was going to ask her when Mike asked Becky, and she ended up without a date to homecoming. Served her right.

That's when the two girls came into my view. They walked into the store I was in, looking like the suburban version of Paris and Nicole with their extremely short skirts and shopping bags galore. "Who cares about Becky," Paige said right on cue. "I'm worried about Ryan. The guy was announced homecoming king and didn't even show up to the dance. He hasn't really been the same lately. Not since the ice queen brainwashed him."

I had to laugh at that. Although, a brainwashing ability might be nice.

"Who does she think she is, anyway?" Paige continued to rant. "I don't care how hot everyone thinks she is. She doesn't deserve a guy as nice as Ryan."

Yeah, and like Paige was any better a person than I was? Ryan deserved way better than both of us put together.

"It's so pathetic the way she's obviously trying to use his popularity to pull herself out of Loserville."

"Psh, like that could ever happen." Tamika laughed. "Ryan may be hot, but he's not a miracle worker. No one can help that poor freak."

Okay, what good are powers if you can't use them for the greater good once in a while? I couldn't listen to any more of this, so just for kicks I casually strolled over to the other side of the clothing rack where Paige and Tamika were sifting through a collection of skirts that were on sale because it was getting too cool to wear them—no doubt they'd both be sporting one tomorrow no matter what the weather forecaster said the temperature would be. They were so engrossed in their conversation that they didn't realize I was standing three feet from them.

As I ran my hand along the rack in front of me, the clothes began to cling to one another. I watched as the static worked its way over to Paige and Tamika, making their hair stand up. I decided to kick up the power just a notch, and soon they both looked like they'd been rubbing balloons on their heads. "I'm sorry," I said, "but did you just call me a freak?"

They both jumped and attempted to cover their shocked faces by scowling at me. "If the shoe fits," Tamika muttered.

"You looked in a mirror lately?"

They glanced at each other and gasped in unison. The looks on their faces almost made having superpowers worth it. I wanted to laugh so badly, but I managed to resist, and it's a good thing too because my mother walked up right behind me.

"More friends of yours, honey?"

"Not exactly, Mom," I said casually. "Did the dress fit?"

My mom is too easy. Her face lit up at the mention of the dress, and she forgot all about Paige and Tamika. "You're right, Jamie. It's gorgeous. I think I am going to have to make your father take me somewhere nice now."

Tamika was still trying to get her hair under control, but Paige scoffed rather loudly, "You came here with your mother?"

She said it like hanging out with my mom was some horribly embarrassing thing, and it wouldn't have bothered me at all except that I could tell that it made my mom feel bad. Insulting me is one thing, but insulting my parents is not okay.

"It's a lot more fun than coming alone," I said, and then plastered a big fake smile on my face. "Speaking of going places alone, how was the dance last night? Do you know who won for king? I didn't actually make it. Ryan and I sort of lost track of time, but I'll bet he'd like to know who won."

My mother didn't know exactly what had just happened, but she shot me a look when she saw how upset Paige was. I ignored it. If Paige and Tamika were going to call me the ice queen, then I should at least get to live up to my reputation sometimes. And Paige was beyond mad this time. She looked like she was going to either vomit or explode. I'm not kidding you. She was so mad that one eye was sort of twitching.

Of course I kept up my sickly sweet act and smiled as big as I could manage as I asked, "So did Ryan win?"

"Stay away from Ryan, you *freak*!"

I was really surprised she had the guts to call me that in front of my mom, but I've never seen anyone so angry.

I was afraid my mom was going to be upset by that, but she wasn't mad at Paige. Well, not once she saw the satisfied look on my face. She waited until Paige and Tamika stormed out of the store to chew me out, but I got a lecture all the way home.

"What?" I snapped when she demanded some kind of explanation. "She's awful. She's just mad because she likes Ryan and he pays more attention to me. Plus, they started it. They called me a freak."

"I don't care who started it, Jamie. I didn't raise my only daughter to act like such a spoiled little brat. The self-pity thing is going to stop right now. We're having a talk with your father when we get home, and you are going to have to start making some serious changes, or there will be some serious punishment."

Sure, I'm a teenager, which means I've fought with my parents same as everyone else, but this was the first time I've ever seen my mother really angry with me when the issue of my powers was involved. I was really surprised by it, and I was even more surprised at how bad she made me feel. I didn't say another word until we got home, and I barely held it together through the lecture my father gave me once he was fully briefed on the situation.

If you can believe it, I got grounded from my computer, the library, and all of my books until I got a job, joined some kind of school club, or went out on a date. Not exactly a normal punishment for teenagers, but it was every bit as cruel.

Worse than the lecture and worse than the grounding was listening to the talk my parents had after I went upstairs. They went for a walk down the street, but I have pretty good range. They would have had to drive across the city if they didn't want me listening in.

Mostly there were a lot of statements like "I'm worried about her" and "she's getting worse," and there was a lot of talk about possible therapy. But the most disturbing part was when they somehow turned to the subject of Ryan. My mom said she thought I was having all this trouble right now because I liked Ryan and I was stressed about it. Okay, maybe she was a little right, but it still made me mad that she knew that.

From there the conversation actually turned into a Ryan love fest. "Such a sweet boy," my mother gushed, "and so polite. And he seems to have taken quite the shine to her."

"And helpful too," my father added. "He helped me reset the circuit breakers before he went home the other night. He seems to have a decent head on his shoulders, for a seventeen-year-old."

After that they came home and spent the rest of the weekend trying to convince me that going out with Ryan would make me feel better.

I knew my parents wanted me to try to live a normal life since we moved to Sacramento, but they were beyond relentless with the Ryan chatter the rest of the weekend. They seemed to think almost as highly of him as he did of himself.

I was so sick of them harassing me about him that when Monday came around and I had to see Ryan at school, the very sight of him made me want to punch something. He was standing out front with all of his football buddies when I got to school, and I could tell he wanted to talk to me, but I was not in the mood.

He started to approach me as I walked past him, but I gave him the most evil glare I was capable of. After that, he didn't try to stop me, and Mike wasn't discrete with his teasing. "Oh! Iced by the queen of cold!" he said, slapping Ryan on the back. "I take it you didn't get lucky this weekend. What's the matter, man—lost your mojo? I thought you were totally in after the way she was all over you before."

I could feel them watching me as I walked away, but I didn't look back. It made me angry that Ryan didn't seem upset by the laughter and the taunting of his friends. And even worse, I hated his response. He actually laughed with them and then said, "It's Jamie Baker, dude. It's going to take me some time to break the ice."

"Ry," Mike said. "I know you're the man and all, but even you can't break Baker. She's impossible."

"Watch me."

Ha! If he thought I was mad at him Friday night… "Watch me"? Someone should tell him it's not wise to make me angry, and after that conversation, angry would be an understatement.

I don't get him! I mean, he'll stand up to Paige in front of the entire school and say I'm not a slut, and then he'll turn around and brag to his buddies about *breaking* me? News flash, Ryan—Mike's right. Never. Gonna. Happen.

I was so mad that I was afraid just looking at him would make me lose control of my powers, so I opted to avoid the cafeteria at lunch, but English had me worried. I thought about skipping, but I didn't want to look like I was hiding from him after he saw me cry this weekend.

Luckily, Ryan didn't say anything to me during class, but he caught up to me like two seconds after I walked out the door. He'd flashed me a small smile as he walked out of the classroom, which he could tell I wasn't happy about, so I thought I was safe. I thought for sure he'd just leave.

I took my time getting out of the room just to be sure. Enough time that Mr. Edwards asked me if I had detention he didn't know about. "Sorry, Mr. E. I was just kind of caught up in my book," I lied.

When Mr. Edwards got up from his desk and walked my direction I started gathering up my things. I wasn't quite fast enough. "Interesting choice," he said as he picked up the biography of Stephen King.

"Hey, you said anyone."

"I'm not saying it was a bad choice." Mr. Edwards chuckled at my defensiveness. "Stephen King is one of the greatest writers of our time."

That surprised me. "You like Stephen King?"

"American literature isn't just Mark Twain, Ms. Baker," Mr. E. said with a wink. "I just find it interesting that you would choose the king of horror as the subject of your book report. Generally, people choose someone they can relate to on a personal level."

Which is exactly why I chose him, I wanted to say. But I didn't want a lecture and a referral to my guidance counselor's office, so instead I grumbled, "He's a lot more interesting than Ryan Miller," as I snatched the book back from Mr. Edwards. I was still a little sore about being forced to have a partner.

Mr. Edwards laughed at me and then stepped out of my way so I could leave the room. "See you tomorrow, Ms. Baker," he called after me.

Mr. Edwards had successfully distracted me enough that I'd forgotten all about Ryan until I walked out of the room and found him waiting for me. I groaned as he peeled himself away from the wall and began keeping pace at my side.

He didn't say anything at first, which I thought was weird, and he was a little cautious when he finally spoke. I was surprised because it was the first time I'd ever heard him sound even remotely nervous. "How are you?" he asked.

"Peachy," I grumbled, refusing to look his direction.

"Oh, come on, Jamie. You're not still mad at me, are you?"

I didn't answer that. I was still furious, just not for the reason he thought. I went back to ignoring him, but he only waited for a second before trying again. "I finished my paper already. Do you want to read it?"

"What, no parties? No hot dates?"

"Yeah." He laughed, a little embarrassed. "I'm not usually such an overachiever, but I was so worried about you after what happened that I didn't really feel like going out. And since I couldn't stop thinking about you, I figured, why not?"

Ryan was really starting to irritate me. I couldn't tell if he really liked me or if he was just trying to score. I mean, Friday night in my room he was this incredible guy. He listened, he cheered me up, he promised not to tell any of my secrets—and so far he'd kept that promise—but then what was all that about earlier, with Mike?

"I'm really sorry for upsetting you the other night." He sighed when I didn't respond. "I wasn't trying to brush off your past. It's just that you seem like an awesome person when you let your guard down. I wish everyone could see you the way I saw you the other night."

I was so touched by his apology that I finally looked at him and regretted it immediately because it turned me all gooey on the inside.

Seriously, how does he do that?

Suddenly I wasn't mad anymore, but that was actually a bad thing. I slapped my hands over my face, rubbing at my eyes as I attempted to control my frustration. It was obvious I was softened a little by his confession, and I expected him to call me on it, but he didn't. Instead he decided to move on to the next tactic he'd obviously thought of before hand. "Are you busy right now?"

Yeah, like I really needed to spend any more time with him right now so that he could break me down completely? "Do I even want to know why you're asking me that?"

"Well, I've got about twenty minutes before practice, and I thought it might be a good time for an interview."

"What do you mean?"

"For your paper. I'm done, but you still don't know anything about me."

"I told you I wasn't going to write one."

"You're just going to blow off the assignment?"

"I have an A in the class. One paper won't make that much difference."

It took him a minute to respond, but finally he grinned. "How come you don't want to write your paper?"

"Why don't you just tell me why I don't," I said dryly, "since you seem to think you already know?"

"You're afraid to find out that I'm not such a bad guy. Because if you were to realize how much you actually like me, that would make it very hard for you to keep blowing me off."

I ignored the fact that he was exactly one hundred percent on the money, and sighed as I burst through the front doors of the school. "You are amazingly self-assured."

He just grinned at me and said, "Yup. So?"

"So I hate to be the one to burst your bubble, if in fact that's even possible, but I am *always* going to keep blowing you off. I'm not just playing hard to get, Ryan. You and I will never happen."

Ryan looked around and lowered his voice even though, since most of the students were in their cars already, the only people near us were a couple of gardeners, and they couldn't hear us over the sound of the riding lawn mower. "Look," he said, "what happened to you was a nightmare. I get that. But you're never going to get over it if you keep pushing people away all the time. Why don't you just give me a chance? I know part of you wants to."

He was almost pleading with me at this point, and I was surprised by his intensity, but after a second his mouth turned up into a crooked smile, and he said, "Haven't met a girl yet that doesn't."

I knew he was kidding this time, but I was also pretty sure he thought it was true. I'm quite convinced that Ryan really does think every girl on the planet would benefit to be in his presence. It was really, really hard not to smile at him, though, so I had to actually glare just to keep from doing it.

It's not that I hated Ryan, because I didn't. Far from it, if the truth be told. But the fact that I liked him, raging ego and all, made things that much more impossible, and it only made me that much angrier about the situation. "I don't need a chance to find out how awesome you are. I already know. You tell me all the time."

"But that's not nearly as good as knowing for yourself."

"You don't get it! I don't want to know you because I honestly don't want people bothering me. And hard as it may be to believe, that includes the one and only Mr. Perfect, Ryan Miller!"

He actually seemed surprised, and I daresay a little hurt by what I'd said. He didn't look destroyed or anything, he just looked upset, but I'd never seen Ryan upset before. Not really.

I couldn't look away from his frown, and he stood there challenging me with his eyes until, suddenly, we heard the sound of tires squealing. The noise startled us, and we both whirled around to see what was going on. It was just Paul Warren showing off his new cherried-out Jeep by peeling out of the school parking lot.

Unfortunately for Paul, the Jeep's ridiculously oversize tires were more than he knew how to handle. He lost control of the truck, jumped the curb, and rammed right into the school's marquee. Which was a big-time bummer for him because that new electronic sign cost the school a fortune and was Principal Huang's pride and joy.

Not that I care about a moron like Paul, but contrary to popular belief my heart is not made entirely of ice. So when that big bulky sign started to fall off its pole, heading straight for the poor guy on the riding lawn mower, I took off running.

My reflexes are just a tiny bit faster than your average human, and when I move as fast as I can, things appear to me as if in slow motion. In only a fraction of a second, and before anyone even knew what was going on, I rammed the guy on the lawn mower out of the way.

Should have been an easy first attempt at heroism, right? Piece of cake? Yeah, I thought so too until I slammed into the biggest guy I've ever seen. I'm not kidding you, the dude had to be four hundred, five hundred pounds easy. I managed to knock him off his seat and to safety, but I wasn't prepared for so much resistance. The impact was so forceful that it knocked me to the ground, and that split second of being completely disoriented was just enough time to bring the marquee crashing down on me.

The blow knocked me out cold for a second, and when I came to I understood how the Coyote felt every time the Roadrunner dropped an anvil on him. Pain. Lots of pain. And here I thought superheroes weren't supposed to get hurt. Life is so unfair.

Okay, so I was new to this whole saving people gig, but it's not like I went to any kind of superhero training academy. I got the crap kicked out of me, but I'm pretty sure that if I hadn't intervened, lawn mower man would be dead right now instead of trying to get to his feet to see if I was all right.

That's when it dawned on me that any normal person in my position would be dead right now. I had to do something, so I ignored the burning sensation in my muscles and used all the strength I had left to raise the sign off me and leaned it against the side of the lawn mower. Then I scrambled into the tiny space beneath it and waited for Mr. Wannabe Sumo Wrestler to catch up.

Within a few seconds three gardeners were staring down at me, shocked that I was still breathing. "Try not to move," one of them instructed me. "I called an ambulance."

What could I do? I couldn't just get up and walk away, but I couldn't stick around to be examined by the paramedics either. After giving myself a moment to calm my panic, I decided to go with the whole pretend-it-didn't-happen tactic. Superheroes do it all the time in the comic books. It all happened in a matter of seconds, and since I was behind the lawn mower, no one had a good view. I crossed my fingers that they were all shaken up enough to believe me. "I'm okay," I said, slowly climbing out from under my makeshift lean-to.

"Impossible," sumo lawn mower guy wheezed. "That thing fell right on you."

"No," I said, ignoring the aches in my body as I pulled myself to my feet.

"Yes it did. It smashed you like a pancake."

"If it had done that I'd be dead right now," I said, trying to hide the fear in my voice. "I ducked. The sign hit the lawn mower, not me." I brushed the dirt off me and held out my hands, half tempted to do a little tap dance or something. "I'm fine, see?"

I could see them all mentally convincing themselves that they'd only imagined it because the outcome was impossible otherwise. Then I relaxed because they were all buying it, whether they wanted to or not.

My relief lasted only a second, though, because the kids that had been lingering in the parking lot were starting to make their way over to us, and they were already debating whether or not it was me in the middle of the chaos. I needed to get out of there, and when the sirens of the ambulance could finally be heard, all eyes turned their direction.

I was gone before they looked back.

I wanted to run. Home, New York City, the Himalayas—it didn't really matter. I was just scared and wanted to be anywhere except where I was, but I knew that wasn't an option. I had to go back to Ryan. Otherwise, I'd never be able to explain my little disappearing act or the fact that half the school thought they had just seen me get crushed.

I went back to the school, but I couldn't just pop back at Ryan's side all of a sudden, and since my entire body felt like a truck just hit it, I took a seat on the front steps. I'd been sitting there for only a few seconds when I saw Ryan do a double take and walk over to me. "There you are," he said, still frowning in confusion. "I didn't see you walk away. I thought you'd disappeared on me or something."

He laughed, but I wasn't feeling very playful. In fact, I wasn't feeling well at all. I thought people with superpowers weren't supposed to get hurt, but my head was pounding, so I buried my face in my arms to block out the light that seemed to be making it worse.

"Jamie? You're shaking. What's the matter?" Ryan asked when he finally realized that I wasn't quite right.

I think I was allowed to be a little shaky after something like that, but I couldn't exactly explain that to him. "I'm fine," I mumbled instead from beneath my arms. "I just don't like accidents."

That was the truth. I really hate accidents, and I probably still would have been upset even if I hadn't just been part of it. It might have a little something to do with one wreck in particular, I don't know, but I'm pretty sure Ryan was now thinking about the same accident, because he crouched down in front of me and ran his fingers through my hair very protectively. "I didn't even think about that. I'm so sorry. Are you okay?"

His voice was so soothing, and the way he was stroking my head felt so amazing that my eyes glossed over with tears. I couldn't help it really. I hadn't been cared about by anyone except my parents in over a year, and Ryan was trying to comfort me because he was genuinely concerned.

"Is there something I can do?" he whispered.

"Go away," I muttered.

I didn't really think that was going to work, but I also didn't expect him to pull my chin up and dry my tears, either. It was an overwhelming feeling, and I was so shocked that I couldn't do anything but gawk at him.

"Jamie—"

He stopped and just stared at me in wonder.

We must have sat there for a full thirty seconds just looking into each other's eyes, but the longer he stared, the more confused I got. "Your eyes!" he finally gasped. "One of your contacts must have fallen out. They really are…"

Ryan tried to say "yellow," but he couldn't form the word. I cursed under my breath and immediately turned my face away from him.

"I'm sorry," he said as I scrambled to my feet. "I didn't mean to stare like that, I've just never seen anything like it. I thought you were kidding."

I tried to walk away, but his voice sounded so desperate that I only got two steps. "Please don't run away from me this time," he pleaded.

I opened my mouth to say something, but someone called Ryan's name from the parking lot, and when I saw Mike and his friend Justin just a few feet away, my heart stopped. I froze, but Ryan smiled at me and then pulled his sunglasses off his face and placed them on mine before turning around to greet his friends.

"Dude!" Mike yelled. "I think your wannabe girlfriend just got crushed by the marquee."

"Do you mean Jamie?" Ryan asked, completely confused.

"Yeah," Justin replied, "and the freak just got up and walked away."

Ryan turned back around to give me a confused look, and when Mike and Justin realized I was standing there they stopped dead in their tracks. "But weren't you just…?" Mike said, unable to complete his question.

"Sorry to disappoint you," I sneered. "But as you can see, I obviously wasn't hit by any falling marquees today. I guess you'll just have to keep wishing, huh?"

"You must have an evil twin then," Justin said, "because it looked just like you."

"Jamie *is* the evil twin," Mike grumbled.

"Back off, Mike," Ryan said.

Not that I was offended by Mike's insult, but it was still kind of nice to see Ryan defend me. Mike just rolled his eyes and then mumbled something about heading to practice. "I'll catch up," Ryan said.

I cringed because I knew he was going to try to make me explain myself, and I had no clue what I was going to say.

Once Mike and Justin were gone, Ryan's face was immediately full of concern again. "Let me take you home."

"I have a car."

"Yeah, but you seemed pretty shaken up a second ago."

"Well, I'm fine now."

"Then can I come see you after practice?"

Okay, this was worse than just asking me why my eyes were yellow. This meant that he wanted time for me to explain it properly. Well, that wasn't going to happen. It couldn't. "Give it a rest already!" I snapped. "No! You can't come over after practice. I wasn't kidding when I said I don't want you bothering me anymore."

"You don't have to be scared of me, Jamie."

"I'm not scared of you," I lied. "The self-exile thing isn't a cry for help. This isn't some ice queen outreach program here, okay? Poor little messed-up Jamie doesn't need you to save her. I'm not your pity project!"

I watched Ryan's face drop as he began to realize how serious I was this time, and he looked so disappointed that I wanted to take it all back. Too bad I couldn't.

"I'm not doing this because I feel sorry for you," Ryan said in almost a whisper.

I was surprised by his tone. I didn't know he was capable of something like humility.

Tears threatened to give away my true feelings when he reached for my hand. I pulled away from him before he could touch me, and out of sheer desperation allowed the energy pulsing through my body to spin out of control.

Nothing makes me angry like feeling what makes me different from the rest of the world, and I needed to be angry right then, so I let myself simmer for a second. I probably would have juiced him if he'd touched me again, so I guess it's a good thing he didn't, but I was tired of fighting him, and I was tired of fighting myself when I was around him. "I'm not going to be your conquest either," I finally said when I was good and mad.

"Excuse me?"

I'd offended him this time, like really, truly offended him, and it stung, but I had to. The longer I encouraged him, the worse I would hurt him, and hurting him was inevitable.

I clenched my fists tightly, praying he wouldn't see right through me, and said, "The first time you talked to me was because you bet someone you could get me to kiss you, and you've tried to put the moves on me every time you've talked to me since."

"Yeah, because I like you. Is that such a bad thing?"

"Oh please, Ryan. Just because I don't talk to people, doesn't mean I don't know what they're saying. Jamie Baker, the freak ice queen, is impossible to crack? So the guy who finds a way to break the ice and nail the queen would be a legend around here, am I right?"

We stood there for a minute, and Ryan was the one to finally break the silence, but his voice sounded angry. "And that's what you think I'm doing?"

No. Not exactly. He may have been joking about me with Mike, but I could tell now that this wasn't just about a hook-up. That's why I hated myself so much for saying what I said. "I know you're 'the man' and all, but even you can't break Baker?" I said, quoting his and Mike's conversation from this morning. I knew he'd recognize it. " 'Watch me'?"

"How did you…?" Ryan's face went pale as he did indeed recognize his own words being thrown at him. "Hang on, now, that's not what I meant! I wasn't just talking about—"

"What's the pool up to now?" I interrupted, purpose-fully not wanting to give him the chance to explain. "Put me down for twenty—I'm good for it. You're never getting into my pants."

I didn't want to hurt him, but I didn't see any other choice. He was never going to leave me alone if I didn't. I've done some pretty mean things in my life, but blowing off Ryan Miller the way I did right then is something that I still feel bad about, even to this day.

"Fine!" he snapped, and then swallowed back his anger. "You win. I surrender."

"Thank you."

He watched me walk away from him until I got in my car, but he did let me go, and I was pretty sure he wouldn't bother me anymore now. I knew I'd made the right decision. It just didn't feel like it.

I cried all the way home from school that day. I'm not proud of that, but I'm not ashamed of it either. I mean, how many people have to worry not about being who they are, but just *being* in general. Being Jamie Baker is a lot of responsibility that I never asked for. It's also responsibility that I wasn't prepared for, don't want, and shouldn't have to deal with. Especially not alone.

I cried because it wasn't fair that I had to reject Ryan. Turning him down was the responsible thing to do. It just sucked. I didn't want to, and I shouldn't have to when all the other kids my age are busy hooking up.

But at the same time, a nonexistent social life isn't the end of the world. I was definitely being a little dramatic, but I think I chose to dwell on Ryan more than I needed to in order to forget about all the other reasons I was crying.

I pulled it together when I got home, though, because I didn't want to have to explain everything to my mom. I'd managed to calm myself and stop the tears, but the minute I walked in the door, my mom knew something was up. She took one look at me and rushed over like a good mom should. She wrapped her arms around me, and I yelped when she squeezed me because even though I'd walked away from the accident, I think I may have jammed my shoulder and bruised myself from head to toe.

"What's the matter? Are you okay?"

"There was an accident," I mumbled, unable to keep it from her, "and I tried to stop it."

I couldn't tell if she was upset with me or not, but she was definitely overwhelmed by the news. I hoped she wasn't angry with me, but I wasn't too concerned about her. Dad would be worse. She simply started with the standard "Are you hurt?"

"Depends on your definition of the word."

"Was anyone else hurt?"

"No, but they would have been."

After I filled her in on the details, my mom sat quietly for a moment, then forced a smile. "Well. I'm very proud of you, honey."

"Yeah but, Mom, I was smashed by a giant marquee, only *I* left the dents in *it*!"

My mom hugged me again, a new wave of fear taking her over. "Jamie, your father and I have talked with you about this."

"I know."

"Sweetheart, you are an extraordinary young woman, but you're not Superwoman. We don't really know how your powers work. What if you'd gotten hurt?"

"But what was I supposed to do? That man would have died. Was I just supposed to watch it happen, knowing I could have helped?"

"It's not your responsibility to save people. If God wants them he'll take them."

"Then why didn't he take me?" I exploded.

I jumped back, putting some distance between us before I could hurt her. I felt bad for losing control, but I wasn't yelling at her, I was just yelling, and I think she knew that. Aside from Derek, if there's any other subject that could cause a citywide power outage, it's God. Considering I'd already fried the circuits once this week, I took a deep breath, but I couldn't help asking, "Didn't he want me?"

I know that sounds like a really juvenile question, but you try being in my shoes for a while and see how much you really know the answer.

"Of course he does."

"Then how come instead of letting me go to heaven like everyone else, he left me behind and turned me into some kind of freak?"

"You're not a freak, Jamie. You're just different. You can still have a no—"

"I can't have a normal life, Mom! I can't go to things like dances and football games like everyone else, because I'm too busy trying not to listen to every conversation around me. I can't have close friends because I'm too worried about what lie I'll have to tell them if they ask me a question I can't answer. And dating is out of the question! I can't even kiss a boy without turning him into the Energizer bunny!"

Okay, so maybe I was a little more upset about the Ryan issue than the whole I'm-not-a-Jamie-pancake-right-now issue, because the lights flickered again after mentioning the kiss that started all my trouble. My mom's not a fool either. She didn't waste a second figuring it out. "Is that what all of this really about? Ryan?"

"I kissed him."

Oops, that one got away from me.

I don't know what bothered me more, the fact that my mom was so shocked I kissed a boy that she nearly fell off the couch, or that she was so excited about it she squeaked, "You did?"

Not wanting to have to go into any details about the relationship Ryan and I didn't have, I decided to get right to the point. "It did something to him."

"What do you mean it did something? What happened?"

"I don't know, Mom. What happens to the lights when I get mad? Why do the fish get pulled across the tank when I walk past them?"

I knew my mom hated it when she didn't have all the answers, and I didn't expect her to, but I still wished she had more than just a sigh for me right then. Her sigh was an exasperated one, and I felt bad for upsetting her, so I dialed back the sarcasm and tried to explain as best I could. "I kissed Ryan, and it charged him up like a freaking Duracell."

"Was he all right?"

Was Ryan all right? I actually managed to smirk at that one. "If I hurt him at all, he didn't seem to mind."

"Thank heavens!"

I wished I could feel as relieved about that as my mom did. "I got lucky," I said grimly, "but the other night I was so nervous that I zapped him pretty good when he tried to touch me."

Just thinking about that wonderful moment brought my tears back. "He keeps asking me out," I said, sniffling, "and the last thing I want to do is hurt him, but how else do I make him stop? I said some awful things to him today. I'm always going to have to be alone."

"No you won't," my mom insisted. "We'll talk to your dad when he gets home. I'm sure he'll have some ideas to get this all worked out."

Oh, he did all right. My father was full of answers when I told him the story that evening. He's always been the more practical of my parents, leaving the romantic notions of happy endings and trustworthy people to my mom. After drilling me for every single detail about the accident, and asking over and over again if I thought Ryan knew I was really involved, he came to the conclusion that I was never to interfere like that again.

He wasn't angry with me any more than I was mad at Ryan, but he was most definitely putting his foot down when it came to pretending I'm Wonder Woman, and honestly, that was more than fine with me. This accident was my first, and I would happily make it my last attempt to save the day.

The only thing I didn't like about our conversation was just how much my dad agreed with me about Ryan. I know it wasn't personal because he'd spent the weekend trying to convince me how being friends with Ryan could be a good thing, but now Ryan knew too much. Now he was a threat. "It may not seem like it," he said, "but you did the right thing by pushing Ryan away."

I knew I'd said those same exact words just a couple of hours ago, but when they came out of my dad's mouth they really made me mad. Then, to make matters worse, he basically forbade me to talk to Ryan anymore. He did it in a nice way, but still, the irrational teenager in me wanted to go to school tomorrow and tell Ryan everything, just because.

"It's best if you just leave things the way they are," my dad said when I told him it didn't matter because Ryan hated me now anyway.

"What happened to 'be a normal teenager, go out, and have friends'?"

"He's a good kid, but we just don't know what he would do if he found out about you." I wanted to argue, but I knew there was no point. "Jamie, you hate having this secret. It's not fair to make him share that responsibility. And it's not safe either, for you or him."

Guilt trip and a half. Not that I was considering the possibility before, but now I was really never going to talk to Ryan again. Of course, it is *Ryan*, so I can't be held responsible if he talks to me first and I give in to whatever he wants. Deep, deep down I hoped that would be the case, but it wasn't. I guess I should say it was lucky for me that Ryan kept his promise to surrender, because I woke up in so much pain the next day that if he even tried to say hello he would have known something was up.

You know how if you forget to stretch before a workout and then you go to sleep, you wake up stiff as a board? Well, apparently, getting squashed by a ton of steel has the same effect, and I guess with supermuscles comes superstiffness. What I needed were some superpainkillers. But how can you go to a doctor for medicine to treat injuries from an accident that you weren't in?

I woke up so sore I could hardly move and could have easily asked my parents for a "get out of jail free" pass, except that it might look suspicious if I didn't go to school the day after half my classmates watched me get flattened, so I ignored the pain and went. Yup, sucked to be me.

I didn't talk to or even look at anyone that day, but I listened to everyone. They were all saying the same things. Someone would say the sign fell on me, and then someone else would dispute it, saying I was with Ryan when it happened. Then of course the first person would ask if Ryan and I were together.

The rumors of Ryan's and my secret love affair spread like wildfire, and by lunch it was all everyone was talking about—everyone except Ryan. He hadn't so much as said my name all day. Not even when Amy Jones had the guts to ask him to his face if the rumors about us were true. He simply said, "Nope."

Then in true Ryan fashion, he smiled at her and said, "Why? You weren't worried that I was off the market, were you?" Poor Amy blushed and Ryan laughed. "I'm afraid I'm still single. In fact, I'm dateless for Friday night. You want to go see a movie or something?"

I had to laugh at the way Amy's eyes lit up at the spontaneous offer. She was literally trying not to squeal as she accepted the date. The way she swooned was almost pathetic, and if I weren't too busy being a normal, jealous, emotional teenage girl, I would have given him a little credit. The boy truly does have a gift with the ladies. Instead, I just wanted to zap them both.

The way Ryan was acting made me so angry. Maybe I really was just a challenge for him. It made sense, I suppose, but he was acting as if yesterday never happened and we didn't fight at all—almost like I never even existed. I kept telling myself that's what I asked him to do and that he was just faithfully keeping a promise, but it didn't help. That day was lousy for me, and the worst of it hadn't happened yet.

I was on my way to English and dreading having to spend the next hour in the same room as Ryan, but when I got to my classroom Principal Huang and two police officers were standing there with Mr. Edwards. As wonderful as this day had been so far, I was sure they were there to talk to me. I didn't even get inside before Mr. Edwards motioned for me to join them.

Principal Huang pointed at me. "That's her."

"Jamielynn Baker?" one of the cops asked.

"I prefer Jamie, actually."

"Ms. Baker, there was an accident in front of the school yesterday afternoon, and everyone involved spoke of a girl matching your physical description."

"That's nice."

I didn't think either of the cops appreciated my response, but I couldn't help giving them a little attitude. Ever since my accident—with the cops and the doctors and the paparazzi all hounding me for information—I don't really respond well to any form of interrogation.

"We also have several eyewitnesses that identified you specifically."

"Well, I'm sorry to squash the lead, but it wasn't me."

The older of the two cops, the one who'd asked all the questions up to this point, huffed in annoyance, and the second guy took over. "You're not in trouble or anything, we're just hoping for a statement to shed some light on a few unanswered questions."

"Yes, we need answers!" Principal Huang interrupted, already on the cops' last nerves. "Mr. Warren clearly ran into my marquee, but the insurance is threatening not to pay because they say the damage doesn't match the description of what happened. Can you believe that!"

Actually, I could believe that. I'm sure the insurance company was very curious about the nice little dent I'd put in his precious sign. I didn't exactly feel bad about damaging the stupid thing. After all, *it* totally attacked *me*.

"And of course we want to make sure that you're okay," the younger cop added, still trying to butter me up.

Unfortunately for him, I hate kiss-ups almost as much as I hate cops. I glanced from him back to the first cop, who was still frowning at me, and smirked. "Good cop, bad cop, huh? I thought that only happened in the movies."

I'm not always a lot of trouble, but I was really nervous, and I was afraid that if they saw that at all, they might figure out I really was involved. I figured being a rebellious teenager would keep them frustrated enough not to see how scared I was.

It seemed to be working with Principal Huang. "This school doesn't have thousands of dollars to replace that marquee," he said, "so if you know something about it, you have to tell us."

"Sorry, Mr. Huang. Don't know what to tell you. Maybe you should think about a wooden one next time."

Mr. Bad Cop was starting to lose his patience. "Ms. Baker," he said, nearly yelling now, "if you're not willing to cooperate, I'm afraid we'll have to arrest you and continue this discussion at the station."

"Arrest me?" I repeated incredulously. Unfortunately, I said that a little loudly, and we instantly started to gather a crowd. I didn't mean to lose my temper, but they were going on some pretty thin evidence, and trying to strong-arm a kid in front of her classmates was pretty low. "Arrest me for what?"

"You are aware that it's against the law to walk away from the scene of an accident, right?"

"Oh, I'm so sorry. I didn't realize that seeing an accident from across a parking lot makes me a material witness."

"Young lady, several of your classmates said they saw you get hit by the sign that fell."

"Well, that would be kind of impossible, considering I hadn't even reached the parking lot when it happened. Ask Mr. Edwards—I was late getting out of class yesterday."

Both men glanced to my teacher, and he shrugged. "It's true. She stayed almost ten minutes after the bell yesterday."

The cops frowned, and when the grumpy one began scribbling on his notepad, Mr. Edwards broke the silence again, addressing the group of students watching us. "And speaking of the bell, everyone get to your classes before I start handing out detention."

The students started to scatter, but Mr. Edwards didn't follow his own advice. As he watched on curiously, the younger cop—Mr. Good Cop—took me by surprise when he asked me if I would take off my sunglasses. I knew exactly where he was going with this, and I wasn't worried about that in the least, so I took off the glasses without hesitation and showed him my eyes. "Maybe she's telling the truth, Vic," he said to his partner. "Both eyes are the same color, and not green or yellow. They're brown."

I hadn't realized that Ryan was also still watching my interrogation until he walked up next to the cop with wide eyes. When I saw him, my heart jumped into overdrive. "Green and yellow?" Ryan said, gazing at me with wonder.

The officer mistook the astonishment in Ryan's voice for confusion. "All three of the landscapers present at the accident described the girl involved as having had one green eye and one yellow," he explained. "They were quite certain."

Ryan looked at me again, and I could see it in his eyes. He knew. And he knew that I knew he knew. We stared each other down—or rather, he stared me down while I panicked like a deer caught in his headlights—until the cop questioned the two of us.

Ryan was much better at shaking it off than I was. He flashed the cop that boyish smile of his and covered for me like a pro. "I was with Jamie yesterday after class. We had just walked out the front door when the accident happened. I'd be happy to give you a statement too, but I doubt it'd be much help. We couldn't really see anything."

"So you were with her at the time of the accident?"

"Yes, sir."

"Lying to the cops is a criminal act, young man," Mr. Bad Cop interrupted. "You're not just covering for this young lady, are you?"

Ryan gave me another knowing glance. "No, sir. I swear she was with me the entire time."

The older cop looked Ryan up and down skeptically and sighed as he began scribbling again. "Your name?"

"That would be Ryan Miller," Principal Huang said, stealing the words out of Ryan's mouth.

"And I suppose you're her boyfriend or something?" the cop asked.

"Um, no sir, we're just doing a project together. She was interviewing me before football practice for her paper."

The grumpy cop seemed disappointed by that answer, and sadly, he wasn't the only one. It reminded me of blowing Ryan off the day before. I felt bad that Ryan had to help me like this after I'd told him to stay out of my life, but I was grateful he did, even if I knew my problem with him was only going to be worse now.

"Was anyone else with you?"

"Yeah, Mike Driscoll and Justin Reader talked to us right after it happened. They can tell you it wasn't Jamie. That's what they've been telling the whole school all day. It had to be just somebody that looked like Jamie."

"All right," the cop said with one last dramatic sigh, "but if these boys' stories don't match up, we'll be in touch, Ms. Baker."

"Can't wait."

Once the cops walked away, taking a highly annoyed Principal Huang with them, I made a mad dash for the classroom. I was safely inside before Ryan could catch me, but I knew he wasn't going to drop the issue this time. I doubt Ryan heard a single word that anyone said in class that day either, because he stared at me from the time we took our seats to the time the bell rang.

I was out the door as quickly as possible, but Ryan actually followed me all the way home. By the time we got out of our cars, I'd convinced myself that I was mad at him. "Don't you have a practice to be at?"

"Yup," Ryan replied with every bit the amount of anger I had just shown. "Coach is gonna ride me pretty hard for missing it too, but I'm not going anywhere until you tell me what is going on!"

I didn't think playing dumb would work, but I had to give it a try. "What? I lost one of my blue contacts and haven't had a chance to get more, so I wore my brown ones. Why do you think I've been wearing your sunglasses all day?" I handed Ryan the glasses. "Here, you can have them back now, thanks."

Ryan took his glasses and I started to walk away again, but he pulled me back. "You were in that accident!"

"Don't be stupid, that's impossible."

"And yet half the school saw you, and the cops are looking for a girl with one green eye and one yellow eye."

I didn't know what to say. I stood there, slowly letting my emotions spin out of control, and Ryan finally cracked. "You have to explain it to me, Jamie. I'm going out of my mind right now! I just lied to the cops for you, and I don't even understand what I lied about. You owe me!"

He looked absolutely desperate, and he basically knew something weird was up anyway. We were past the point of pretending, so I figured at this point it was probably better just to tell him everything rather than let him try to figure it out on his own. I glanced back at my house and listened for my mother. When I heard her inside, doing what sounded like aerobics, I figured she hadn't heard us, and I looked back at Ryan.

"Please?" he begged.

"Fine," I said as I pushed him back toward his car, "but not here."

And once again I gave in to Ryan Miller.

I used to wish on stars that one day I'd be able to escape the tiny hick town I grew up in. But I guess I wasn't specific enough, because Sacramento suburbia? Big step down. Driving through its dull brown neighborhoods is a lot like passing through all those cornfields I used to hate so much in Illinois, only not so glamorous.

Yup, there's nothing like an endless row of tract homes rolling past your window to make a long stretch of awkward silence seem even longer. When we finally reached the end of my neighborhood Ryan broke the quiet with a measly "Where to?"

The sound of his voice startled me so badly that I accidentally let out a burst of energy that not only blitzed the radio and the lights on his dashboard, but actually revved the engine of the truck. Ryan tapped the gauges on the dash with a frown and started to say something, but I screamed before he could get any words out.

"Stop the car!"

Ryan looked at me, a little stunned, but pulled the truck to a stop. I immediately jumped out before I fried the car and him along with it. As I started walking away I felt electricity pulsing through my body, and I was too upset to stop it.

"Stop!" I screamed when Ryan came running after me. "Don't touch me!"

He stopped only for a second because I'd startled him, but then he slowly reached out for me.

"I mean it, Ryan! Don't come any closer!" I backed away from him again. "I don't want to hurt you!"

Ryan didn't just look confused; he looked scared. Sadly, he was right to be afraid. I was dangerous. "What do you mean, 'hurt' me?"

"I can't control it!"

"Control what?"

The more upset Ryan got, the more frantic I became. I clenched my hands into tight fists when I felt them start to heat up, and suddenly the streetlight I was standing under lit up and exploded.

After Ryan ducked the shower of glass, I watched him make the connection between his truck, the broken lamp, and me. The way his mouth dropped open made me feel sick. It was probably one of the most awful moments of my life, and I wanted to run. After all, what did it matter at this point if I just disappeared? Ryan clearly knew I was different.

But for some reason, I couldn't make myself move. I couldn't think straight. I couldn't even breathe. In fact, Ryan was the first to come to his senses. He held his hands out and slowly stepped back. "Okay, I'm backing up now." His voice was low and forceful but very soothing, and the distance he put between us helped a great deal. "Take a deep breath," he instructed, "and let's try to stay calm."

Ryan inhaled deeply as if he was coaching himself to breathe and not actually talking to me at all, but I obeyed his orders anyway. I could feel my muscles start to relax when I focused on the sound of his breathing.

As I calmed down, the low hum of the streetlamp faded, and eventually I was able to take that deep breath I desperately needed. It felt good to breathe. It was also easier to settle down now that I could see that Ryan wasn't panicking or anything. I closed my eyes and took several more deep breaths.

"Are you ready to talk to me?" Ryan asked when he was sure that speaking wouldn't set me off again.

I was as ready as I would ever be, so I shrugged my defeat. I headed back to his truck in a bit of a daze, but when I started to climb back into the passenger seat I realized that Ryan was still standing a good ten feet away. He swallowed uneasily, like he didn't want to have to ask me his next question but had no choice.

"Is it safe?"

I was too out of it at the time to get upset about the fact that he was scared of me, so I simply nodded. He got in the truck very slowly, and I noticed him hesitate before he started the car.

I'm not sure why I felt the need to apologize, but I whispered a weak "I'm sorry," to which he didn't respond. Instead, he glanced up at the fried lamppost once more, and then drove us back to his house without saying another word.

"It's just us," he eventually promised when I hesitated to follow him inside.

He couldn't take his eyes off me as I walked in, but I couldn't meet his gaze. I looked everywhere but his face because I didn't want to see the expression on it. I didn't want to see him watching me like he was afraid of me, or like he thought I was some kind of freak that belonged in a cage. A lot of people look at me that way, but I'd gotten used to Ryan looking at me like I'm a person. He usually watches me as if I'm someone he likes, or someone he really cares about. To see all of that taken away because he'd learned the truth would hurt too much.

I stood in the entryway, looking around, surprised by the earthy decor of the house. Even though the place had such a peaceful feeling to it, I somehow felt like I was marching to my death when I heard the door shut behind me. The rope was around my neck, and the crowd was just waiting for the floor to drop from beneath my feet. I realize that's kind of a morbid analogy, but having to tell Ryan the truth about me really felt like the end of life as I knew it.

I watched the scene play out in my mind, until I finally had the guts to look at Ryan. Instead of asking me if I had any last words, he quietly asked, "Does stuff like that happen to you all the time?"

Yeah, the situation sucked for me, but Ryan's voice sounded so weak that I realized I was not the only one struggling at the moment. Ryan was freaked out. He was trying his very best to hide it from me, but that classic, cocky Ryan smile was nowhere to be found.

I thought that seeing him afraid would hurt somehow, but it actually made him seem vulnerable, like me. It felt good to not be the only weak one, and I was able to answer his question without getting distraught again. "Only when I get upset."

"So what happened to my truck? And the other night at your house, when the lights went out?" Ryan swallowed hard, like he didn't want to believe what he was thinking, but somehow knew it was true. "That was you?"

I shrugged. "People are right to call me a freak."

Ryan flinched when I used the word "freak," giving me a tiny glimmer of hope that he didn't agree. But he didn't turn into my mother and tell me I'm not one, he just stared at me for a second and then asked, "You're not gonna, like, blow up my house, are you?" He was honestly a little concerned, and I couldn't blame him for worrying.

"The whole house?" I shook my head and failed at an attempt to smile. "No. But I can't promise I won't fry the circuit breaker if I get too upset."

"So it only happens when you're angry?"

"Angry, nervous, scared, excited... It's there all the time. It's just harder to control when I get emotional."

There was silence again, and I was terrified as I watched him stare at me. He wasn't meaning to be rude, he was just trying to absorb everything I was saying. When he finally snapped out of his trance he spoke in a slightly more relaxed tone. "Let's try to keep calm then, huh?"

The corner of his mouth twitched like he was trying really hard to smile, even though he was totally overwhelmed. It wasn't much, but it was enough to keep the electrical storms at bay for the time being. I nodded but could manage only a weak "I'll try."

"Here." Ryan dropped his backpack to the floor. "I've got something that might help."

I followed him into the kitchen and watched, intrigued, as he put a teakettle on the stove to boil. I didn't say anything as he pulled some homemade concoction of leaves from the cupboard, but when he set out two pretty little teacups on tiny saucers, I finally cracked a smile.

"You should have warned me we were having a tea party," I teased. "I would have brought my Barbies."

I was really surprised when the always-confident Ryan Miller turned a deep shade of red, but he was so cute that I could no longer give him a hard time. "My parents are on this all-natural kick lately," he explained nervously. "Like herbal remedies and stuff. This one is supposed to be stress relieving."

"Does it really work?"

"I hope so," Ryan said with a laugh as he poured steaming water over the dried leaves. "My mom uses those eco-friendly lightbulbs. They're expensive, and I'll have to work for a month in order to pay her back if you blow them all up."

I gave him a strange look but finally laughed, and for a second we were just two normal kids enjoying each other's company, just like the other night when he tried on my crown. I couldn't believe we were joking about my powers, but it was such a relief to have the tension broken. I think for him as much as me because once we finally laughed, he became that relaxed, happy Ryan that I've secretly come to crave.

As I stood there watching Mr. Star Quarterback happily slurping tea from a tiny cup with flowers on it, as if drinking tea was something he did all the time, I finally realized that, aside from the football thing, I really knew nothing about him. I was suddenly curious to know every detail.

"So your parents are hippies?"

I loved the way he cringed. I know it's probably mean to take pleasure in making Ryan blush, but I couldn't help smiling at his obvious embarrassment. It was nice to have the upper hand on him for once.

"Not exactly hippies. They're more like super new age health nuts. My mom's a yoga instructor, and my stepdad is a motivational speaker. So instead of tree hugger meetings and protest rallies, it's self-help seminars and meditation."

"And relaxing herbal remedies," I teased, holding up my teacup.

"So the tea's working?" Ryan's voice sounded very hopeful. "You're feeling better?"

"Maybe a little."

"Enough to tell me what's going on without blowing me up?"

My heart jumped in my chest at his request, but he already knew I was different and was willing to joke about it, so I don't know why it was so hard for me to explain it. Maybe because I've never said it out loud to anyone other than my parents before. Plus, he didn't know the full extent of what we were talking about either.

"I'm working up to it," I finally replied, sipping the last of my tea.

Ryan stared me down for a moment, debating whether or not to let my answer slide, then shrugged and led me through his house to the backyard. At first I thought he figured I would do less damage if I were outdoors, but when we walked into his backyard it was like stepping into a whole different world.

I've never seen a yard more beautiful. There were so many flowers and trees, and even a koi pond with a nice little fountain in the middle. I was so surprised by my surroundings that I just stood there gawking until Ryan grabbed my hand and led me through the garden to a tiny gazebo.

"Sorry there's not really a place to sit," he said as I took a seat on a thin mat. "This is where my mom does her yoga."

"I can see why. It's beautiful out here."

"My stepdad calls it a Zen garden. I wasn't kidding about the meditation thing."

I was a little amazed when Ryan lit some incense—again, as if he did that kind of thing often. "Your stepdad sounds like an interesting guy."

I knew I was in trouble when Ryan's confidence returned, but I wasn't sure yet why.

"Yeah, he is kind of different," he said, plopping down right next to me. "But then, I always seem to like people who are a little out of the ordinary."

So much for having the upper hand. Ryan actually winked at me, and just like that, he was back on top. He not only managed to bring the conversation back to my powers, he was able to hit on me while doing it. The worst part about it was, the way he said it sounded so sweet that it made me blush!

What was it with him? If I wasn't careful, I'd be kissing him within five minutes, and he'd be dead in six. I wasn't ever going to go through the whole killing someone thing again, so I shook myself from his spell and whispered, "I shouldn't be here."

I tried to get up to leave, but Ryan immediately pulled me back down. "Okay, okay. I'm sorry, all right? No more flirting. I promise. Please don't leave."

Ryan gave me this look that was so sad and desperate…and cute. How anyone could ever resist such a pout is beyond me. No, really, I can't say no to the guy.

"I'm not a bad guy, you know," he said when I made myself comfortable again. "You don't have to be afraid of me."

I knew I would never get out of there without explaining everything to him. I also knew it was time to quit stalling, but I had no idea where to start. I let go a deep sigh and looked down at my feet, because there's no way I'd be able to get through it while staring into his eyes.

"I have to be afraid of everyone," I whispered. "Even myself."

I managed to glance up briefly, and I could see that Ryan wanted to argue, but he didn't dare interrupt me now that I was finally talking. "It's not safe for people to know about me. And until I figure out how to control it all the time, it's not even safe for people to be around me. You saw it yourself. It's dangerous."

"What exactly is...*it?*"

"I don't really know for sure. I emit some kind of weird energy. And as you've noticed, sometimes I have a hard time holding it in."

"So you're blowing stuff up with some kind of psychic mind powers?"

He was one hundred percent serious. And I know I am the last person who should be talking, but psychic mind powers? Come on, it was funny. "No, it doesn't work like that," I said, managing one tiny laugh. "It's like electricity."

"Electricity?"

So far so good. Ryan didn't seem freaked out at all anymore. If anything he looked really intrigued, so I took a chance and held my hand above his head. "Yeah." I smiled again when all of his hair began to stand up. "Electricity."

When I pulled my hand away Ryan reached up to feel the static in his hair. He played with it for a minute before smoothing it back down, and then looked at me in complete awe. "That's kind of cool," he whispered.

His admiration was so intense that it made me forget about everything around me. My heart started to flutter, and I wanted him to kiss me so badly it hurt. Of course, when he leaned toward me like he might actually do that, I clammed up again and said whatever I could that would keep me from throwing myself at him.

"When I lose control, some kind of power surge explodes from me, and anything electrical in my vicinity gets cooked. That's when it gets scary."

Ryan leaned back a little, disappointed, when it was clear that the moment was gone. "Makes sense," he said. "But why are you so afraid of hurting me? It's not like I run on batteries."

"You're kidding, right?" Ryan just gave me a blank look. "Yeah, I can't zap you from across the room like the lights, but that doesn't mean I can't hurt you if you touch me when I'm all charged up. Didn't you pay any attention in science class?"

"I may have fallen asleep once or twice." Ryan pouted as if my comment had offended him, but I knew better, and he grinned right on cue. "Hey, I can't be good-looking *and* a genius. Wouldn't want all the girls in school to fight over me or anything."

"Oh please! They all do that already, and you know you love it."

"Okay, fine, maybe I do." Ryan chuckled. But then his face became completely serious. "But it's really frustrating that the one girl in school who doesn't need to fight for me won't even get in the ring."

Okay, he did *not* just make me blush with a lame sports metaphor. What is wrong with me?

Sweet-talking jerk.

"Ryan." I sighed. "You only say that because I'm the first girl who's ever said no."

"I know you think that." Ryan shook his head forcefully. "But it's just not true."

"You mean you've actually been rejected before?" I didn't hold back any of my doubt.

"Well, no," Ryan admitted, that cocky grin creeping into the corners of his mouth. "But you know that's not what I meant."

"Either way it's never going to happen, so you need to stop trying. Please!"

"But why? I already know about you now, so what's stopping you?"

"Did you ever consider the possibility that I'm not interested? That maybe I just don't like you that way?"

Ryan looked at me like I'd just said the impossible. "What's not to like?"

I gave him a less than enthusiastic look, but he never once considered backing down. "How about I make you a deal," he said, and I had to admit, this had me curious. "I'll take you out this weekend on a proper date, anywhere you want. But you have to go with an open mind and give me an honest shot. If I can't make you fall madly in love with me by the end of the night, I'll never ask you out again."

And there he went again, breaking me down. Like he would need till the end of the night? He didn't even need till the end of this conversation. I could feel my head starting to bob up and down, accepting the offer without my approval. "No!" I shouted, trying to stay strong. "We are never going to go out on a date. We can't! Remember that part about me being dangerous?"

"So you fry small electronics, big deal. I just won't stand next to anything that can explode."

"You still conduct electricity!" I didn't mean to yell, but I was just so desperate to make him see how serious I was. "All it would take is one touch. If you reach out to me when I'm really upset, or take me by surprise and startle me, I could roast you. Trust me, accidents happen, and if one ever did, I wouldn't even be able to stop myself. I'd freak out, and it would only kill you quicker. I'm sorry, Ryan, but I just can't risk it."

That seemed to do the trick. Ryan released a huge frustrated sigh. "Well, if we can't ever be friends or anything else, then what are you doing here? Why did you come with me? Why are you telling me all this?"

"I didn't want to, but I didn't have a choice." The confusion in his eyes made me want to cry. I lowered my voice so that he wouldn't notice how unsteady it was. "You knew I was in that accident. I was afraid that if I didn't come, you'd get mad and tell everyone about me."

"Well, that's one thing you don't have to worry about. I'm not going to tell anyone. I promise."

I was surprised by how hurt he looked. Again! It seems like every time I talk to him I hurt his feelings in one way or another. I felt really bad about that, but I also felt just as deflated as he did at the moment. I barely managed an audible "Thanks."

He nodded, I shrugged, and then we just sat there.

I looked at the garden around me again, and it really is true what they say about finding tranquility in beautiful places. The garden was so beautiful, and I had so much on my mind, that it was hard not to just let my thoughts run away with me. I don't know how long Ryan let me sit there and think, but it felt like it had been an eternity when he finally spoke.

"Jamie?" I pulled my eyes up to meet his. "How exactly were you in that accident? It doesn't make any sense. Electricity can't put you in two places at once. And how come you didn't get hurt? Mike said that marquee landed on you."

I knew this was coming. In fact, I was surprised it took him so long to ask. But even though Ryan already knew I was different, and miraculously seemed to be okay with it, I was still scared of having to tell him *everything*.

"*Hurt* is a relative term."

I felt the butterflies return to my stomach, so I took a deep breath before I shyly pulled my shirtsleeve as far off my shoulder as it would go, giving Ryan more than enough of a view of the bruises that covered it. "I should probably be dead right now, so I guess in a sense I didn't get hurt, but I jammed my shoulder pretty good, and my head still feels like it's being smashed against pavement repeatedly."

Ryan's mouth was gaping open at this point. He couldn't seem to tear his eyes from my black-and-blue shoulder, so I kept talking in order to avoid any more awkward silence.

"Whatever this power inside me is, it makes me different. I wasn't in two places at once. I just got from one to the other very fast."

"You ran?"

I nodded, and he got quiet again. Then, though he was already stunned, something else occurred to him, something that had nothing to do with how fast I could move. "You ran underneath a giant falling sign?" he gasped.

I nodded again.

"Why?"

This time I shrugged. I honestly didn't know why I did it. At the time I didn't even think, I just reacted. "The guy on the lawn mower was about to be toast. I guess I couldn't watch him die. I would have been standing safely back at your side by the time the thing hit the ground if that guy hadn't weighed more than Shamu."

"So you're like Superman?"

I smiled, but I don't think Ryan was trying to be funny. I think he was still trying to grasp the concept. I can't blame him. It is a lot to absorb, and I gotta tell ya, he handled it a lot better than I did. When I figured it out, I had a total breakdown that lasted for weeks. I'm glad Ryan is a lot more easygoing than me.

"I'm pretty sure Superman doesn't bruise," I joked, wanting to keep the situation light, "and he probably wouldn't have biffed it, but, yeah, I guess that's one way of looking at it."

Ryan was quiet for a minute, but he eventually looked at me with those big curious eyes. "How did this happen to you?"

That was the dreaded question of the hour. I didn't want to have to explain this part. I didn't even want to have to think about it, but I found myself telling the story anyway. "It was my accident."

My voice turned to a whisper, and then I fell into the story as if I were reliving the nightmare all over again. "It was the night of the pageant. I was so tired of all the congratulations, so Derek and I went for a drive someplace quiet. The car was parked on the side of the road, and this big tanker truck full of hazardous waste came barreling up the highway. The driver hit his brakes when he saw us, but he was moving too fast. The truck jackknifed and slid right off the road.

"The side of the tank slammed into my car and pushed it nearly fifty feet, into an electrical tower. It was a nice night so we had the top down, and when everything smashed together the car ripped a hole in the side of the truck. This smelly green liquid started spraying all over the place. It burned, but I was pretty banged up and I couldn't really move. The last thing I remember was the electrical tower falling on top of the car, frying everything, and the truck exploding."

Ryan's gasp brought me back to the present, but he really startled me when he picked up my hand and squeezed it. I gave him a tiny shock, but he refused to let that stop him. I let him hold my hand for only a second before pulling away to wipe away the tears that were escaping down my face.

Ryan gave me a moment to pull myself together and then asked the only logical question. "How did you survive?"

Unfortunately, there was no logical answer. I shrugged my shoulders and pulled my knees tightly against my chest. "I should be dead," I croaked. "Just like the truck driver. Just like Derek."

Saying Derek's name opened a floodgate for my tears, and I buried my face in my knees as I cried. Within seconds I felt Ryan's arms around me. Being pulled tightly against him was probably the best feeling in the whole world, so I sank heavily into his embrace, forgetting all about the possible consequences of such an action.

Right then I wasn't a freak. I wasn't an ice queen. I didn't have powers. What I had was a friend comforting me when I needed it most. Right then I was just a normal girl, and Ryan was the superhero.

I buried my face deep in his chest and wrapped my arms around him. He squeezed me tighter in return, and my tears came more forcefully, but the reason for their being there had now changed. You have no idea what a good feeling normal is until it's taken away.

I was quite prepared to stay right where I was forever, but it didn't exactly work out like that. My bliss was interrupted by a faint noise. "Jamie?" It sounded like Ryan, but the voice was unsteady. "Jamie?" he said again, a little louder.

I opened my eyes to see Ryan's arms trembling around me. He was covered in goose bumps and every hair he had was sticking straight out from his body. I would have shrieked, but I was so terrified that my voice failed me. I scrambled a safe distance from him, my nerves completely shot, and energy began to pulse through my entire body again. "Ryan!" I choked as soon as my throat allowed.

Ryan looked disoriented the same way he had after I kissed him. "It's okay, Jamie... I'm fine... I promise..." He stumbled over his words as he spoke them. "Whatever you did, it didn't hurt me. I'm just a little...um...overwhelmed? I think I need a minute."

I felt sick to my stomach, thinking about what could have just happened. I knew better, and I let it go too far. But more than that, I was horrified that I had done something to him. He said "overwhelmed," but judging from the way he looked, he meant completely freaked out. "I am so sorry!" I pleaded while the tears returned with full force.

"It's okay," he promised again.

But it wasn't okay. It was far from it. I'd done it. I'd officially scared him. And I just couldn't face him any longer. "I should go" was the last thing I said before I disappeared from his sight.

Every time I closed my eyes that night, Ryan was there, holding me so tenderly that I felt as though I'd died and gone to heaven. Then I would pull away, and instead of his carefree smile I would see nothing but charred black flesh. That's when he would crumple into a pile of ashes around me.

I used to have nightmares all the time, right after my accident. But I hadn't had one in so long now that my parents actually came to check on me when I woke up screaming this time. I told them to forget about it and go back to bed, but sleep was a luxury I couldn't give myself. Not after that.

As if my nightmare weren't enough to make me feel sick, Ryan was not at school the next day. Aside from my obvious worry about the timing of his absence, I was filled with disappointment. It had been weeks since I hadn't come into the cafeteria and met his curious eyes. I couldn't believe how accustomed I was to being greeted by his smile, and even worse, how much I needed it to get through the rest of my day. I wanted to kick myself for feeling so addicted to his presence, but oddly enough, I wasn't the only one suffering from his sick day.

Only Ryan Miller could have such an effect on an entire school. He was the sunshine in this crappy prison, and without him a dark, dreary force loomed over the entire cafeteria. Or at least the popular kids' table.

On the bright side, it was nice to know that I wasn't the only one he had cast under his spell. Mike would grumble something to Justin every time he looked at the empty seat next to him—which nobody dared fill in Ryan's absence—and Paige sat across from them, sulking rather pitifully. The strangest difference, however, was the empty seat next to Paige. Of course Tamika was sitting on her right, hanging on her every word as usual, but the seat on her left, Becky's seat, was as empty as Ryan's.

"He'd better be dying," Mike was grumbling when I finally decided to see if they knew anything more than I did. "Coach was pissed when he ditched practice yesterday."

"Is that why you guys had to run so many laps yesterday?" Tamika asked. The scowl on Mike's face was an obvious yes.

"He must be really sick," Paige said. "Maybe we should go over to his house after school and check on him."

As much as I hate to agree with Paige on anything, I'd also thought about running over to Ryan's house between classes. I just wanted to see if he was there and make sure he was okay, but I chickened out. If I didn't know why he wasn't at school, I could pretend that his parents just dragged him to some Buddha convention or something, instead of the more likely answer—that he was hanging out at home because he was too scared of me to come to school. If that were the case, it wouldn't help any if he caught me super-stalking him.

"I don't know, Paige," Tamika argued. "If Becky's gone too, maybe it's contagious. We have our first cheer competition next weekend. We can't all get sick."

"Becky's not sick." Paige had so much edge in her voice it startled everyone present, myself included. "She sat next to me in calculus this morning. I don't know why she bothered, though. She barely even said hi."

"Then where is she?"

"Avoiding us, obviously. She has been all week."

"You know?" Tamika looked as if she were just now realizing the truth in Paige's statement. "She *has* been acting really weird ever since the dance." She giggled flirtatiously at Mike and added, "What'd you do to her?"

"I didn't do anything." I was surprised by the defensiveness in Mike's voice. "I don't know what her problem is. We had a great time at the dance."

"And an even better time after the dance, from what I hear." Justin laughed.

"What? So, Mike, are you two, like, a thing now?" Paige asked.

Paige seemed pretty excited by the idea of Mike and Becky. She was obviously hoping she didn't have to worry about Becky as competition for Ryan anymore since everyone knows that "Ryan and Becky" is only a matter of time, but Mike burst her bubble pretty quickly. "She wishes," he said.

"Ugh, so it *was* you. Thanks a lot."

"What was me?"

"You're the reason Becky's been pouting all week. She's mad that you turned her down."

"What can I say? I asked her to go to the dance with me, not marry me. I can't be tied down like that. There are way too many beautiful ladies at this school."

Mike winked at Tamika as he bumped his fist against Justin's. Tamika's back was to me, so I couldn't be sure, but judging from her silence, I'm sure she swooned. I, on the other hand, threw up in my mouth a little. The guy makes me sick. I can't believe I used to think he and Ryan were on the same level.

I couldn't listen to any more, so I left the cafeteria and spent the rest of my day trying to block out everyone. Usually the best way to do that is to get lost in my own thoughts, which wasn't hard today. With Ryan not in school I was crazy with worry. Worried that I'd scared him so much he transferred schools, or that whatever I'd done to him somehow made him sick enough that he was in a hospital somewhere. Dying. Right now. Because of me.

As I walked to English my worry expanded beyond just Ryan's well-being. I started to fear that maybe he'd told his parents. That maybe they'd gone to the police. And maybe, just maybe, the government was planning a secret operation right now to take me away to Area 51 or some secret place like that.

My paranoia was disrupted when I reached the classroom and Becky was already there, with her head down on her desk. For the first time since I came to this school, I felt a hint of sympathy for her. What Mike did to her was pretty lousy. I couldn't believe I was thinking this, but when it was just the two of us in the room, I considered talking to her. I knew I shouldn't get myself involved in the mess—I already had more than enough trouble on my hands with Ryan, and I didn't need anyone else curious about me—but for reasons I simply can't explain, when she felt me staring and looked up, I actually smiled at her and said, "Hi."

Becky looked confused for a second, but she quickly turned her surprise into a brutal glare. The look stung. Not that she had any reason to be friendly to me or trust me, but it was the first time I'd made any attempt at all to reach out to someone since my accident. I was shocked that I'd done it, but I was way more surprised that her reaction to me hurt.

"There you are! I've been looking all over for you."

Paige's interruption startled us both. Paige glanced back and forth between the two of us and started to question what was going on, but then decided Becky was more important. "How come you didn't tell us what happened?"

she demanded with bland sympathy. "Mike told us about Friday night."

"What do you mean?" Becky gasped. "What did he tell you?"

"He's telling everyone that you guys hooked up after the dance, and you freaked out when he said he didn't want to have a girlfriend."

There was something eerily familiar about Becky's expressionless eyes, and the hollow tone in her voice, as she replied to Paige. "Mike's a liar."

"You mean you guys didn't do it?"

Even if Becky's silence hadn't given away the truth, the tears in her eyes would have. She put her head back down on her desk, and Paige put her hand on her shoulder. "You got played, Becky, but you can't let him beat you. Everybody in school knows what happened. You've got to suck it up and not let them see that he hurt you. Otherwise you're going to..." Paige glanced at me and lowered her voice. Not that it mattered. "Otherwise you're gonna end up like *her*."

Becky's eyes naturally drifted back to me, and for the first time in my life, I looked away, feeling scared and ashamed. Scared of what Becky thought of me and ashamed of what I'd let myself become. The feeling almost brought tears to my eyes, and I was horrified that I might actually cry in front of them, but luckily, students began drifting into class, breaking the tension.

When the bell rang, Paige finally sat down in her seat. "Why don't you and Tamika come over to my house after practice today, and we'll think up a great smear campaign for the jerk. You know, Scott Cole is single and completely gorgeous. If you go out with him, it will make Mike so jealous he'll be begging your forgiveness within a week."

"Can we please not talk about this anymore?" Becky snapped. "I'm not going out with Scott, and I'm definitely not going to forgive Mike! Look, it's nice of you and Tamika to want to help, but please just let me deal with this on my own. Okay?"

"Fine. Dig your own grave."

Paige was clearly insulted, and as much as I wanted to take pleasure in her misery, I couldn't. I was still stuck on the nasty look Becky had given me. I don't know why, but it rattled me inside and out. I didn't think it was possible anymore, but Becky Eastman had actually hurt my feelings. I tried not to think about it through the rest of class because I shouldn't have let her get to me, but I just couldn't stop. It wasn't until on the way home from school that I managed to think about Ryan instead of Becky, but that didn't make me feel any better.

"I HATE HIM!"

I slammed my bedroom door so hard that it blew through the doorjamb and straight into the wall across the hallway. Then of course I flung myself down on my bed as if the world was coming to an end. "I hate him! I hate him! I hate him!"

I heard the sound of debris crunching beneath my mother's feet as she crossed the now-doorless threshold into my room. "Jamie? What's wrong?"

"I hate him!"

"Hate who?"

"Why did he have to do that? I was doing just fine on my own! I was finally starting to forget all the things I was missing out on. Getting used to being a loner. Accepting my fate! Now, one little dirty look from Becky, and I'm spilling more water than Niagara Falls. I HATE HIM!"

"Sweetheart, you've got to get a grip on yourself. The neighbors don't know to trip their circuit breakers when you're upset, and I don't want to be the only house on the street with power tonight."

"I don't care about the neighbors anymore!" I screamed, ignoring my mother's warning. I knew she had a very valid point as much as I knew why the sound of her voice came from across the room, instead of right beside me. But I didn't want to be calm this time. "I'm seventeen years old—I'm *supposed* to get irrational! I want to be a normal, hormonal teenage girl! I want to be able to love OR HATE whoever I want, as *much* as I want!"

When I screamed, the entire house shook around me, forcing my mother and me both to freeze. She'd cut the power to the house the minute she heard the door slam—a useful trick we'd picked up over the last year—so I'm not sure how I was having an effect on the walls.

The power inside me was stronger than it ever had been. It was so terrifying that my rage vanished in an instant. "I should leave for a while, until it's safe. I'll be back by dinner." My mom just nodded her blood-drained face, and I took off before she could warn me to be careful.

Where was Ryan's Zen garden when I needed it? I was on top of Mount Rushmore, one of the most beautiful places America has to offer, and yet I didn't feel even a tenth of the serenity I'd felt in Ryan's backyard.

"That's because it wasn't the flowers that made you feel better, idiot!" I sighed in defeat. "But I can't help it!"

The talking out loud seemed to help. "I love every single thing about him. Even the things I hate. His confidence. His persistence. That stupid grin that's plastered on his face twenty-four, seven." I could feel the smile breaking out on my lips as I spoke. "I love his stupid witty comebacks, even if he is way better at them than me. I love his ridiculous nonchalant attitude, even if it always makes me want to scream."

I closed my eyes, and I could see Ryan's face so clearly that I could practically feel him there. My smile faded, and I didn't have the heart to say the last one out loud, but I couldn't not think it. *I love the way he held me, even though I'd just warned him that doing so was extremely bad for his health.*

I tried to push the memory from my mind, but one point kept resurfacing. He'd held me *after* he knew the truth. I'd scared him, sure, and rightfully so. But he didn't run away screaming. No, that was me.

After coming to the conclusion that there was simply no way for me to get over Ryan, I decided that if he could risk electrocution to try to make me feel better, then he deserved that same kind of courage from me. If he wanted a relationship, then he was going to get one. It was time to give in to Ryan Miller.

Well, not entirely. I still couldn't kiss him. After all, I couldn't turn my only friend into a pile of ashes. But I was sure that if I explained the necessity of a strictly platonic relationship, he would understand. Hopefully, he could be happy with the compromise.

Being able to let go of my fear and admit that I could be friends—just friends—with Ryan was the stress breaker I had been praying for. I felt so much better that I practically skipped all the way home, and then I burst through the door with a giant smile on my face.

My mom gasped when I appeared behind her in the kitchen and hugged her as tight as I could without breaking her in half. "Feeling better?" she asked, eyes sparkling with happy relief.

"Much!"

"I'm glad. That means at least one of you is in a good mood."

My mom nodded her head toward the living room, where my dad was absorbed in something on ESPN, and suddenly my great mood was right back to scared and grumpy. My mom seemed encouraging as I debated facing my father, but I couldn't help feeling like I was marching to my doom as I stole his attention from the game.

"Dad?"

"Jamielynn Baker, where on God's green earth have you been for the last four hours!"

He literally roared. Like a bear. And when he jumped out of his seat, I could see the veins in his neck popping. I knew he wouldn't exactly be thrilled about the condition of the upstairs hallway, but I hadn't expected him to fly off the handle like that. I mean it really wasn't my fault. Well, it was but not completely. It's not like I ripped the door from its hinges on purpose.

"Don't worry, Dad." I couldn't help but get defensive. "I wasn't at the library. Or on a computer or reading a book. I'm grounded, okay, I get it."

"Grounded or not, you can't just take off like that! Not without telling us where you're going."

Okay, I'll admit it. I was being a little facetious as I pulled my cell phone from my pocket and waved it at him. Sue me. "More bars in more places?" I spat. "That's why you got me the stupid thing, remember? Mount Rushmore has surprisingly good reception. Not that you bothered to call to see how I was doing. Forgive me if I was afraid I was going to blow up Mom."

I was aiming for guilt, but I was surprised when I received compassion. My dad sighed and pulled me into a grip that resembled a bear more than his yelling had. There's nothing better than one of my dad's bear hugs, except for maybe one of Ryan's hugs. I was putty in his arms, and I sighed deeply. "I'm really sorry about the door, Dad. I'll help you fix it. I swear I really didn't mean to—" I cut myself off when my dad chuckled. "You... not mad?"

My dad's embrace tightened. "Not at you, honey. You're my baby girl—how could I be? But wait till I get my hands on the boy who has you so upset you're throwing doors through my bathroom wall." He wasn't kidding.

"Oh no, Dad! It's okay. Ryan's actually a super nice guy. It's not even him I was really mad at. Okay, it was, but it wasn't his fault. See, there's this girl at school and—"

"So it *was* the Miller boy then?" His compassion was slowly turning to frustration. "Jamie, we talked about this."

"I know, but, Dad—"

"No buts. He knows too much. It's too dangerous. You have got to stop talking to him."

Ha! If he only knew. "Yeah but, Dad, I was thinking about that. Don't you think it might be better if I just explained things to him?"

My father's eyes bulged from their sockets, but I took a deep breath and continued with my theory. "I mean, he obviously knows something's up. He's not just going to let it go. He likes me, Dad, and I trust him. He could keep this secret." I hope...

"Absolutely not!"

So much for frustration. We were officially back to anger.

"I don't get it. You say you want me to make friends, and then you ban me from the only one I've got. I like Ryan, Dad. I like him a lot. I think he could handle it. Think how much easier it could be if I just told him the truth."

"No one can ever find out about you! No one! Don't you understand what would happen if people learned about the things you can do?"

"Yeah," I grumbled bitterly. My dad wasn't the only one who'd come full circle with the emotions. "I'd end up in some secret government lab somewhere. But aside from the possible needles, I don't see how I'd be any worse off than I already am. It's not like I don't basically live in a cage now anyway, with only my books to keep me company. And I don't even have those anymore!"

That was a low blow. Dad was hurt, I could tell. But he kept his composure. "I'm putting my foot down," he said in a voice so cold I figured out who I get my ice queen tendencies from. "You are not to talk to that boy ever again. No one is going to take my daughter away. Not now, not ever."

"What's it matter if I can't have a life either way?"

"Promise me, Jamie." He was pleading with me now. "Don't throw your life away over a boy. Make friends, go out, have a life. You know that's all I've ever wanted for you. Just promise me you won't ever tell anyone. You may not care, but I can't lose my baby girl."

My dad's veins were popping out again, but his eyes misted over with tears. They were nothing compared to the flood streaming down my mother's cheeks, but still, if he was going for guilt, it definitely worked. Too bad he was asking for a promise I couldn't make. A promise I'd already broken.

"Dad." I refused to cry, but I couldn't disguise the hurt in my voice. "I promise I will keep my secret safe."

That was the best I could do. And it was the truth. Ryan told me that he would never tell anyone about me, and I believed him. Ryan may know the truth, but my secret was still safe, and I wasn't about to do anything that could jeopardize that.

I had my usual front row seat on the Grand Canyon's edge, waiting for another spectacular sunset. I sighed when the sun hit the horizon, painting an array of vivid colors throughout the canyon's depths below me, and a brilliant orange and purple sky above. "It's almost perfect," I breathed, still taken aback by the earth's natural beauty even though I'd seen many desert sunsets before this one.

"Almost?" whispered a voice behind me.

My heart pounded in my chest as I turned to face my surprise company. My first instinct was to ask him how he got here, but I was immediately distracted by the perfect smile on his face and the clump of wildflowers he was holding out to me.

Ryan pressed the flowers into my hand and chuckled when I couldn't stop staring in disbelief. "You're going to miss the best part," he said, and then gently turned me back around to face the scenery.

His hands caused a burning sensation inside me as they slid around my waist and pulled me securely against his perfectly sculpted body. I couldn't believe how naturally I seemed to fit there. It was as if my body had been made specifically for the purpose of being close to his.

I shuddered from the chills that ran through me as he buried his face in my hair to inhale my scent. Then he pressed his lips softly against the side of my neck right behind my ear. "What would I have to do to make it absolutely perfect?"

Another round of shivers made me go completely weak in the knees, and I barely found enough breath to reply. "Nothing could make this more perfect now."

We were silent until the sun dipped completely from view, and then Ryan whirled me around so fast it made my head spin. Or maybe it had already been spinning. To be honest, I wasn't really sure of anything except how close Ryan's face was to mine.

"You do know it's against the law to pick wildflowers in a national park, don't you?" I mumbled nervously, gulping when his face began slowly sinking toward mine. Ryan didn't respond except to pull the corners of his mouth up into my favorite cocky little smirk.

I gasped when he threw his lips on mine so passionately. The feeling was so incredible that I was unable to back away from him like I knew I should. I waited for him to pull away. I waited for him to scream out in pain. I waited for that image of the black, crispy face twisted in agony. But none of that came. Instead his passion intensified. I forgot all about waiting for my nightmare, and my arms locked around his neck as if they planned on never letting him escape. It was the most perfect, passionate kiss of my entire life.

And then I woke up.

I knew there would be no more sleep that night. This dream had been every bit as real and intense as my nightmares. While it lasted, kissing Ryan was a much better way to spend my sleep than roasting him alive, but when the dream was over I couldn't decide which was worse.

It was after this dream, while I was waiting in bed for the sun to rise, that I finally mulled over my father's request—demand, really—to never speak to Ryan again. After thinking about it long and hard, I came to the conclusion that my father was probably right. Being friends with Ryan and sharing my secret with him was probably a huge mistake.

I also decided that I absolutely, positively did not care. This wasn't my father's secret to keep, it was mine, and I could decide who to trust with it. I knew I'd feel a little guilty for defying my dad's wishes, but it surely wouldn't kill me. I wasn't really doing anything wrong, and Ryan's friendship definitely wouldn't be the only secret I'd kept from my parents. Or the worst.

So, with that attitude, I got ready for school, feeling a little anticipation. I got out of bed a full hour early, taking extra care as I touched up my ever-annoying green roots and eyebrows. I even fussed over my outfit and makeup for once. I couldn't help being a little excited. Until this point, I'd only ever been stressed out over what to do about Ryan, but now, today, seeing him was something to look forward to.

I was still a little worried that I'd really freaked him out the other day, but I'd come up with so many different things I could say to him to help him through it. I was sure he'd have more questions, but now I was ready to answer them all. I was prepared for every possible thing he could say to me. The only thing I wasn't prepared for was him saying nothing at all. Which was exactly what he did all day long.

I'd come up the front steps, relieved to see that his truck was in the parking lot. I didn't think I could handle him being gone two days in a row. I saw him gathered with his usual posse in the quad as I headed toward my first-hour class. My heart fluttered a tiny bit when I saw him, and I waited for that big goofy grin. But it wasn't until Mike saw me and said, "For someone made of ice, Baker's looking particularly hot this morning," that Ryan's eyes flicked to mine for the briefest moment.

There was no smile, no wave. No internal struggle as he debated whether or not to approach me. He looked away as quickly as he'd looked up. They were all watching me—Mike, Justin, Scott, the entire varsity starting lineup—all of them except Ryan. Ryan grabbed the backpack at his feet and walked off in the opposite direction.

Mike was confused by the reaction, but I was downright startled. My eyes stung as my disappointment threatened to cause a breakdown, but then Mike looked at me again with a look of utter disgust, and it was easy to forget my disappointment and return the gesture.

A moment later, Mike went catching up to Ryan. I didn't want to hear what he possibly had to say, but I couldn't stop myself from listening. "Shake it off, buddy," Mike said to Ryan. "Everyone gets burned by the ice queen eventually. If I were you, I'd be more worried about Coach Pelton ripping your head off today."

Ryan was quiet for a moment, but when he started talking his voice sounded just as cheerful as ever. "Nah, Coach is fine. My mom talked to him yesterday. But if I were *you*, I'd be worried about Paige. She called and gave me an earful last night about you. What's up with that, anyway? I thought you were into Becky."

"Too much drama."

"You want to trade?" Ryan laughed. "You think Becky's drama? Try having Paige in love with you for five minutes."

When Ryan and Mike burst into happy laughter together I got so angry I had to skip first period in order to avoid a school blackout. I just didn't understand how everything could be back to normal. Pre-kiss normal. I had gone against every instinct I had, made a life-altering decision to tell him the world's craziest secret, and he was acting as if none of what we went through the other day had ever happened. I didn't understand it, but more than that, I was completely crushed.

I'd thought lunch was bad when Ryan wasn't there, but it was way worse now that he was back and was intentionally avoiding me. He nearly threw the entire Rocklin High universe out of whack when he didn't sit in his usual seat, but rather shoved between Paige and Becky, conveniently putting his back to me.

He threw his arms around Becky. Not quite the same way he did to me in his backyard, but it was still like rubbing salt in an open wound. He finally found out that I really am a freak and went straight to her. I should have known, I guess, but I had really believed that Ryan was different.

"Paige told me what happened," he said to Becky.

"Of course she did—she told everyone," Becky mumbled under her breath.

"Come on, Beck. We all know Mike's destined for bachelorhood," Ryan continued.

"Amen, brother." Mike laughed.

"Not helping, dude," Ryan said, and then turned back to Becky. "If he says he's sorry, you think you could forgive and forget?"

I was almost glad I couldn't see the look on Becky's face, because I bet it was a lot like the one she gave me the other day.

"Want me to punch him?" Ryan asked, rolling off her glare just as easily as he always did mine. "Avenge your honor and all that?"

"You can try," Mike said, "but you know I'd whoop you."

"Would not."

"Would too."

"So would not."

"Everyone knows a quarterback can't take a hit."

"Bring it on." Ryan laughed.

"Oh, it's on," Mike said with equal enthusiasm. "Today during practice. I owe you anyway for all those laps Coach made us run when you ditched."

"There you go," Ryan said, giving Becky another hug. "I'm going to smear Mike into the ground for you at practice. Then you'll have to feel better. You know, you should even come out with us on Friday after the game. We could get a group together and all go bowling or something."

I waited for the swooning that usually occurred when Ryan unleashed his magic on someone, but no such response followed. "Save the knight in shining armor crap for Jamie," Becky snapped, shrugging Ryan's arm off her. "I'm not buying it."

My eyes snapped immediately back to the food in front of me, but I don't think anyone looked my direction. They were all too busy watching Becky leave the room. "Just let her go," I heard Paige grumble.

A few minutes later I felt a pair of eyes on me. The minute I looked up Ryan turned back around, but not before Paige noticed the brief interaction. "What exactly is going on with you and Jamie anyway?" she hissed.

"Nothing," Ryan said. "Same as Jamie and everyone else in this school."

"Trust me, dude. It really is better that way," Mike interrupted.

"She said you were with her during the homecoming dance," Paige continued to accuse.

"You talked to her?" After the way Ryan had just brushed me off so casually, I didn't understand the concern in his voice at all, but it was definitely there.

"We had an unfortunate run-in with her at the mall," Tamika explained. "She was way harsh to Paige, for no reason. There is something really weird about that girl, Ryan. Seriously, I don't know why you bother. You can't help her. She's a total freak."

"I'm not trying to help anyone. Jamie and I aren't dating. We're not even friends. We had a paper to do. It was the only time she had free. That's it. My paper's done now."

"Why'd you kiss her in the first place?"

"It was nothing. Mike bet me I couldn't get her to do it. I knew he was wrong."

It was *nothing*? He *knew* Mike was wrong? What a jerk!

"And I'll never doubt your skills again, play-uh," Mike said solemnly.

The lights in the cafeteria flickered. Just once. Ryan's back stiffened, and that was my cue to leave the cafeteria.

English went by in much the same fashion. I had a feeling every now and then that Ryan was looking at me, but I didn't dare find out. I was having a hard enough time controlling myself as it was. If I looked at him even once, they'd be calling the fire department to put out the flames when I spontaneously combusted in my chair.

I was out of there as soon as the bell rang and ended up doing my homework at Lake Tahoe for a few hours before going home. (I had to find a new spot since now the Grand Canyon was tainted for me.)

The weekend was endless, and by Monday I'd come to the conclusion that even though Ryan had clearly kept his promise not to tell anyone about me—easy enough when I didn't really exist, right?—he was still the world's biggest jerk, and I was going to hate him for all eternity.

On the bright side, I didn't have to disobey my dad's request, and most of the tension at home was finally gone. I was back to being the ice queen, and I'd kicked Jamie Baker under the rug again.

There were advantages to being in ice queen mode again. For instance, Becky's nasty looks no longer invoked door-destroying emotional outbursts. The painfully delicious make-out dreams about Ryan finally stopped haunting my sleep. And when the obnoxious reporter that used to stalk me in Illinois showed up in the parking lot after school Friday, I managed not to have a complete mental breakdown in front of everyone. Barely, but I managed.

I'd just come down the front steps of the school, headed for the parking lot, and I stopped dead in my tracks when he spoke. "Jamielynn," he called in a low, urgent tone.

The voice came from behind me, but I knew without looking that it was Dave Carter, tabloid journalist extraordinaire and the majority of the reason my family had had to flee cross-country to California.

My blood immediately boiled, and I whirled around to face him, half tempted to zap him accidentally on purpose. When I tensed up, about to explode, he held his hands up defensively. "Now, hold on! Don't go overreacting, Jamielynn. This is not what you think. We need to talk."

"The only thing we *need* is a restraining order."

"Jamie, about the accident you were recently involved in, you—"

"Check the police reports. I wasn't involved."

"I have checked the police reports, and your name comes up quite a bit."

"If you're looking for a story, you should ask the people that were *involved*."

"I'm not here for a story this time."

"Ha!"

I walked away, not about to give this creep the time of day, but as I turned my back on him he said, "I know the truth, Jamielynn. I know the toxic waste changed you."

My blood froze in my veins, making it impossible for me to take another step. Never in all those countless articles he wrote back in Illinois had he ever once come even close to the truth. Oh, he knew every intimate detail of my life, down to the brand of toothpaste I preferred and my weakness for reality TV. But he'd never even hinted at the idea of my powers.

When I stopped walking, Carter immediately started in again. "The gardener in Monday's accident claims he watched that sign smash you, and that you just pushed it off two seconds later. There was also some unexplained damage to the marquee. A mysterious dent just about the size of, well, *you*. It doesn't take a genius to figure it out."

I turned back around and glared at him. "I don't know what you're talking about," I said. I'd meant to sound fierce, but my statement came out in a whisper.

"If you want people to believe you're just a normal kid, you really should stop miraculously walking away from accidents. You shouldn't be so sloppy."

Okay, he was totally right about that. It was sloppy. And he was spot-on about my powers too. But clearly he had no solid proof. He wouldn't be here hounding me if he did. So I took the route that every superhero takes. I called him crazy. And why not? To anyone but me, what he was saying *was* crazy. "You're insane," I said with a hard laugh. "You followed me all the way here just to accuse me of what? Having *superpowers*? Was homicidal ex-girlfriend not enough? Am I the Incredible Hulk now?

"You can deny it all you want. But that doesn't make the evidence any less true."

"You call that *evidence*? A mangled sign and one eyewitness who was in shock from nearly being a sumo pancake? That's pretty thin, even for you. Go ahead and print your stupid theory. It's not like anyone will believe it anyway, since it will be smushed in between a story about an alien abduction and a baby born with three heads."

I must have hit a sensitive spot because Carter suddenly looked as angry as me. "I told you it's not about a story this time!" he yelled, frustrated.

I wasn't sure what his angle was, but I knew one thing was certain. "Everything is *always* a story with you, Carter!"

I was suddenly reminded of my final months in Illinois. I could have eventually moved on from Derek's death if it hadn't been for all the rumors. All the pictures and the stories. This man had single-handedly destroyed me. He turned everyone I loved against me and forced me to leave the home I grew up in.

Angry tears sprang up in my eyes. "YOU RUINED MY LIFE!"

I'd been so preoccupied with Carter's being here that I had forgotten we were in public until Mike Driscoll, of all people, stepped into the middle of the argument. I furiously batted at my eyes, horrified that Mike would notice the tears in them, but his attention was completely focused on the stranger. "What's the problem here?" he demanded, his voice hard.

"No problem that concerns you, Johnny Football," Carter said, brushing him off. To me he said, "Can we go somewhere more private?"

Before I could tell Carter where exactly I thought he should go a voice sang out, "Bow chicka wow wow!"

The comment startled me. I looked over my shoulder to see Paul Warren grinning like a moron. "Creepy old dude's diggin' on the Bake-ster!" He nodded at Carter and said, "Take a number, bro."

Unable to find any words, I just watched as Scott Cole called Paul a tool and kicked his knees out from under him.

When Paul dropped to the ground, Paige was suddenly directly in my line of vision. The expression on her face not only made me forget about Paul, it caused my adrenaline to spike.

It took me a moment to recognize my fear. I quickly looked from Paige's face to Becky's, next to her, and then to the entire circle of people who surrounded me. Half the school was now watching, and all of them were wondering who Carter was and what he wanted with me. I could see it in their eyes. Curiosity. Suspicion. Right now they would all believe anything Carter told them.

And there was a lot that he could tell them.

I looked back at Carter, my eyes pleading rather than angry as panic began to set in. "I'm not going anywhere with you," I said. Unfortunately my voice faltered, so I added, "Leave now, before I call the cops and explain to them that you're stalking me from clear across the country."

As I pulled out my cell phone Carter rolled his eyes at me and said, "You can't afford to act like a teenager right now, Jamielynn. You will be sorry if you don't hear me out, I promise you that."

Carter's threat caused another surge through my body, as did the way he reached toward me like he was planning to pull me by force from the parking lot. But this time the surge I felt was not adrenaline, it was electricity, and it was pulsing rather violently through me. "Don't touch me!" I shrieked, imagining what would happen to him if he did.

The horror in my voice made Carter draw back his hand curiously, and Mike stepped between us. "All right, dude," he said, getting in Carter's face. "Time to leave."

Carter's face flushed with anger. "Or what? You're gonna give me a wedgie?" he snapped, taking an aggressive step toward Mike.

Mike met his advance, and the two started arguing back and forth like a couple of sixth-graders. Immediately all the guys from the football team lined up, ready to pounce on Mike's command, and Paul Warren started chanting, "Fight! Fight! Fight!"

I was going to use the distraction to make a run for it, but a single word brought everything to a halt.

Ryan Miller had spoken my name.

That's all. Just my name. But that was enough. I whirled around and he was *right there*. His eyes lingered on me for an agonized moment, and then his expression turned murderous. "What," he asked in a controlled but dangerous voice, "is going on here?"

Even Mike gulped before he spoke up. "This dude was harassing your woman," he explained. Then he turned back to Carter and added, "He's about to get a beat-down if he doesn't take off. Right now."

Ryan flashed a glare at Carter but couldn't keep his eyes from returning to me. "Jamie?" he asked again.

My heart spun out of control as Ryan looked at me for the first time in a week. The overwhelming sense of relief was just one too many emotions for my poor body to handle at the moment. I shut my eyes before tears could spill from them and didn't open them again until I heard Carter sigh. I'd had enough, so I looked helplessly into Ryan's eyes. "Get me out of here?" I whispered.

Ryan didn't even hesitate, but as we started to leave Carter grumbled, "I hope you know what you're doing, Jamielynn. Because these *accidents* seem to follow you around, and if something happens to your new Derek Witters, here"—he motioned to Ryan—"I'll be the least of your worries."

My knees buckled under the weight of his statement. Ryan was too stunned by the reference to my dead boyfriend to catch me before I fell, but not too stunned to ball up his fist and throw it so hard at Carter's face that it knocked Carter on his butt. Carter's nose started bleeding everywhere—definitely broken.

"Whoa, Ryan! What is going on here?"

Of all the teachers to witness Ryan bloodying the jerk, I was glad it was Mr. Edwards. He's cool. He kind of gets me. Or at least doesn't bug me. He's also the only teacher that wouldn't take Ryan directly to the principal's office. Fighting, even if it is with a sleazy reporter and not another student, gets you suspended at Rocklin High, and I didn't want Ryan to get suspended. Sure, he was reigning champ of the jerks for ignoring me all week, but he was defending my honor. Plus, it's Carter. I've wanted to pound that man more times than I can count.

Okay, maybe Ryan was forgiven.

"Jamie?"

I shook myself from my thoughts and blushed a deep red because judging from the bemused look on Ryan's face, I had been staring, probably dreamily, at him while deciding I didn't hate him anymore.

I scrambled to my feet just about the same time Mr. E. reached Carter. "Is someone going to tell me what's going on here?"

Mr. E. seemed unnecessarily angry with Carter. He must have seen more of the spectacle than I thought.

"Just a misunderstanding," Carter told Mr. E. absently, then turned his attention back to me. As he wiped at the blood starting to dry on his face he said, "We'll talk later, Jamielynn."

"Not if you know what's good for you," I warned.

He became irritated again, and his eyes deliberately flickered to Ryan. "I'm not the one you should be worrying about."

I don't know why I got so angry. Okay, I do. Because his subtle warning that I should be concerned about Ryan hit a little too close to home. But even still, I shouldn't have lost it the way I did. Energy blitzed from my body like an invisible shock wave, and suddenly the lights throughout the student parking lot flicked on. It was only for a second, and most people didn't even see it, but I noticed, Ryan noticed, and even Mr. Edwards noticed. He was staring up at the lights completely puzzled.

But more importantly, Carter noticed. His eyes grew really wide for a minute as he was unable to mask his shock, but he recovered quickly and gave me a knowing glance before he walked off. "See you around, Jamielynn." There was no mistaking the threat in his tone.

Once he was gone and the shock of everything that had just happened wore off, Mr. Edwards was the first to speak. "Everything all right, Jamie?"

He was going to ask something else, but I cut him off. "Don't worry about it, Mr. E. I'll take care of him."

I finally looked up to see half the school now staring at me. I took a deep breath and then met Mike's gaze. "Thank you."

"Don't mention it," he muttered, clearly surprised by my sincerity. "Who was that guy? What was he talking about? Who's Derek Witters?"

"Look, I appreciate what you did, but it's really none of your business."

"Whatever," Mike grunted, and then immediately headed for the parking lot.

"Are you sure, Jamie?" Mr. Edwards pressed again. "I think maybe we should call the police. That man should not be harassing you."

"Just forget it—I'm fine. His harassment is second nature to me by now."

"Who is he?"

"Nobody, all right!" I was beginning to lose my patience. Carter just has that effect on me.

"Okay. If you're sure."

My expression was ice cold again. "I'm sure."

"In that case," Mr. Edwards said with a sigh, "Mr. Miller, I'm going to pretend I didn't see you break anyone's nose."

With that, Mr. Edwards headed back inside, and the rest of the crowd slowly began to disperse. Soon enough the only person still there was Ryan. "Are you all right?" he asked when we were finally alone. "Is there anything I can do?"

I went against my better judgment and met Ryan's gaze, instantly getting lost in it. There *was* one thing he could do. He could pull me into his arms again and magically make me forget everything bad in my life the way he had in his backyard.

Remembering the magic of that moment reminded me of how abruptly it ended and how Ryan hadn't so much as looked my direction since it happened. Suddenly the magic was gone.

"Ryan, you don't have to do this."

"Do what?"

"Pretend like you care." I tried not to snap, but Ryan was still startled by my sudden hostility. "You were right—your paper's done now, and you solved your mystery. I told you the truth about me, so there's no need to keep up the charade."

"You heard all of that?"

I tapped my ear with my finger. "Like Superman, remember?"

"I'm sorry, Jamie. I didn't realize you could hear well too."

"So you're only sorry because you got caught? Is this a joke to you? Do you have any idea how big a deal all of this is for me? I didn't just disclose intimate details of my life to you last week. I put my entire family's lives in your hands by telling you the truth. It's bad enough that you ignore me so that your reputation won't be tarnished by association, but to trust you like that and then actually hear you say that it meant *nothing*? That we're not even *friends*?"

"But I didn't mean what I said!"

"Which part?"

"Any of it!"

I instantly regretted everything I'd said the second I saw his face. He looked so desperate for me to forgive him, so I relaxed as much as I could.

"I was just trying to get them off my case because I was scared," he finally explained.

"Scared? Of what? Afraid they were going to get mad if you admitted we were friends?"

Ryan blushed guiltily but shook his head. "It's more than that. After you left my house, whatever you did to me, it was just like when you kissed me. I was bouncing off the walls with all this crazy energy that I just couldn't explain. My mom started asking me all these questions, and I didn't know how to answer any of them. She wanted to take me to the doctor, but I freaked out and wouldn't go. I wasn't hurt or sick or anything. It actually felt amazing. But I didn't know how all this stuff works. I was afraid a doctor might find something weird, and I didn't want it to be able to come back to you."

My anger was temporarily replaced with horror over the idea that I'd hurt him, and I gasped. "Are you sure you're okay?"

"Oh yeah, I'm great! I mean, once it wore off I kind of crashed and slept for like eighteen hours, but other than that everything's fine."

I don't think I've ever been more relieved in my life than I was to hear that I hadn't really hurt him. I was honestly convinced I'd killed him when he didn't show up to school that next day.

"Anyway, Jamie, I realized that you were right. All those times you told me it was better if I didn't talk to you—I get it now. So as hard as it was for me, I stayed away from you all week because I'm scared of people figuring it out. I see why you don't put yourself out there. It's too big a secret. It would be too easy to make a mistake."

All I'd wanted was for Ryan to understand. Yet having him agree with me somehow vaporized any hope I had of a normal life. Ryan had been the one thing that ever made me think my life might still be worth living, but now that was gone.

Surprise tears filled my eyes. Ryan reached out to wipe them away but once again decided not to touch me. "Your safety's what's important," he whispered. "If that means staying away from you, then that's what I'll do. I give up. You really do win this one." He gave me a smile that didn't quite reach his eyes. "Feel honored. You're the first girl to ever successfully reject me. I didn't think that was possible until now." He stared at me for another long moment with a lot of regret in his eyes, and then sighed. "See you around, Jamie Baker."

Letting him walk away from me was the right thing to do. It was the out I'd been looking for, and it was what my dad wanted. It was the safe thing for sure, the smart thing. But in case you haven't noticed yet, I sometimes lack some serious common sense. That, and Ryan Miller seems to be my Kryptonite. He got only about ten steps.

"Ryan, wait."

He whirled around a lot faster than I expected, and his hopeful expression made me nearly forget why I was stopping him. "Yes?" he prompted when I forgot to speak.

"I don't deserve that honor. I haven't really earned it."

"What honor?"

"Rejecting you."

"What are you saying?"

"I wasn't right. It *is* too big a secret. It's too big to try to keep it alone. It's dangerous and completely unfair of me to push this responsibility onto you. It's a lot to ask, and I know I don't deserve it, but if you're not too freaked out by me, is it too late to accept your offer to be friends?"

I've never seen anyone look more stunned than Ryan did right then. It was as though finding out that comic book characters can actually exist was nothing compared to the possibility of me wanting to be his friend. Nice. Real nice. I must have been more of an ice queen than I realized. On the bright side, it was a good kind of surprised. He was definitely happy with my confession. Once he gained his composure, his smile turned into that infamous smirk of his. "Friends?" he asked skeptically, taking a step closer to me.

"Friends," I warned seriously.

His face was only inches from mine now, and he was smiling down at me as if he owned the entire world. "I knew you secretly wanted me."

Way to kill the moment. "Oh, would you get over yourself already?"

"I can't." His grin grew even wider. "I just won the heart of the world's only superhero. I'm the man!"

"Ugh. Okay. I'm going home now, before I get sick."

"All right, all right, I'm sorry. I'm just kidding. Kind of. But seriously, you like me. I can tell. I'm man enough to say it. I want you, Jamie. So bad I'm going crazy over it. Why won't you just admit that you want me too?"

"I want to keep you alive—that's what I want."

"That's it?"

"That's a pretty big thing, don't you think?"

"Well, yeah, not killing me is a pretty good goal to have, but I meant, is that all that's keeping us apart?"

"Duh."

Once again Ryan was so close to me that all I'd have had to do was pucker and our lips would meet. I felt my heart speed up, and then suddenly he was leaning in. "You're not really trying to kiss me, are you?" I breathed just before his lips touched mine.

"You're not really trying to stop me, are you?"

You know? In the end? I swear it's going to be Ryan's cockiness that saves him. It's a lot easier to say no when he's so sure he's getting his way. I sighed and then lightly tapped my index finger to his stomach. The jolt didn't hurt him, but it definitely didn't feel good.

"Ow!" he grunted, and then frowned at me. The pout didn't make me feel sorry for him. "Did you just do that on purpose?" he whined.

"Didn't have any choice. What you were about to do to yourself would have hurt a lot worse."

"But you kissed me before."

"Yeah, and I was completely, one hundred percent calm then because (a) I had no idea that it could hurt you, and (b) that kiss was just a bet. It meant absolutely nothing."

Ryan's frown disappeared. "So you admit that kissing me would mean something to you now?"

"No." I'm stubborn, what can I say?

"You're killing me, Jamie. Killing me!"

"Look, Ryan, if you can't handle being just friends, we can always go back to the me-rejecting-you option."

The angry glare Ryan gave me was priceless. "Fine," he grumbled, "just friends. But just for now."

"Just for always."

"Just until you learn to control it."

Ryan raised his hand to my face again. I started to back away, but he refused to let me, so I took a deep breath before he ran the back of his hand slowly down my cheek. It felt so good that my eyes fluttered shut.

"All it will take is some practice," he whispered.

You have no idea how much I hoped he was right.

Eight o'clock Saturday morning I was up in my room—yes, watching cartoons if you must know— when Ryan's voice suddenly caught my attention. Wherever it was coming from, it wasn't that far from my house. "That's great, Mom," he was saying.

I turned off my TV and tried to concentrate on his conversation. Invasion of privacy? Maybe. My moral compass usually points pretty north, but I do have my moments of weakness, and let's face it, a teenage girl spying on her crush is not exactly front-page news. I can't help it if I'm better at it than most. Besides, I was curious as to why he was in my neighborhood.

I could hear his mother's voice coming through the receiver of his cell phone. "Well, we wanted to come home and take you to lunch to celebrate, but we're going to be a little longer than we thought. I'm sorry, Ry, but it looks like you'll be on your own today."

"That's okay. I actually have plans for the rest of the day. Well, hopefully. I haven't asked her yet, but I took the day off work."

"Something I should be worried about?" his mother teased.

"Only if I get caught, in which case the police will fill you in, I'm sure."

Ryan laughing with his mom had to be the cutest thing I'd ever heard. What a momma's boy. It's no wonder he got along so well with my parents. "Actually, Mom," he said, becoming excited, "remember that girl I was telling you about, Jamie?"

Wait, what?

I was at my window now, trying to see if I could spot him driving down my street. I couldn't.

"Oh, honey!" his mom gushed with sudden excitement. "She's finally letting you take her out? Ry, I'm so proud of you! You see? I told you no girl could resist you."

"Oh sure!" I laughed out loud to myself. "Throw gas on the flames, why don't you?"

It's no wonder he has such a giant ego.

"Well, actually," Ryan said, "she hasn't agreed to a date yet, but I've got a plan that I think will work. I'm headed over to her house right now."

"Good for you, honey. Good luck."

"Thanks, Mom. Have fun with Gene, and tell him congratulations for me."

Ryan was on his way to my house? Not good. If he showed up, acting like we were friends now, my father would have a conniption. Especially if he realized that Ryan knows about me. I had to cut Ryan off before he could reach the front door. I ran downstairs, but then I saw my reflection in the china cabinet and headed back to my room.

I know I could break a lot of world records if I wanted to, but even for moving at superspeed, I took the world's fastest shower, brushed my teeth, and threw on the first thing I could find. I came flying down the stairs, but my parents are all too familiar with that faint breeze rushing past them.

"Jamielynn, you get back here right now and tell me where you're going, young lady!" my mom called out to the thin air, knowing I could still hear her.

"Sorry, Mom." I was out of breath because I was slightly panicked, not because I was tired. "I was just going to go for a run. I've been cooped up too much, and I need to get some of this energy out. You want me to bring back a souvenir from somewhere?"

You should see our refrigerator. I'm not sure if having so many magnets is really healthy, but I can't help picking them up from the random places I stop at when I'm bored. I like the look my mom always gives me when I come home with one and she realizes that I was just in Nebraska or wherever.

"Jamie, sweetheart." Oh great. She was in one of those lecturing moods. Not exactly the best time when Ryan was going to show up any second. "I don't think going for a run is what you need. Why don't you try to find where all the kids are hanging out? Isn't there a school football game to watch or something?"

"The football games are on Friday nights here," I answered dryly.

"Oh. Well, there has to be something going on. Jamie, when your father and I said you needed to get out more, we didn't mean running around the country all by yourself. You should use all this energy to be with kids your age. You need to be social."

"Okay, fine. I'll go see what Ryan's up to."

"Jamie."

I could tell my mom wanted to say yes, but I suppose I couldn't blame her for worrying.

Just then I heard Ryan's truck pull up to the curb of my house, and I nearly had a heart attack.

"All right, fine," I said, not having any more time to argue. "I'll go out and look for a job. Will that make you happy?"

My mother's face lit up with a glimpse of hope that actually made me feel very guilty all the sudden. "Very!" she exclaimed, clapping her hands together. "But you can't get a job wearing that. Go put on something nice."

I frowned down at the jeans and T-shirt I'd pulled off my floor in my haste to stop Ryan. I disappeared so fast that I was standing in front of my mom again in a business-like skirt and jacket before she could even shake her head. "Better?"

"Beautiful," my mom said. "Good luck, honey. You won't regret this, I promise!" She was calling out to the air again because I was already gone.

I tugged on Ryan's arm just before he had the chance to knock on the door. If I weren't so paranoid about my parents seeing him there, I would have enjoyed the confused look on his face as he realized I'd just appeared out of thin air and was dragging him off my porch. The only words he seemed capable of spitting out were "What the—"

"I'll explain in a minute," I grumbled. "Just get us out of here before my parents see you."

Ryan frowned but obeyed, obviously happy that even though I was making him leave, at least I was going with him.

"Good morning?" he finally said, very unsure of himself for once in his life as he rounded the corner, putting my house out of sight behind us.

"I'm sorry." I sighed. "It's just that I heard you pull up, and I didn't want my dad to have an aneurism if you mentioned something about knowing my secret."

"They don't know about your powers?"

"Oh, no. They know about me. They don't know that you know. I would have told them, except my father sort of banned me from ever speaking to you again."

"What? But I thought your parents liked me." I don't know what was cuter, the surprise in his voice, or the wounded look on his face. "Your dad told me to come back anytime. You're mom actually hugged me."

That confession made me cringe. "Yeah, she gets a little excited sometimes—sorry about that. But it's not you. They just freaked after I mentioned the accident and you helping me out with the cops. They're afraid you're going to figure me out and expose me to the world. My dad went into his usual secret-government-lab-testing rant."

"But I don't want anyone to take you away any more than he does."

"He's a great dad. It's his job to be overprotective."

Ryan's face slowly straightened out of its frown. "I guess if you were mine, I'd be crazy overprotective too." He sighed and then smiled at me. "I'd probably be worse, judging by how I felt when that reporter showed up."

I couldn't believe my heart was fluttering over that, but it was, and even worse, I liked the feeling. "That was quite a punch you threw." I laughed, trying not to let myself blush.

"Yeah, I was quite impressed myself."

"I'm not surprised—you're always impressed with yourself."

Ryan laughed but didn't deny the accusation. "I've never really been a fighter, but I'll admit I wanted to kill that guy."

Ryan wasn't the only one. I wanted to put Carter six feet under too. The only difference between me and Ryan is that I could have. All too easily. My power scares me, but sometimes the feelings that come with that power are a lot scarier. I can almost understand how supervillains get the way they are, because it's so hard not to want to use your power to hurt someone when they're hurting you first. Of course my conscience always gets the better of me, but if I had to deal with guys like Carter all the time, forever and ever, eventually I'd crack.

I shuddered at my train of thought, and when Ryan questioned it, I quickly changed the subject. "Where are we going?"

Ryan grinned, successfully distracted. "I hope you didn't have any plans today."

"No, but you obviously do. Would you mind filling me in?"

"Practice."

"No offense, Ryan, but I'm not exactly excited by the idea of watching you and Mike smear each other into the ground for hours."

"Not me—you. You're going to learn how to control your power."

"And how do you suggest I do that?"

"Practice," he said again. "Haven't you seen *Smallville?*"

"Everyone's seen *Smallville*," I said, not amused that he was now comparing my life to a TV series about a fictional town full of freaks.

"Every time Clark gets a new ability, he practices. It never takes him very long, so if you're as much like Superman as you claim, then I bet we could be making out by next week."

I gave him a sideways glance, but he just laughed. "You know you want to."

"This plan is right up there with your plan for getting to take Becky to homecoming."

"Hey! Technically, that plan worked."

I was annoyed to high heaven that he was right about that. "Okay, Einstein, then do you have a strategy for this game plan?"

"Interesting choice of words," Ryan said, and then intentionally changed the subject. "You look so hot, by the way. Very Lois Lane."

"Oh, shut up!"

"Sorry, it's just a little ironic, considering what we're about to do."

"And that would be?"

"A surprise."

Ryan wouldn't tell me his plan any more than he would tell me where we were going. Of course it wasn't really a mystery when he turned off I-80 toward Tahoe City. I wondered why he was taking me to Lake Tahoe, but I have to admit, after that dream I had about the Grand Canyon, I wasn't exactly opposed to being alone with him in the wilderness.

We wound through the mountains, and there was nothing but forest to see out the windows until suddenly we were pulling up to a big log house with a huge veranda that wrapped all the way around the side. I couldn't help but stare at the beautiful structure. It seemed to be hidden so perfectly from the world that I felt like Ryan and I were the last two people on earth. Again, not complaining.

"You like it?" Ryan asked, seeing the smile on my face.

"It's hard to believe that something so beautiful can be so close to Sacramento. It looks like a jigsaw puzzle."

"Close. It was featured in a wall calendar once." Ryan chuckled. "It's my stepdad's cabin."

"You call this a cabin?"

"Gene does. When he married my mom, he moved into our house so that we would feel more comfortable because the house he used to own was a good three times bigger than this."

I blinked. I couldn't help it. My dad manages a sawmill in West Sacramento. He makes enough to afford our nice little cookie-cutter piece of suburban heaven, but he'd have to win the lottery to own a house like this.

"A lot of screwed-up people in this world need motivating," Ryan joked. "Come on, the view from the back is better."

He was right; the view from the back was much better. The deck hung over the side of the mountain, granting a view of the entire lake. I actually recognized the back of the house. I'd seen it from across the lake on the many trips I've made here to do my homework in a little peace and quiet. It was one of the nicest houses visible from the lakeshore, and I'd often wondered what kinds of people own a place like this. It felt strange to be standing there now.

"Thank you for bringing me here, it's absolutely beautiful, but what exactly are we doing here?"

"Well, if we're going to unleash these powers of yours, then we need to be someplace where no one is going to see us. This was the most private place I could think of."

"You want me to 'unleash' my powers?"

"Yeah, show me whatcha got."

"What do you want, a front-row seat to the freak show? I'm not going to stand here and do tricks for a handful of doggie biscuits."

"Jamie." Ryan rolled his eyes at me like I was the one being ridiculous. "I get that you're self-conscious about being different, but you're really not going to scare me away, so stop worrying so much. I'm not looking for cheap entertainment. I'm just trying to help you. If we're going to practice, then I need to know what you're capable of first. Like tryouts."

"Tryouts?"

"Yeah." Ryan reached into a duffel bag he'd brought with him and retrieved a lightbulb. "Then, after I know what you can do, we start with the fundamentals."

Ryan grinned really big. I hate it when he does that. It's so not fair! He was being too cute, and I was eating it up. I couldn't stop myself from humoring him. "What is that for?"

"Can you light it up?"

I glared at him, but he waited for me to do as he asked, so I grabbed the lightbulb out of his hand and pumped the thing so full of power that it exploded.

"That's what I thought." Ryan laughed, pulling a second light bulb from his bag. "Now, can you hold this one without lighting it up?" I was still not amused. "Well, can you?"

I took the bulb and closed my fist around the bottom. "Satisfied?" I asked when the light stayed dark.

Ryan smiled bigger than I'd ever seen him smile before. "Completely," he admitted, and then stepped closer to me. "You see? You do have *some* authority over it. You just have to figure out what that feels like, and then try doing it when you start to lose control."

Ryan slowly took my free hand in his, and the minute his fingers touched my skin I could feel butterflies in my stomach.

"Like right now, for instance," Ryan said, looking at the dim glow now shining from the light in my hand. "You're starting to lose control. See if you can turn it off."

I was dying of embarrassment, but I was also curious to see if I could do it, so I played along. I kept my eyes focused on the lightbulb because looking at Ryan's face as close as it was to mine now was sure to be a guaranteed repeat light-bulb explosion. After a moment the light slowly started to fade. I felt a tinge of excitement, and it started to glow again, so I concentrated even harder. Again the light faded.

Ryan dropped my hand with a proud smile on his face that screamed, "I told you so," but I was too amazed to care. Even though it was on a tiny scale, I was actually controlling myself.

I smiled at the dark lightbulb, but then, without warning, Ryan put his hand to my cheek and started to bring his lips to mine. He took me by surprise and I jumped back, shocking Ryan's fingers when I pulled away from them. The lightbulb lit up so bright it was nearly blinding.

Ryan laughed. "Okay, okay. I'm sorry. I won't do that again. But you can't blame me for wanting to make sure."

I didn't think it was so funny. My hand tightened on the light until the brightness was squelched, and the bulb lay in tiny pieces on the deck.

"I'm sorry," Ryan said again, more seriously this time. "I promise, no more surprises. But did you see that? You controlled it. If we keep working on it, you're only going to get better and better. And we could do that with all of your powers."

"Fine." I sighed. "You want to see what I can do?"

"I'm dying to see everything you can do."

"Be careful what you wish for," I grumbled, and then took off running.

I was gone for probably about ten seconds. When I got back, Ryan still looked dazed from seeing me disappear.

"Here." I dumped a fistful of sand into his hand.

Ryan looked down with wide eyes. "Is that…" He cast his gaze down the mountain behind us at the lake. "Did you just go—"

I looked over his shoulder at the lake below and shook my head. "Nope. That would be Pacific Ocean sand. Carmel Beach, actually, in Monterey." I shrugged when his mouth fell open. "Nothing but the best."

I waited for Ryan to do or say something. It took him a minute, but as he'd promised earlier, he didn't freak out. "You just went all the way to Monterey? That's like a five-hour drive from here."

I shrugged again. "I'm fast. Of all my powers, speed is the strongest, then probably the hearing. Those are the ones I use the most. All the others I can't do quite as well."

Ryan was still trying to keep his game face on, but he had that overwhelmed look in his eyes again. He couldn't stop staring at me, so I leaned against the porch railing and looked out over the water to avoid his gaze. After a minute he joined me. Once he was looking at the lake and not me, he was able to speak a lot easier. "So, you're fast, you can hear, and you could murder me with a single touch. And you're saying there's more you can do?"

"Not much. Aside from the walking battery part, everything seems to be strictly physical. My dad has a theory about that."

"I love theories!" After I gave him a peculiar look Ryan explained himself. "Remember the one about you and the mafia?" He shrugged, guilty. "That wasn't my first."

I don't know how Ryan managed to keep a straight face because I sure couldn't. I cracked up, but that made it a lot easier to tell the story. "The truck that was carrying the waste I was doused in had come from a fertilizer plant. My dad thinks that the electricity from the power lines cooked all that fertilizer stuff into my body like some sort of super Miracle-Gro cocktail. We think it's enhanced me physically, just like it would grass or whatever."

"So is that why your hair grows in green now?" he asked with a devilish grin.

"Ha, ha," I said.

"Is it a grassy green? Or more of a neon green?"

I ignored him.

"Sorry," he said, laughing at himself. "I just can't picture you with green hair. You'll have to show me sometime."

"Yeah," I said, snorting. "Right."

"Why not?"

"Uh, maybe because I'd have to let it grow out for you to see it, and I'd look like a major freak. I might be able to get away with it in Los Angeles, but Sacramento?"

Ryan frowned and then tried to negotiate. "Okay, fine. But the eyes. You have to let me see the eyes."

I cut my gaze back to the water. Unlike with the hair, I didn't really have a good excuse not to show Ryan my eyes. But I'm not just self-conscious about my post-accident looks—I'm *super*self-conscious. My eyes were the most freakish thing about me, and no way was I going to let Ryan win this one. "You've seen them," I said, my mind made up.

"I barely saw the one, and only for a few seconds. That doesn't count."

"Does too."

"So does not!"

Whatever look I gave Ryan just then was enough to make him throw his hands up in defeat. "Okay, okay, fine," he said. "We're talking about the accident. Your dad's theory about you being Miracle-Gro Girl..."

I glared at him again, but decided to let the stupid nickname slide. This time. "The chemicals I was doused in somehow amped up all my physical senses. Speed and agility, sound, sight, strength, smell, taste."

"You have supertaste?" Ryan asked.

"It's not my favorite superpower. Basically my taste buds are supersensitive just like everything else. Mostly it just makes me superpicky. Drives my mom insane."

"The world's first superhero food critic. Watch out, Wolfgang Puck."

Ryan laughed again, and I felt myself being intoxicated by his laughter. I've never joked around about my powers before. The only people I've ever talked about them with are my parents, and then we're always so serious. I've never thought about the possibility of them being fun before, but standing there with Ryan, laughing and joking around, I was starting to see how he could be optimistic.

Optimism obviously isn't one of my stronger qualities, but it seemed to be a superpower for Ryan. "How come you are the way you are?" I asked when the laughter died down.

Ryan was surprised by the question. He smiled a little warily and then asked, "What way am I?"

"I've never met anyone like you before. You're so laid-back all the time, and you can find the bright side of everything. You never let people upset you. You're just so... happy. All the time. And it's contagious. No one can light up a room the way you can."

"No one can light up a room the way you can either," he joked.

"I'm serious! No one can be as relaxed as you are all the time. How do you do it? If I could be half as calm as you are, I wouldn't need to go through your superpower boot camp."

"In that case, I'll never give up my secret."

"Seriously, though, Ryan, tell me something about yourself. You know everything about me, but you're as much of a mystery to me as I am to anybody else." I felt my neck heat up and looked away, hoping he wouldn't notice the blush. "Please?" I whispered shyly. "I want to understand you too."

I glanced back at Ryan when he didn't say anything, and he seemed to be a million miles from where I was all of a sudden, lost in his own world.

Just when I thought he wouldn't open up to me, he said, "It's because of my dad." His eyes stayed glossy, and they never left the water.

"I should have figured. Self-help guru and all."

"Not Gene—my real dad." Ryan finally broke his stare to smile at me. "Gene's a great guy, and I guess he has helped me a lot. That's probably where I get my confidence. But the mild temperament comes from my father."

I suddenly realized I didn't know what had happened to his dad. I didn't know if his parents were divorced or if he had died. I didn't even know how long ago Ryan's mom got remarried. I was afraid I was bringing up really painful memories, but I was so curious I couldn't tell him to stop.

"My dad isn't a bad guy necessarily, but he was so miserable when he lived with us. Everything was such a big deal to him, and he would pick a fight over the tiniest things. If my mom somehow looked at him funny, if she answered the phone while they were talking, if I spilled my juice on the table or dropped a pass when we were playing catch... He was always yelling and making my mom upset over the most ridiculous things. By the time my parents got divorced they were fighting with each other ninety-nine percent of the time. I spent most of my time hiding out at friends' houses or in my room.

"Mom joined a yoga class after my dad left, as a way to deal with everything, and this woman in her class dragged her to one of Gene's seminars. Gene changed my mom's life, but it's the memories of my dad that make me the way I am. It's just not worth it to be so stressed and angry about everything. Life's generally not so bad—most people just choose to see the negative."

Ryan stopped for a minute, smiled nervously at me, and then said, "It's kind of like you. You've been through a lot and have legitimate problems to worry about, but do you even try to see the good things? You were given a second chance at life, Jamie. Everything about you is a walking, talking miracle, but you're wasting it."

And I thought my parents were good with the guilt trips...

I started to cry, and to be honest I don't think Ryan was surprised at all. "You're right," I said. "I am wasting it. I hate my life. Every single day a part of me wishes I didn't survive that accident."

"It doesn't have to be that way."

"Yeah but, Ryan, I'm not like you. I don't know how to just shake things off like they don't matter. What if I can't change?"

Ryan grabbed another lightbulb from his bag. "You've already started the process."

Tears were falling fiercely down my face, but I smiled through them and even let go this half sob, half laugh. I wanted to throw my arms around him, but the last time I did that he missed a day of school, so instead I wiped the tears from my cheeks.

"How many of those did you bring?" I asked, pointing to the lightbulb.

Ryan smiled, grateful to see my good mood return. "Let's just say I came prepared."

Having to find excuses for all the time I spent with Ryan over the next few weeks wasn't really much of a problem—since my accident I'd constantly been taking off for hours at a time, claiming I needed a little peace and quiet—but my parents' fridge was becoming even more crowded. Every time I had "practice," as Ryan called it, I made sure to take a minute to collect another magnet. I don't know if I was trying to produce a stable alibi, or if I was just hoping to ease some of the guilt I felt for lying to my parents.

I felt bad, but I hung out with Ryan anyway. Aside from the fact that I was sort of addicted to him, he really was helping me, and that was too important to ignore. The more we tested my powers, the more aware my body became of them. I physically felt like I had a better understanding of how they worked and what my limitations were.

Still, no matter what I did, I couldn't seem to separate the power from all my stupid emotions. With every little mood swing all control would fly out the window. If Ryan looked at me the wrong way, I lost it. If Ryan looked at me the *right* way, I lost it. And whenever he tried to kiss me, something usually blew up. Someone ought to teach *him* a little control.

So we gave the powers a rest, and instead Ryan taught me some of his stepdad's theories on stress management and herbal supplements. He also showed me proper meditation techniques. We did yoga together, and even though I felt ridiculous, I couldn't deny the positive effects living a healthier lifestyle were having on me.

My dad noticed the changes too, and completely floored me one Saturday evening with a hefty gift certificate to Barnes & Noble, of all places. "What's this for?" I asked, unable to fathom his reasons for giving it to me.

"Well, I know technically you still haven't made any friends or gotten a job, but you've been a different girl these last few weeks, so I'm letting you off the hook."

"What's the catch?" Yeah, I was suspicious. My dad doesn't just back down from stuff. I totally get my stubbornness from him.

"No catch," he insisted. "We only wanted you to do those things because you seemed so miserable, but you've been so much happier lately that even though you didn't do it my way, you still earned your freedom."

"So I'm not grounded anymore?" I was still waiting for the punch line.

"Not grounded anymore."

"And what about Ryan?"

"What do you mean?"

"Am I still forbidden to talk to him?"

"Jamie, I wasn't grounding you from Ryan as punishment, it's just that it's too—"

"Dad," I interrupted, not needing to hear what I knew he was going to say. "You've got to see that there are going to be risks no matter who I choose to talk to. Whether it's Ryan now or someone else who gets to know me in the future. Either I stay locked up in this house forever and make sure that no one ever learns the truth, or I make friends and risk someone finding out. I can't have it both ways. But believe me, if there's anybody that doesn't want the world to figure out I'm a freak, it's me."

My parents both frowned at my use of the word "freak," but I never broke my concentration. I gave my dad the most earnest smile I had in me. "I'm the one this happened to. It's my secret, my life. You've got to give me a little more trust that I know what I'm doing."

This seemed to make my dad think about it, but he was still clearly not convinced. I knew I couldn't just drop it and hoped I could get through this speech without blushing. "You said you wanted me to be happy." I shrugged sheepishly when I had both my parents looking at me intently. "Ryan makes me happy. It's not even his fault. The kid just has a gift. He makes everyone happy. He's my best friend, my *only* friend, and I need him."

So much for not blushing. I felt my face heat up, and my shyness on the subject finally unlocked the tears of joy my mother had been trying so hard to hold back. Talk about embarrassing. "Oh, for heaven's sake, Stan!" she whined.

My dad was quiet for a minute, and then finally sighed. "Honey, if he's responsible for the changes in you," he said, giving me a wary smile, "then I'm grateful to him. I guess if it's really what you need, then I trust you. Just promise me that you'll be careful about this."

I managed not to squeal in my moment of bliss, but I bounded into his arms and practically knocked him off his feet. "Thanks, Daddy!" I squeaked as I kissed his cheek. "I promise my secret will stay as safe as it's always been."

I kissed him on the cheek again. I couldn't help it. I was just so relieved to have my dad's approval. This time he chuckled lightly and hugged me back.

"So, can I go over to Ryan's for a little while?" I asked when I pulled away from him. "Tell him the good news?"

After another long sigh, my dad's smile finally faded. "Fine, go," he said. "Just be careful!"

This time I rolled my eyes at the warning. "Ryan's a really, really good person, Dad. You'll see. There's nothing to be worried about, I promise."

"That's not what I mean," he said, putting on his best dad face. "He's still a seventeen-year-old boy."

I laughed when I realized what he was talking about. "Don't worry, Dad. If he doesn't keep his hands to himself, I'll just zap him." I winked, and then I blew out the door before he could change his mind.

I was so giddy that I didn't bother driving to Ryan's house. I had no need to keep up appearances with him, and a car just wasn't fast enough. And since this was the first time I'd made the effort to see him without him practically forcing me to, he was pleasantly stunned when he found me on his doorstep. "Jamie! What are you doing here?"

"I have good news."

Ryan responded immediately, with an excited puppy-like quality. "You're finally ready to promote me to boyfriend status?"

"Of course not." I laughed. "Don't be ridiculous."

"You're going to show me your eyes?"

"Nice try."

He pouted for only a second, but then his face lit up again. "You learned how to fly?"

That one was so unexpected it stopped my train of thought. "What?"

"Come on—that would be awesome and you know it."

"Well, I am pretty amazing," I teased, "but I doubt even I could ever defy gravity."

Ryan laughed as he pulled me into his house. He then immediately locked the door behind us like he was trying to keep me from escaping. "Okay, then," he said cautiously. I think he wasn't quite convinced yet that I was actually there. "So what is this really good news?"

"I came to let you know that you are no longer off limits."

"Really!" Ryan's eyebrows flew up with excited curiosity, and the next thing I knew, his arms were secure around my waist.

"Don't get any bright ideas, Romeo. We're still star-crossed lovers." I peeled his hands off my hips and laughed when he frowned at the distance I put between us. "*I* am still completely off limits to *you*. I just meant that my dad has lifted the Ryan ban, and I'm now technically allowed to hang out with you."

"Oh."

I don't think my news was as good for him as it was for me. He was pouting rather pathetically.

"I don't have to lie anymore," I said, trying to get the excitement back. "I have to admit, though, practice probably won't be nearly as fun now. The sneaking around was kind of hot."

Ryan had no witty comeback this time. He just gave me one of those looks. The dangerous kind that turns my brain to mush and makes me agree to whatever he wants. "Whatever this mood you're in is," he said, taking a step closer to me, "I really like it."

I would never have admitted it to him, but I really did too. I was in a great mood, but I surprised even myself with my reply. "Well then, you're going to love this," I said, closing the distance between us for once. "Let's go out."

"What?" Ryan was so sure he'd heard me wrong that the look of shock didn't come until after I'd repeated myself.

"Let's go out," I said again. "All we ever do together is practice. We never just hang out. Let's forget my powers for once, and go see a movie or play minigolf or something."

Ryan actually staggered backward. If it weren't for the fact that he was completely speechless and couldn't close his gaping mouth, I would have thought he was trying to be funny. The fact that he was serious made it not just funny but hilarious. I couldn't help my laughter. "If you're not in the mood," I teased, "maybe another time."

I reached for the handle on the front door, and Ryan's fingers fell on top of mine before I could twist it. "Are you asking me to take you on a date?" he asked, still staring very wide-eyed at me.

"If you call spending the evening with me having fun in a very platonic, strictly hands-off, absolutely-no-kissing-at-the-end-of-the-night kind of way a date, then yes. I believe that's what I'm asking you to do. That is, if you don't have anything better to do tonight. I do realize that this is Saturday night, and you are Ryan Miller."

Ryan pulled my hand away from the door and said, "Actually, there's this big party tonight and it would be a great chance for you to—"

I put my finger to Ryan's lips. He was so surprised by my casual touch—unnecessary contact was usually his job—that his words caught in his throat.

"Not a chance," I said. "I know all about Mike Driscoll's party, and I am *not* going."

I removed my finger from his lips and he immediately started to argue, so I clamped my whole hand over his mouth. "No way," I warned. "I understand if you need to be there—he's your best friend and all." Ryan nodded his head vigorously beneath my fingers. "But, practice or no practice, if I had to spend an entire evening with Mike, Becky and Paige, I'd probably kill someone. On purpose."

Ryan's face fell at my statement and I felt myself starting to melt. So I took a page out of the Ryan Miller handbook and pouted. Pathetically.

I released a sigh that would have made even my father give me what I wanted. "It's okay," I said. "We can go out some other time."

I reluctantly pulled my hand away from Ryan, and he reached out—as I'd hoped he would—to stop me from leaving. "Mike does throw parties all the time," he said hesitantly. "I'm sure he'll understand if I miss just one."

I smiled at my victory. But when Ryan matched my smile and brought my fingers back to his lips to kiss them, I blushed.

That was the last time I blushed that whole night, though. Ryan was the perfect "strictly platonic" gentleman. I admit he handled himself way better than I thought he could. He opened every door, refused to let me pay for anything, and didn't lay a single finger on me all night. Absolutely no physical contact whatsoever, which is definitely not the norm for him.

He was so well behaved that it was almost disappointing. But then, the California State Railroad Museum isn't exactly the most romantic place in the world. That's right, for our first date Ryan took me to Old Sacramento, where we pulled taffy, panned for fools gold, and, you guessed it, toured the railroad museum.

Ah, Sacramento—the city of love…

All right, the horse drawn carriage ride past the capitol was pretty romantic. But even then Ryan made no attempt to touch me, much less kiss me. I think he looked at this date as some sort of test or maybe some kind of barrier he'd finally gotten over, and he didn't want to lose any ground.

I didn't mind having to settle for only kissing Ryan in my dreams afterward because that one night of normalcy was more than I could have asked for. I had such a great time—only Ryan Miller could make hanging at the train museum on a Saturday night cool—that I was sure my awesome, carefree mood was going to last forever.

I was wrong. My bubble burst the minute I got to school on Monday. Ryan was already there, and he was talking to Mike and Paige in the quad. I heard them from the parking lot, and yeah, I have superhearing, but after a few minutes anyone could have heard them from the parking lot. Well, heard Paige anyway.

It started out simple enough, with Paige in her sickeningly innocent—which never fools anyone—voice, asking Ryan how his weekend was. "Missed you Saturday night."

"Thanks. It's always nice to be missed."

Ha! That response was so Ryan. I don't think Paige appreciated it like I did, though, and Mike clearly wasn't happy with it. "I can't believe you bailed on my party," he grumbled.

"Sorry, dude, something important came up," Ryan said, seeming unfazed by Mike's anger. "I'll make it up to you, though. I'll see if I can talk Gene into letting us take the boat out to the lake this weekend."

"I called you like fifty times. What was so important that you had to ditch your best friend?" Mike demanded.

"I was out with Jamie."

I was surprised to hear Ryan get defensive, and I think Mike was too, because he quit pushing. Paige, on the other hand...

"You weren't home on Sunday either," she said pointedly. "I was going to see if you wanted to do something."

Ryan's voice was almost too polite when he said, "Sorry I missed you. I was at my stepdad's cabin all day Sunday. Another time though, I promise."

That's when Paige snapped her cap. It was quite shocking actually. Years of trying so desperately, and failing so miserably, caught up with her, and she simply couldn't take it anymore. "Yeah, right," she grumbled bitterly.

"What?" I could hear the confusion in Ryan's voice as well as the hurt.

"I said, yeah, right!" she yelled. "That's just your way of blowing me off again. Ryan, if you don't want to go out with me, then just say so."

There was silence for a moment and then Ryan said, "I'm sorry, Paige." He was being sincere, but that wasn't going to help him any. Not with Paige. "You're a great friend, but I'm not really looking for anything else."

"You mean just not from me! You're not looking for anything else from *me*."

I could hear Ryan swallow a lump in his throat. The poor guy was probably sweating. "Yes," he said calmly. "That's what I mean."

Individually, every gasp that followed Ryan's confession was relatively quiet, but there were apparently enough people watching the spectacle that collectively the sound practically shook the walls. Well, that and Paul Warren yelling, "Oh, snap!" loud enough to rattle my focused ears.

Paige was obviously too upset to speak, but Mike came to her defense. "That was harsh, dude. What's your problem?"

Ryan sighed. "She asked for the truth."

I cold hear Paige sniffling, and then Ryan turned his voice to almost a whisper. "I'm sorry, Paige. I just don't see anything ever working out between us."

"You've never given us a chance!" Paige sobbed.

"What do you want from me, Paige? You're just not the right girl for me." Ryan said, trying to make his voice sound strong again.

"And the freak is?" Paige screamed. She sounded like she'd stopped crying now, and her voice was so full of anger that even I would have been afraid of her. "Oh, don't deny it, Ryan! It's so obvious it makes me sick! You like Jamie! The girl's a freak! An ice queen! She's not capable of having feelings! She's just using you to hurt me and trying to make herself popular. Was that one kiss really worth giving up all your friends to try to hook up with some slut who will never care about you anyway?"

"Jamie's not a freak—stop calling her that. And you're not losing me as a friend, Paige. I've always been your friend. I'm still your friend. Why can't I be Jamie's friend too?"

"I don't know, man. Paige has a point."

I'd almost forgotten Mike was involved in this fight, but now, even though he wasn't yelling, he seemed even angrier than before.

"What? What have I done that's so bad?" Ryan finally sounded exasperated. "I said I was sorry I missed your party on Saturday."

"The party on Saturday? Try everything for the last two or three weeks! Loner chick is rubbing off on you. You're losing major points, bro."

"Oh, *I'm* losing points? Becky won't even look at you now."

"At least I gave her a shot."

"You didn't give her a shot. You used her to get a little action, then dumped her the next day."

"If Becky didn't want a hook-up, then she shouldn't have gone to the dance with me."

Paige suddenly exploded back into the conversation. "Who cares about Becky? This isn't about Becky! It's about *you,* Ryan. You're changing, and it's all because of that freak, Jamie Baker!"

"Can you blame me?" Ryan yelled. "All I ever get from you guys anymore is this crap!" There was a pause, and then Ryan let out an angry breath. "Forget this."

I'd never seen Ryan lose his temper before. Okay, *heard* Ryan lose his temper. I still hadn't seen this because I was hiding in my car. Not that I'm a coward, but I seriously doubt my showing up just then would have made things better for anyone.

Suddenly Mike's voice rang out. "Hey, Miller!"

There was a loud smack. The sound of fist hitting bone sent a chill through my heart, and I immediately got out of my car.

"You have no idea how long I've wanted to do that. It's good to finally have a reason," Mike said, confirming my fears that Ryan had just been punched.

"It's a good thing you did," Ryan spat in the most menacing voice I'd ever heard. "It's nice to know who my real friends are. Jamie may be antisocial, but at least she doesn't pretend to be your friend to your face and then trash you when you leave the room."

"Don't worry. I won't bother to wait till you're gone anymore. Have fun in Loserville with Baker. We're done!"

The commotion ended. I could hear the crowd dispersing, and as people made their way to their classes, they were murmuring about the scene they'd just witnessed, all trying to decide who was right.

It sounded like the school was about to be split into two opposing forces. I already knew which side I was on, but as I made my way through the parking lot I was torn up inside. I was happy that Ryan had finally realized what Mike and Paige were really like, but I knew he was hurt, and I hated that. I loved that he'd defended me, and even chosen me over them, but I hated that I was the cause of his fight. He'd done so much for me, and here I was tearing his happy little world down.

None of my happiness was worth Ryan's pain and suffering. I was just like Paige. I could be every bit as mean as she was, and I wasn't worthy of Ryan. I didn't know what to do about it, but I knew that Ryan shouldn't be alone right now, so I headed straight for the quad and prayed that Paige and Mike would be long gone before I got there. They were, and so was most of the school because first period was about to start, but Ryan was not alone. Becky beat me to him.

I froze when I saw them together. They made such a beautiful picture that I nearly cried. They weren't saying anything, just hugging each other in an embrace so intimate it could have been a Hallmark card. Ryan was trembling—with anger or hurt, I couldn't tell—and there were tears streaming down Becky's face.

I wanted to be jealous, and I was, but not for the reason most girls would be. Their hug was one of old friends, comforting each other because they were hurting equally. I wasn't jealous that Becky was hugging Ryan, I was jealous that she *could*. I couldn't hold Ryan like that. I couldn't be close to him. Ryan was dying for a relationship, but I couldn't give that to him.

Ryan and Becky stood there for what seemed like forever. And for as long as they held each other, I stood there, watching. I felt like I should give them their privacy, but I was unable to make myself look away. Becky was the first to move.

"Are you okay?" she asked, pulling back from Ryan's arms to assess his eye. It was already turning purple.

"I'm fine." Ryan sighed. "Shiners are sexy, right?"

Becky laughed once through her tears and shook her head, forcing Ryan to sigh again. "At least he didn't break my nose. I can't believe he hit me."

"He's a jerk," Becky argued.

"I guess I deserved it. I shouldn't have gone off like that."

"You didn't say anything that wasn't true."

"But they've been my friends for so long."

"Forget them, Ryan," Becky whispered, hugging her arms tightly around his waist again. "They deserve each other. And you deserve better friends."

"You're still my friend, right?"

"Only the best since second grade." Becky pulled back and smiled up at Ryan. "That's never going to change."

They laughed as they hugged each other again, but Becky's smile quickly faded. "Thanks for sticking up for me."

"Mike's an idiot. I should have kicked his butt weeks ago. But I thought it would all just blow over, you know?"

"Yeah."

"Sorry."

"No." Becky sighed. "I'm sorry. I didn't mean to cause a fight."

"Don't worry about it. That fight was really about Jamie anyway."

A sharp pain ripped through me as I watched Ryan drag Becky off in the direction of her first class. It was one thing for me to think I was ruining his life, but it was entirely another to hear him confirm it.

I had to get out of there. I turned around and headed right back to the parking lot. I could still hear Ryan and Becky talking as I walked. "Ryan, about Jamie," Becky started to say. It was clear from her tone that she wasn't exactly thrilled with our friendship either.

"Let's not talk about Jamie right now," Ryan interrupted her. "I've already had enough arguments for one day."

"But she's…"

I don't know what made her stop her sentence, but instead of repeating all the things Paige called me earlier, all she said was, "I'm just worried about you."

"Don't be" was the last thing I heard before I started my car and sped away from school.

I went home, and my face was so pale it was easy to convince my parents that I didn't feel well. I might as well have had a legitimate illness because I was miserable all day. Sure, it was self-inflicted suffering, but I doubt even the nastiest virus could have made me feel worse.

I fell asleep after lunch and didn't wake up again until there was a soft knock at the door. I said, "Come in," assuming it was my mother checking on me for the millionth time, and didn't open my eyes until I realized that the hand pushing my hair back was much too big to be my mother's. "How are you feeling?" Ryan asked softly when my eyes flew open. "Your mom said you're sick."

I had too many questions to figure out which to ask first, so instead I just reacted on instinct and gasped at the awful bruise covering the right side of his face. "Your eye!"

He gave me a lopsided grin. "Sexy, right?"

I couldn't even laugh—it looked that awful. "It looks painful."

"It's not so bad."

Ryan didn't elaborate at all, and I didn't know what else to say, so I started asking my questions. "What are you doing here?"

"You weren't at school. I was worried."

After everything he'd been through today, he was worried about *me*? It was so sweet, and yet it made me feel that much worse. How could he still be giving me that carefree smile? He had to be hurting. I wanted to ask, but I didn't want to be the first to bring it up. "Shouldn't you be at practice right now?"

Ryan's smile turned sheepish, and he pointed to the bruise on his face. "Driscoll and I got suspended for the rest of the week. That includes all school-related activities. Coach was so mad he burst a capillary in his eye."

I couldn't believe he was laughing. I didn't think it was funny. "Why did you get suspended? Mike was the only one who punched anybody."

"How do you know I didn't beat his butt to the ground for it? You weren't at school today."

Oops. "I was until your best friend punched you on account of me. After that I was pretty sure nobody wanted to see me there."

"I did."

"You don't count."

Instead of a pout, Ryan gave me another smirk. "I thought I was the only one who *did* count."

I sighed. "Ryan." I was upset, and it took me a minute to steady my voice. "Mike was right. Not about you being a jerk, but you have been spending a lot of time with me lately. You're losing your friends over me, and I can't handle that. Maybe we should stop hanging out."

Ryan gave me a very no-nonsense look, but he wasn't angry with me. "You'll have to kill me first."

Again, I didn't think it was funny, but this time he wasn't joking. "Nobody is losing anything. Paige is just jealous, and Mike's always looking for a fight. They'll get over it as soon as they get to know you. Everything will be fine, you'll see."

"What do you mean, when they get to know me? Nobody's getting to know me."

"I thought that was the reason for all the practice, so you could have enough control to be safe around people. You're doing so much better now that I just assumed you'd want to start meeting other people."

"Wrong."

"But why? I thought you wanted to have friends. Live a normal life."

"If that means hanging out with Mike and Paige, then thanks but no thanks."

"Jamie." It was his turn to sigh. "You've got to get over yourself. You can't just hate everyone all the time. You're just scared, but there's really nothing for you to be afraid of."

"Easy for you to say. You're Ryan Miller! You're perfect! I'm a freak, remember?"

"I wish you would quit saying that."

"Why deny what I am?"

"You're not a freak, but I meant I wish you would stop calling me perfect. I've got plenty of issues."

"Like?"

"Like my need to be perfect? I make people like me because I care so much what they think about me that I do whatever it takes. I put up with Paige even though she drives me crazy because I'd rather go nuts than have her not like me. I don't even really like football all that much, but I play because I know it's what my dad likes best about me, and even though he left, I still need his approval."

I couldn't believe what I was hearing. Ryan? Self-conscious? It couldn't be.

"It's sick the things I do just to make other people happy. I've always admired you, Jamie, since your first day of school here. I was standing next to Mike when he asked you out, and you laughed at him like he was crazy. I didn't understand how anybody could do that, but you really didn't care what he thought of you. You didn't care what anybody thought. You have no idea how much I wish I could be more like you."

I was stunned speechless. Literally. Without speech.

"You must be rubbing off on me," Ryan teased after it was clear I wasn't going to respond, "because I'm not giving you up for anything, no matter how many people I make unhappy over it." He smiled playfully, but the look faded quickly. "I really wish you'd make an attempt to get to know my friends. I know it's hard to believe, but they really aren't bad people."

He smiled at me and then quickly pressed his lips to my forehead before standing up from my bed. "Think about it, please. Besides the fact that it would be good for you, they mean a lot to me, and I would love for you to know them."

When he said that, all I could see was him and Becky in each other's arms. *They* didn't mean a lot to him, *she* meant a lot to him. Maybe she should.

Ryan had come over to see if I was feeling any better, but all his visit did was make me feel worse. "Get some rest," he said, concerned by the new look of despair suddenly prominent on my face. He waited for a moment before stepping out of my room, hoping I might tell him what I was thinking, but when I didn't, he forced one last smile. "Don't forget we said practice on Sunday. I'll pick you up at ten."

Thanks to Mike and his itchy punching fist, I hadn't seen Ryan all week, and I was stuck with nothing but my thoughts to entertain me at school. Not good. All I could think about was his fight and how it was my fault.

And then, of course, there was Becky. She was still just as withdrawn as she'd been for weeks now, but she seemed more content to be that way. I knew the change could only be because of what happened with Ryan, and that got me thinking even more.

By the time Ryan showed up Sunday morning, just as he'd promised, I was completely out of it. Seeing him should have cheered me up, not depressed me even more, especially when he demanded we work out together. You see, there's Ryan Miller, and then there's Ryan Miller working out. Shirtless, sweat glistening on his hard skin, slow focused breathing forcing his chest to expand just as his abdomen tightens around each individual muscle in it… It should have been enough to scorch my eyes and render me useless, but I didn't even notice the perfection in front of me.

I didn't realize just how somber I was until Ryan pulled me from my thoughts with a chuckle. "You know," he said, now merely using his bench press as a front-row seat to witness my workout. "I think you were right. Making you work out was a really bad idea."

"Why?" I frowned at the truck I was bench-pressing. Ryan had spent the last three weeks trying to convince me that I needed to work on my super-strength. He said that for a superhero I was "superwimpy."

"Aside from the fact that the F-250 you're pumping is making me feel extremely inadequate," Ryan said, "I'm afraid that if you don't stop doing that, you're going to end up throwing it at me."

"Why would I throw a truck at you?"

"Because you usually get really cranky when I try to kiss you, and if you don't stop looking so downright sexy, I'm going to have to do just that."

I took a slow breath, lowered the truck, and pushed it high above me again. As I did, I could feel my ponytail sticking to the back of my neck. I was sure I looked anything but sexy, and Ryan seemed to be able to read my thoughts. "I've never seen you break a sweat before," he confessed. "It's got my mind in the gutter big-time."

The heat I felt in my neck now was from embarrassment instead of a raised heartbeat. I sneaked a quick glance at Ryan's face and suddenly felt like the sports bra and work-out shorts I had on were not nearly enough clothes. On the bright side, I forgot about sulking. "Quit objectifying me right now, or I *will* throw this truck at you! Go take a cold shower or something while I finish."

"I've got a better idea. Why don't you call it quits and come in the hot tub with me."

"Oh yeah, that's a brilliant idea. Why don't you just take a soak with a blow dryer?"

Ryan gave me an annoyed glare, but dropped the subject and gulped down a bottle of water before throwing himself down on the patio swing and closing his eyes.

I continued my workout in silence for a few minutes. It was so peaceful at Ryan's cabin that I never minded when things got quiet between us, but as I listened to the nature around me I noticed a strange noise that didn't seem to fit in with the sounds of the woods. "Do you hear that?" I asked before realizing what a dumb question that was. Of course he couldn't hear it; I could barely hear it.

"Hear what?"

"A really quiet humming noise. I can't exactly place it, but I've never heard it out here before." I set the truck carefully back on the ground and listened again.

"It's probably just a boat down on the lake," Ryan offered.

It didn't sound like a motor to me. It almost sounded electronic. But as soon as I'd put the truck down it stopped. "The lake is behind the house—this noise was coming from out there."

I pointed to the forest in front of the house and scanned the trees again, but I didn't see anything. Whatever it was, it was gone now, so I joined Ryan on the front porch with a heavy sigh. "Maybe my mind is just playing tricks on me. I tend to get a little paranoid when I'm doing things like lifting trucks out in the open."

Ryan sat up, making room for me next to him on the swing. When I sat down he put his arm around me, and I didn't fight him. We'd been practicing so much lately that I was less of a stickler about him touching me, and I knew I was okay at the moment.

"All right, then," he said, obviously happy that I hadn't shrugged him off, "why don't we work on something a little more subtle if you're worried? How about your hearing? I'll start singing, and you go for a jog. Call me when you can't hear me anymore. That's not so obvious as bench-pressing my truck."

Ryan gave me a squeeze, and having his arm around me reminded me of the mood I'd been in all week. A flash of him wrapped up in Becky's arms instantly made my heart drop into my stomach. "I don't feel like practicing anymore today," I said.

Ryan heard the disappointment in my tone. "All right. It's lunch time anyway, and I've officially worked up an appetite."

I could tell by his careful tone, that Ryan was resisting the urge to ask me what was wrong, but he's good at that for only so long. I didn't want to explain it to him, so I decided to try to distract him. "You like New York–style pizza?"

Ryan instantly perked up. Mission accomplished. "I'm a guy. I love all forms of pizza."

"Well, I happen to know where to find the best pizza in the country, so why don't you point me in the direction of a bathroom, and once I'm cleaned up I'll run get us lunch."

"Aw, come on, Baker. I'm digging that post-workout look."

"More like post-workout *stink*. Don't forget I have a heightened sense of smell."

I laughed when Ryan wrinkled his nose. Obviously he hadn't thought of it like that. "Gross."

"I know, so make sure you shower up while I'm out getting the pizza."

"Yes ma'am." Ryan saluted and marched me inside to the bathroom.

Forty-five minutes later I returned to the cabin with a hot pie from Ricci's. I plopped it down on the patio table, where Ryan had barely sat down to wait for me, and his eyes grew really big when I lifted the lid.

"I'm telling you, best pizza in the country." I said.

"This looks amazing! Where did you get this from?"

"This little town in Illinois."

"You mean that state clear on the East Coast?" Ryan asked incredulously.

"Well, technically it's the Midwest. Did you sleep through geography too?"

"Whatever. I just meant that it's not exactly around the corner." Ryan stared at the slice of pizza in his hands for a moment as if it were magical, but when the smell reached his nose, he snapped out of it. Once he was on his third or fourth piece, he finally slowed down enough to carry on a conversation politely. "I can't believe you just went all the way to Illinois."

"It is kind of surreal sometimes when I think about what I can do," I admitted.

"I wish I had powers too. How much fun would it be if I could just go tromping around the country on a whim and still be back in time for dinner? I'd be at Miami Beach all the time. Or New York."

I knew what he meant, but I couldn't stop his comment from ripping at my stomach. I would never wish for something so awful to be placed on anyone, especially not Ryan. But then, my powers hadn't seemed like nearly as much of a burden since I'd told Ryan about them, and part of me agreed that it would be amazing to be able to drag Ryan off to my favorite spot with me.

"The Grand Canyon," I whispered.

"What?"

I blushed as I remembered the first dream of mine Ryan ever starred in. "If I could take you anywhere with me, I'd take you to the Grand Canyon, not New York. Best sunsets on the planet."

Ryan considered this for a minute and then smiled. "We'll plan a trip sometime. You'll just have to go by plane like us mere mortals."

"Like you mortals?" I groaned. "Oh please! Shut up and eat that last piece."

Ryan laughed but did as he was told, and was quiet as he polished off the last of the pizza. When he was finished he finally broke the silence. "Can I ask you a question?"

"Sure."

"But you have to promise not to freak out."

That made me a little nervous, but my curiosity got the better of me. "Okay," I agreed slowly.

"I was just wondering..."

"Yeah?"

"Well, I was just thinking about how you got your powers."

I felt butterflies in my stomach as I remembered the accident. "And?"

Ryan gulped nervously, but he looked determined to spit out whatever was on his mind. "I was just wondering why...Derek"—he stumbled over the name—"didn't end up like you."

I couldn't hide my shock, and Ryan's face paled when he realized he might have upset me. "I don't mean to pry," he said shyly. "It's just that, well, if it was the waste from the truck combined with the electricity that gave you your powers, then shouldn't Derek have gotten them too, instead of... you know..."

I felt like I was going to be sick. It was a logical enough question. Obvious even, if you really thought about it, but I still never expected Ryan to make that connection. It was part of a secret I'd sworn to take with me to the grave. But I had to answer him somehow. I watched Ryan's face carefully as I spoke, unsure of what I was searching for exactly but terrified all the same. "Derek wasn't in the car when the truck hit me. He wasn't sprayed with the chemicals, just electrocuted."

Ryan was quiet for a minute, and I wondered if he could see me trembling. "What was he doing if he wasn't in the car with you? Where was he?"

"We were coming back from this place we liked to go to sometimes. An old bridge over a big irrigation canal hidden in the middle of a cornfield. It's a nice quiet place for stargazing. I beat him back to the car, and right after I got in, that's when the truck appeared."

This answer seemed to suffice for the time being, and when he hesitated I became desperate to change the subject. There were still questions he could ask. Questions that I knew he would ask if he had time to think about them. Questions that I knew I wasn't prepared to give answers to. Not even to Ryan.

"Can I ask *you* a question?" I asked quickly when he started to open his mouth, another question dripping from his lips.

He choked on his words, surprised by my request, and then nodded. "Sure, anything."

"What's the story with you and Becky? Why haven't you guys ever gone out?"

That one floored him. And rightfully so. It was way more out of the blue than the one he'd asked me. I hadn't been planning to pry into this subject, but I was curious, and my question accomplished its purpose. Ryan forgot all about my accident and my dead boyfriend.

"Um…" he stuttered, still a little startled. "Well, actually we did for a while. Kind of. If sixth grade counts." The smile that subconsciously spread across his face was tragically beautiful. "She was my first kiss."

"Oh."

"You're not worried about Becky, are you?" Ryan asked, looking up at me with an anxious expression. I guess my disappointment was poorly disguised. Of course I had no reason to be jealous, no right to be, but I was. "There's nothing like that going on between us anymore. There hasn't been for years and years. I promise you, Jamie, you have nothing to worry about."

Ryan's promise tore my heart into pieces. Why was he declaring his faithfulness to me when we weren't even in a relationship? When we could never be in a relationship? Ryan deserved so much more than to waste himself on an impossible crush, and I couldn't take advantage of him like that.

I'd asked the question casually, but this conversation seemed anything but casual all of a sudden. "That's exactly what has me worried though, Ryan—the fact that there's nothing going on. Becky is so pretty, and aside from how she feels about me, she seems really nice. You obviously care a great deal for her. She could be the perfect girlfriend for you. That's something that I could never be. You deserve the things she could give you, all the things I can't."

I was horrified when my eyes betrayed me and filled with tears. I batted them away quickly, but the damage had been done. Ryan was already on his feet and scooping me out of my chair, into his arms. "But she can't be you," he insisted. "Don't you understand that you're the one I want? You. Not Becky or Paige or any other girl that may or may not be able to make out with me. Just *you*."

Ryan was doing his very best to win me over, and I was so close to giving in. Too close. I couldn't remember why I was supposed to resist him anymore. I just knew that I should. I began to chant *No! No! No!* over and over in my head until I gained some of my strength back. "No," I finally managed to say out loud, only it came out as a faint whisper. "You shouldn't want me, Ryan."

I pulled myself out of Ryan's grip and started to run. I don't know why I didn't take off at superspeed. Still feeling the fuzzy effects of his "just me" speech, maybe. I only got as far as the front steps. Ryan grabbed me by the wrist, whirled me around, and pulled me down onto the porch swing we'd been sitting on earlier. "Oh no you don't. You are not running away from me this time."

"Ryan, please!"

"No!" He clamped his arms around me and held me down beside him on the swing. Not in a scary aggressive way, just so that I couldn't get away without going super-Jamie on him. "If you don't want to be with me because you're not ready for another relationship or you don't like me that way, then that's fine. I can respect that. I could even deal with the excuse that you're just too scared. That's a lame excuse, but it's one I could live with. What I can't live with is you playing the martyr because you don't think you're good enough for me, understand?"

I took that as a rhetorical question, but I stopped straining against his grip. He felt me relax and narrowed his eyes at me as he let me go. I slumped back in my seat and didn't fight him when he slid his arm around me and tucked me securely into his side. He let out what sounded like a sigh of relief and then rested his head on top of mine.

I wondered what he was thinking about as we sat there, but I didn't ask. I had a feeling I was better off not knowing this time, because he buried his nose in my hair and inhaled really deeply before planting a kiss on the side of my head. Then the arm he had around my shoulder dropped down my back and slid around my waist in order to pull me even tighter to him.

For a split second his fingers slid across the bit of my skin that was exposed between the bottom of my T-shirt and the top of my low-rise jeans. I wasn't sure if he'd noticed the contact, but I sure did, and the brief touch sent a shock wave through me.

Ryan did notice. His fingers quickly found their way back to my skin, and then he slid his free hand firmly across my stomach, making sure to catch as much of my bare skin as he could before lacing his fingers together, locking me in his arms. The action raised goose bumps on my skin. "Ryan." I sighed reluctantly. It was meant as a warning.

He cut me off with gentle authority. "Shh. We're just going to sit here for a minute."

He didn't say anything more because he knew he'd won the argument. Not that I'd put up much of a fight this time.

Ryan was beginning to learn where my weaknesses were and was artfully figuring out how far he could push me before I hit the panic button on him. He waited a few minutes until I was completely relaxed again, and then he unlocked his hands and began grazing my skin with his fingertips. His touch caused a burning sensation that left a trail everywhere his fingers roamed. My whole body shuddered. As I gasped, trying to find enough breath to tell him to stop, he cut me off with a whisper. "Jamie?"

I could barely think straight anymore. "Hmm?" I breathed in a voice so small I wasn't sure if he'd heard me.

"Kiss me."

I shuddered again at his request. "No."

I answered his question but didn't have the strength to tell him to stop the torture his fingers were inflicting. I shuddered again, forcefully enough that Ryan stopped what he was doing and locked his hands back together. "You're ready," he insisted. "If you can handle this, then you can handle just one kiss."

Suddenly I felt his nose brush against my jaw. His lips fluttered across my ear as he whispered a faint, "Please?"

My pulse was racing and I felt almost faint, but I concentrated on my breathing, willing myself to stay calm. I wasn't strong enough to resist him, so I had to try my hardest not to hurt him. And then his hand was under my chin tilting my head up to his. Our lips met before I even realized what was happening, and that was the end of it. Every logical thought I had slipped right from my mind.

Just like the first time we kissed, my body pulled me to him like a magnet to iron, and my arms wrapped themselves around his neck. I felt the flow of energy pass through us, and Ryan responded by pulling me closer to deepen his kiss. I felt the hairs begin to rise on the back of his neck and started to pull away. "No," Ryan gasped, refusing to let me go. "No, it's okay."

Ryan's a persuasive guy, and an even better kisser, so when his lips crashed down on mine again, I kissed him back with full force. When I lost complete control of myself, the flowing power became more intense than ever, and I realized I was not giving off energy, but rather pulling it to me.

I could feel my body sucking power right out of the atmosphere around me. The electricity from the house, and the power lines that fed it, came rushing at me in all directions. Everything felt so warm, and a whirlwind of energy began to circle around us whipping my hair about in a wild frenzy.

When Ryan's entire body finally began trembling against me, my passion was quickly replaced with panic. I meant to simply push him back enough to separate us, but all of the energy I'd channeled had made me much stronger than normal. When my hands pressed against his chest, I accidentally knocked him back a good twenty yards. He went flying off the swing and over the porch railing, where he landed on the dirt driveway.

I'd thrown him so far that I was sure I'd hurt him, and I started to rush to his side. But as I bounded down the steps, I could feel that something was really, really off with me.

Not wrong necessarily but definitely not good either. I felt scary powerful. All of the energy I'd sucked in was bouncing around inside me like atoms in a nuclear bomb.

I stopped, afraid that if I moved a muscle I would lose control of all the wild power inside me. Holding still didn't seem to help. The energy flowed through my body causing my arms and legs to shake with fury. My hair began flowing away from my head as if the energy was trying to escape through each individual strand. Heat began to rise to the surface of my skin, and my palms felt like they were on fire.

I was momentarily distracted from my situation when I heard a groan. Ryan had regained consciousness and sat up holding a hand to his head. I was confused because as far as he'd flown there should have been some damage done, but he looked merely shaken up, not really hurt. He looked around in a daze for a moment until his eyes fell on me.

"Jamie!"

The way he screamed, as if he feared for my life, startled me from my trance, and the fire beneath my palms suddenly exploded from me like bolts of lightning. The blasts shot straight out from my hands, whizzing over Ryan's head by only a couple of feet, and zapped a gigantic pine tree behind him. With a blinding light and a deafening crack of thunder, the base of the tree exploded out from under itself.

Ryan hollered my name again, but not as loudly as I screamed his, because the tree behind him was starting to fall. Unable to make myself move, all I could do was scream, "Look out!" and point at the three-foot-thick trunk falling directly toward him.

With no time to pick himself up and run, Ryan threw his hands above his head in an instinctive move to shield himself. My heart stopped beating as the tree crashed down, but to my astonishment, Ryan caught the massive trunk and held it steady above his head.

We stared at each other in disbelief for a moment. It should have been impossible. How had it happened? *What* had happened? I was worried, but I watched that infamous beautiful grin spread widely across Ryan's face, and he threw the tree behind him in much the same manner as I'd tossed him just moments before.

"That was freaking awesome!" Ryan laughed as he rose to his feet, but I couldn't follow his lead. Relief, shock, and fatigue all caught up with me in that moment, and I realized that the explosion had left me feeling completely weak. My muscles were like Jell-O, and my knees buckled.

When Ryan came rushing to my aid, I screamed, "No! Wait!" But it was too late. Ryan grabbed me and electricity surged through his body. The jolt kicked him hard, knocking him on his back. His muscles contracted in wild spasms for a second, and then he fell lifelessly against the dirt.

It could have been worse, I guess. Though at the time I couldn't see how. But at the time I thought he was dead. He sure *looked* dead, which meant I'd killed yet another boyfriend. Not that Ryan was my boyfriend, you know, technically, but he was close enough.

I screamed at first—so loud that I'm surprised the neighbors didn't come to investigate even if they did live nearly two miles away—but the screams morphed into sobs when I noticed him breathing.

A wave of relief washed over me, but it wasn't nearly enough. He was still unconscious, his hair was standing on end, and his skin looked grossly pale. I had to do something. If I hadn't been sure I'd fry him all over again, I'd have carried him to a hospital already, but as it was, I couldn't touch him.

I hated feeling so helpless. I tried to calm myself down, but it was useless. The crazy emotions were rebuilding the energy I'd exerted with the blast of lightning. I was already starting to feel strong again, and that made me dangerous. All I could do was sit there with him and wait.

I cried, begging Ryan to wake up, until my ears caught the sound of the faint humming I'd heard just before lunch. I sucked in my sobs and turned my eyes to the forest, focusing all my attention on the sound. It was definitely electronic. A video camera maybe? And it was coming from way off in the distance, up the side of the mountain, deep in the trees.

The harder I listened, the more things came into focus. Wind pushing its way through the pine needles. Tiny feet scampering in the branches. A nondescript rustling in the bushes. Breathing. And a heartbeat. I wasn't sure I was hearing a human—a deer would breathe and have a heartbeat too.

At first I saw nothing, but the tiniest glint of sunlight reflected off something up the hill, and as I strained my eyes everything came into focus. The bush looked normal enough, but within its branches the colors blurred together a few shades darker. There was definitely a figure hiding there.

"Carter," I breathed. I was frozen in fear at the possibility that someone was watching me. I couldn't tell for sure, but what else could it be? The sound? The reflected light?

As I frantically tried to figure out what to do, I was startled by a horrible coughing fit. It was the most beautiful sound I'd ever heard. "Are you okay?" I asked, tears returning to my eyes. "Oh, Ryan, I'm so sorry!"

Ryan pulled himself up. As soon as he had his wits about him his eyes focused on me. I was so sure I'd finally pushed him over the edge, freaked him out beyond repair. I was convinced that he'd run away screaming and never speak to me again. I was also convinced that that wasn't such a bad idea, but Ryan surprised me. The corners of his mouth slowly crept upward and he said, "That. Was. Awesome!"

His voice was a little gruff, but I could still hear the unmistakable excitement. The jolt had clearly fried his brain. "What?"

"Let's do it again!"

If my face was pale before, now it was white as a ghost, and Ryan laughed at my expression. "I don't mean the whole getting zapped part," he said. "Though I always wondered what it would feel like to get Tasered. FYI? It sucks. But you are seriously the best kisser in the entire world. So worth it. And did you see that? For a minute I was strong like you!"

Ryan grunted as he got to his feet. After stretching all his stiff muscles, he stepped toward me with open arms.

"Are you suicidal?" I screamed, putting a good twenty feet between us instantly.

Ryan blinked. "You're not calm yet?" he asked.

"Calm?" I screeched. "Calm? Ryan, I nearly killed you! How could I possibly be calm?"

Ryan studied my face for a minute and then rolled his eyes. His smile turned to a frown. "You're not going to let me kiss you ever again, are you?" It wasn't really a question.

"And you say you're not that smart."

"Aw, come on, Jamie. Getting zapped was my own fault. I shouldn't have touched you—I figured you didn't have any juice left in you when you collapsed. Maybe we need to figure out a way for me to know when you're charged up, but the kissing didn't hurt anything. You can't go ice queen on me over that."

"Hello? Did you see the part where I shot lightning out of my hands?"

"Yeah, coolest thing I've ever seen."

"Lightning that missed your head by mere inches and then exploded a tree?"

"But it missed me, and I caught the tree when it fell. No harm done."

I opened my mouth to speak, but it took a minute before any words could escape it. "You *are* suicidal."

"What are you doing?" Ryan asked when I headed around to the back deck and gathered up my things.

"I'm leaving. Playtime is over. No more practice."

"Jamie, you can't just quit."

"Watch me."

I ignored his pleading and zipped up my backpack. He chased after me as I bounded down the front steps. "Jamie, wait! At least drive back with me because we should really talk about this."

"There's nothing to talk about."

"Okay, fine, then just humor me. You may be able to get home in a few seconds, but I have an hour-and-a-half drive... Please?"

Ryan gave me a ridiculous puppy-dog face, but his eyes seemed genuinely desperate. I wanted to take off, but since when have I been able to really walk away from him?

We were silent all the way back into town. A couple of times Ryan opened his mouth to say something but then thought better of it. We both knew that what he wanted to say would only cause an argument.

Eventually he found a way to bring up the subject without raising my blood pressure. "You know, right before you did the thing with the lightning you looked kind of freaky. You're hair was flying all over the place, except there wasn't any wind, and your eyes were glowing."

"Glowing?" I gasped. Something about that image was very disturbing.

Ryan nodded and then cautiously asked, "What do you think happened out there, exactly? Not just the glowing and the lightning, but the thing with me and the tree. Have you ever done that before? Like accidentally given your parents your powers or something?"

I wanted to keep quiet, but I couldn't help the smirk that appeared on my face. "I've never exactly made out with my parents, Ryan, so, no. The lightning and the glowing and the *you* thing… all firsts for me."

"Okay," Ryan said, laughing. "But that is what happened, right? When we kissed, you gave me your powers."

"It would appear so."

"How is that possible?"

I shrugged, but then I really thought about it for a minute and said, "It must be the energy. Remember how I told you that the energy makes me feel different? I'm obviously transferring a little of that energy to you, and it must have the same effect on you as it does on me. That's got to be why you were so wired after we kissed that first time, and that day after I told you about me. I bet you probably had powers then too, at least on a small scale. You just never thought to use them."

"Do you think I had all your powers and not just the strength?"

I shrugged. "Probably."

"Cool."

I was about to explain to Ryan just how *not* cool that was, when he distracted me with another thought. "I wonder why it wore off so fast this time. Maybe the shock canceled it out."

"Shock?" I repeated dryly. "I think you mean electrocution. I guess it could be. Or maybe it's because you used it up quicker. It took superstrength to catch that tree and toss it the way you did. That probably takes a little more energy than running on a treadmill."

"Maybe. It'd be easy to test the theory, though. I'll bet we could go to the Grand Canyon after all. We should try it again next Sunday and see if I could keep up with you."

"No! No way! We're never doing it again. I mean it—no more practicing!"

"But you have to keep trying."

"Oh no I don't! This isn't football practice, okay? We're messing with something neither of us understands, and if I screw up you *die*. You may not care, but I really don't want to kill you, so we're done. End of story."

I was done having the discussion so I clenched my jaw and crossed my arms over my chest. Ryan, however, was far from finished arguing with me. "So you're just going to give up?"

"That's exactly what I'm going to do."

"You're going to give up on having a normal life? Give up on your own happiness?" Ryan paused a moment and then added in a surprisingly soft voice, "Give up on *us*? Am I really the only one who cares about that?"

His voice cut through my heart like a knife. I was hurting him again. I really hated doing that, but I didn't have a choice, and he refused to understand that I was doing it for his own good. "Of course you're not the only one who cares about us," I admitted in as gentle a tone as I could. "I wish we could be together too. Probably more than you do. But we just can't. Don't you see that?"

"You really want to be with me? Really? Like the way I do? Like boyfriend and girlfriend?"

Suddenly all of my concern for his feelings vanished. "Don't act so surprised," I groaned. "You've been saying all along that you knew I liked you."

"Well, sure, I hoped, but I didn't *know*. You're very good at that whole acting detached thing."

"Yeah, well, I'm not detached. Not in your case, anyway. Happy?"

Ryan still looked like he didn't quite believe me, so I sighed. "Ryan, I like you a lot more than I care to admit.

I was a lost cause from the minute you told me the truth about your bet with Mike. I heard your conversation before you came up to me, you know. I knew what you were up to. I was ready to chew you up and spit you out, but somehow you completely worked me over. I'm still surprised that you managed it."

He was truly shocked now. "You've liked me since the first time I talked to you?"

I rolled my eyes, but I still turned red in the cheeks. "I would never have kissed you if I didn't."

"Then why are you always so..."

Ryan didn't finish his sentence, but he didn't need to. I knew what he was asking. "I didn't want you to know how I felt. I figured if you knew, you would only get more... Ryan-ish."

"Ryan-ish?" Ryan liked the sound of that. And worse, he liked how annoyed I suddenly was.

"Yes," I grumbled. "And when you start acting all Ryan-ish I can't seem to say no to you. It gets worse every day! You get harder and harder to resist every time I see you."

Ryan's confidence returned, and he had that stupid cocky smile on his face. It was very Ryan-ish, actually. "Well, if it's so hard," he said smugly, "then just stop resisting."

"Aghhh! You don't get it! I have to resist! No kiss, no matter how good it is, is worth killing you for. I've already lost one boyfriend. I am *not* going to lose another one! Do you understand me?"

Ryan didn't answer my question, but he was positively glowing. "You just called me your boyfriend!" he accused.

"I—" My mouth dropped all the way to my lap. "I did not!"

"Yes you did! You said you weren't going to lose another boyfriend, and that would be me—the other boyfriend you don't want to lose."

"But...I...I..."

"Ha! You said it, and you can't take it back! You are *so* my girlfriend now!"

"I am not!"

"Are too!

"Am not!"

"So are too!"

"Aghhh!" I screamed again. "You are so impossible!"

When I screamed, I lost control for a second and let out a burst of energy that stalled the truck. Ryan just grinned at me. He was lucky the car stopped right then, because I was contemplating knocking the stupid cocky smirk right off his face. Instead, I flung the door open.

"Bye, honey!" Ryan called playfully as I jumped out of the truck. "I'll see you at school tomorrow!"

I was slamming the front door to my house shut not two seconds later. "Jamie?" My mother called nervously.

"Why are boys always so pigheaded?"

My mother's worry was replaced with a laugh. "It's just genetic, hon. What happened?"

My mom was making cookies, and when I spied the open bag of chocolate chips on the counter I grabbed a spoonful of peanut butter. "Nothing. Ryan's just delusional," I explained, my annoyance quickly draining—peanut butter dipped in chocolate chips always makes me feel better. "He's got this crazy idea in his head that he's my boyfriend and won't let me tell him otherwise."

"Oh?" My mother was trying really hard to play it cool, but her voice cracked.

"Anyway, it doesn't matter because he's not."

My mom turned on her mixer then, but she'd been so distracted by the thought of me having a boyfriend that she'd put too many cups of flour in the cookie dough, and the beaters jammed up tight in the thick goo. When they got stuck, the roar of the mixer morphed into a low hum.

Something clicked in my head, and I gasped. The noise from the woods. How could I have forgotten!

"Jamie?" My mother was now just staring at me, her face a mixture of surprise and concern.

I didn't know what to say. Like I was going to tell her about Carter. If she knew he was back, the first thing she'd do was tell my dad, and then one of two things would happen. He'd either be in Folsom Prison by the end of the night for killing Carter, or he'd be there for murdering me when he found out I was having super practices with Ryan.

"Jamie?" My mom asked again. She was taking her apron off now.

"Sorry!" I blurted out. "I was just—" I reached up lightning fast and yanked off one of my earrings. "I lost one of my earrings," I mumbled. "They're my favorite."

My mom took a visible breath of relief but still gave me a sympathetic smile. "Oh, I just hate it when that happens. Remember the pearl stud I lost in Chicago the last time we went? I'm still irked about that."

I nodded absently, telling myself that I wasn't stupid for completely forgetting about Carter. I was justifiably preoccupied with having fried my boyfriend.

Not my boyfriend! Ugh! Now he had me thinking it! Anyway.

"I think I'm going to go look for it," I said quickly. "I mean, if anyone can find it, it's me, right?"

My mom smiled proudly as I ran out the door. "While you're at it, you should do a sweep of Chicago and find mine too!"

I actually got to Ryan's house a minute before he did. He was clearly startled when he pulled up to the curb and saw me waiting on his porch. He jumped out of the truck and I bounded across the lawn to him at superspeed.

"Jamie?" Ryan asked when I stopped just short of his open arms. "What is it? What's wrong? Are you hurt? Are your parents okay?"

"Ryan, that reporter that showed up here? He didn't go home after you broke his nose. He knows my secret! He has proof!"

"What? How?"

"He was at the cabin today! I thought I saw him, but it was right after the lightning thing, and you were lying there unconscious so I didn't go see, and then I completely forgot! And now it's too late! And he's going to expose me! And now I've got you involved, and he's going to ruin your life too!"

The more I spoke, the more upset I became. But now that Ryan knew what was going on, he curbed his own anxiety. "Okay," he said gently. "Okay. It's okay. We'll figure this out. But you need to calm down before you completely lose it."

Ryan took a deep breath, prompting me to follow his lead. It took me several tries before I was able to really fill my lungs and exhale slowly. When I finally managed it Ryan reached out and asked, "Am I gonna get fried?"

I shook my head. I was by no means calm, but I had a grip on the power. For the moment, anyway.

"Good." Ryan pulled me into his arms and squeezed like there was no tomorrow, then said, "I hate not being able to do this when you're upset."

Okay, I would never ever in a million years say this out loud, but I'm sure I hated it much worse. Having his arms around me was like magic. It worked to calm me down way better than any of his hippy breathing—no offense to his parents or anything.

Every muscle in my body relaxed, and I slumped against him with a sigh. "This doesn't mean that I'm your girlfriend," I mumbled, but unfortunately I was too comfortable to really sound like I meant it.

"Whatever you say." He chuckled.

Great. Like I was ever going to convince him now.

We stood there a moment longer, and then Ryan got down to business. "So this guy..."

"Dave Carter."

"Right, Carter. You saw him taking pictures? Filming us?"

"Well, I didn't *see* him, exactly. But I know he was there."

Ryan's concern turned into a patronizing smile. "I'm not paranoid!" I yelled before he had the chance to say anything. "You don't know him like I do. The guy is completely insane! He used to follow me everywhere, and he would make up all these crazy stories. I had to *move* just to get away from him. Trust me, he's here."

"All right," Ryan relented, though he clearly thought that a year and a half of keeping secrets was causing me to suffer from paranoid delusions.

Whatever. He's the deluded one, convincing himself that we're a couple.

He grinned at me like he knew exactly what I was thinking, and then grabbed me by the hand. "Come on," he said, and then dragged me toward the house.

I stopped when we got to the porch. "What is that smell?"

Ryan sniffed his shirt and with a smile said, "Armani. You like it?"

"Not you," I said. "It smells like someone is frying up dog vomit in your house."

This took Ryan by surprise. I guess it was pretty random. "You're really sick sometimes, Baker," Ryan said. "You know that?" He opened the front door and inhaled deeply. "Smells like lasagna to me."

"That is not lasagna!" I whispered.

"Tofu lasagna," he clarified, shrugging. "It's good for you." He laughed at the look on my face—which was totally disgusted—and then called out, "Hey, Mom! I'm home! And I've brought you a surprise!"

The thought of meeting Ryan's parents had never occurred to me. I was *so* not in the mood for that. I glared at Ryan, but that only ever seems to encourage him. He pulled me into the kitchen and said, "Look who wants to join us for dinner!"

That dirty little…! I couldn't even argue, because when his mom looked up, she was so utterly excited. The woman was absolutely tiny and had brown hair, but she was definitely Ryan's mom. She had his same crystal blue eyes, and her entire face was lit up with the very smile that I can never say no to. It was so unfair!

"Smells delicious," was all I could say.

"Jamie! I'm so glad to meet you!" she said, wiping her hands in order to shake mine. "Ryan has been talking about you for so long I feel as if you're already part of the family."

I couldn't find my voice to respond. I actually blushed! There was just something about her. Ryan may have got his attitude from his father, but his charm? That was all his mom.

Eventually I croaked out, "Nice to meet you, Mrs. Miller."

"Oh, it's Rosenthal now, Jamie," she said, waving dismissively when I turned a deep red. "But please, Julie is fine."

"Good news!" Ryan interrupted, throwing his arm around me. "We're boyfriend and girlfriend now."

I whipped my head his direction so fast it may have actually been superfast. I would have been concerned that his mom noticed, except I was too busy willing myself to develop Superman's nifty heat vision so I could blow up Ryan's big fat head. When it didn't work I turned back to Mrs. Rosenthal and as calmly as possible said, "I'm not his girlfriend."

"It was her idea," Ryan argued. "She's just having a bad day and taking it out on me."

"You're going to be the one having a bad day in a minute!" I snapped. I didn't care that his mother was standing right there.

She didn't seem to mind though. "You poor thing," she said, scooting me gently over to a barstool. "Why don't you sit down and relax? I'll make you something to help you feel better, and you can tell me all about yourself."

I recognized the concoction she pulled from the cupboard and was actually looking forward to some of her magic tea, but Ryan pulled me up just as soon as I sat down. "We'll be in my room," he said, and then tugged me down the hall.

"What is the matter with you?" I hissed before he even had the door shut. "Are you *trying* to cause a power outage?"

I was surprised to see the smile gone from his face. He looked almost sad as he apologized. "I'm sorry, Jamie," he said. He meant it too. "It's just that you seemed really upset about this Carter guy, and my mom can smell stress like a dog smells fear. I had to distract you. If she knew you were really upset she never would have left us alone until she knew everything." He shook his head and added, "If you think that reporter is nosy…"

You ever notice how Ryan always makes it impossible to stay mad at him? I *hate* that.

I stood there so completely chagrined that Ryan finally cracked a smile. He pulled me against his chest, which of course I couldn't resist at that point, and whispered, "Forgive me?" against the side of my head.

"No," I replied in the most pathetic pout ever, even as I was wrapping my arms around his waist.

"Thanks," Ryan said, relieved. Then he kissed the top of my head and pulled his now trembling arms away from me. He shook off a shiver, smoothed down the strands of hair that were starting to stick up, and then clapped his hands together. "Okay," he said, clearly getting back to the problem at hand. "So, did you call this guy?"

"Oh, yeah, I keep his number in my speed dial, Ryan."

Ryan was not deterred by my sarcasm. He sat down at his computer and clicked on the Internet. "Well, did you look it up?" he asked. "You know where he works in Illinois, right? Did you call to see if he's back there now?"

"No," I answered grudgingly. "He works for the *Chicago Reporter*."

Ryan typed the name into the search engine and asked me, "Have you done *anything* to try to find him yet?"

"I haven't had time," I said, exasperated. "As soon as I remembered, I came straight here."

Ryan turned to face me before clicking on the results. I didn't like the way he was suddenly looking very suspiciously at me. "You were really upset..." he prompted, but I didn't know what he wanted me to say.

"Your point?"

"My point is, when you freaked out you came straight to me for help. That is the most girlfriendy thing ever. I don't know why you won't just accept what you are."

"Would you just find me a phone number already!"

Ryan found me a number, and I called the rag Carter writes for in Chicago. I mean, Ryan did have a point. If Carter's been there, busily writing stories and ruining other people's lives this whole time, then he couldn't be here stalking me. Right?

"Yes, hi. I need to speak with one of your staff journalists, Dave Carter."

"Oh, I'm sorry," a female voice said. "Dave Carter's no longer here."

My heart sputtered in my chest, and I quickly told myself that it was Sunday evening in Chicago and he'd just gone home for the day. "Well, it's very important. Do you know what time he'll be in, in the morning?"

"No, you misunderstood me. Dave Carter no longer works here. He left weeks ago."

Weeks ago. As in right after I tried to play superhero and got beat up by my school's marquee. "Oh." I took a deep breath. It wouldn't help any to panic. "Um, well, do you know where he's working now?"

"I'm sorry. He didn't leave any forwarding contact info. It was quite sudden."

"Please!" The hysteria was starting to break through my voice. "You have to know something."

"Miss, is everything all right? Are you in some kind of trouble? Can I put you in touch with someone else here? Another journalist?"

"No! I just… I have to find him."

I heard the woman on the other end of the line sigh, and then she said, "The last time I saw him he was saying something about a company called Visticorp. I assume he got the job since he quit so suddenly."

"Visticorp?" That just didn't make sense. "What kind of a job? That doesn't sound like a newspaper."

"I'm sorry. I don't know anything more than that. If you want to leave your name and number, I can call you if he ever contacts us again."

"No! No, that's okay. Thank you."

I hung up before she could ask any more questions. She'd given me enough information anyway. "Carter isn't in Chicago anymore—he quit," I told Ryan. "I told you I'm not paranoid. He's still here. He's probably been watching me ever since I blew him off at school that day. I just don't know why he hasn't gone to the papers about me already. We've been practicing for weeks."

"Well, obviously he doesn't have any proof. If he did, he'd have released it already, wouldn't he?"

I thought for a minute, and even though I knew Carter would never sit on information that could make him rich and famous, I found myself disagreeing. "I don't know. He was so weird that day at school. Pretending like he wasn't there for a story? Warning me not to be sloppy? I can't figure out what his angle is."

I thought for a minute and then pointed at Ryan's computer. "May I?"

"How do you know he's got an angle?" Ryan asked as he moved.

"Because he's Carter," I said, typing in the name the woman on the phone had given me. "He's essentially the devil. He comes under the guise of concern and then profits from your misery."

According to Google, the company called Visticorp had its own website. I clicked the link, and up popped a picture of a bunch of guys in lab coats. I choked on a gasp, and the special low-wattage light bulb in Ryan's lamp couldn't handle the surge of energy that hit it.

"What is it?" Ryan asked, startled by the sudden pop and shattered glass.

I was already skimming the "About Us" section by the time Ryan looked over my shoulder.

"It's not about a story," I breathed.

Things began to spin out of control around me. I nearly fell out of the chair as I tried to rise to my feet.

"Jamie, breathe!" Ryan was warning me.

But I couldn't. I was way too freaked out. I mean an article in the tabloids would suck for sure, but scientists are way worse. They don't just expose. They experiment. And according to my dad, you're never seen or heard from again.

"It's a genetics research company in Las Vegas," I mumbled as the heat started burning through my body. "He's going to sell me out to a bunch of scientists."

"Jamie, focus! Your eyes are doing the glowing thing again. You have to calm down. You can't be shooting off any lightning here."

My body started to tremble, and Ryan backed as far away from me as he could. "Jamie," he said again. It was the fear in his voice that caught my attention. "You could really hurt yourself. You could hurt me. You don't want me to get hurt, do you?"

No. Not again. I really didn't want to hurt him again. Once was bad enough.

Ryan seemed to notice when I started thinking coherently again because he started encouraging me. "Focus, Jamie. Deep breaths."

I could do that much. I pinched my eyes shut and sucked in a huge breath, thinking that maybe if I could hold my breath inside, then I could hold the electricity in the same way.

I tried to focus on the power itself. Everything felt so much clearer to me now because when I'd kissed Ryan the power had been stronger than ever before, and as distracted as I was by the anxiety, I could still feel the power separate from the emotion. They were definitely separate. I just had to figure out how to do one without the other.

Keeping my eyes shut tight, I held my hand out in front of me. I tried to push all the energy inside me to my hand, hoping to manipulate the direction of it. As I concentrated on the flow, I was suddenly very aware of my body and the strange electrical force inside it. I couldn't seem to tell it where to go, but I could feel it everywhere it flowed.

In that moment of extreme concentration I felt something I'd never noticed before. I suppose it had always been there, because it didn't really feel different, but I'd just never paid this much attention before. I could feel the electricity in the atmosphere around me. It was stronger near the lamp, and Ryan's computer, and strongest near the electrical outlets in the wall.

The tingling sensation felt natural to me, and my body seemed to gravitate to it. So, keeping my eyes shut and my breathing slow, I held out my hand to the place where the power felt the strongest and tried to pull the warmth to me. At first nothing happened, but after a moment I felt energy flowing into me. I was sucking it right out of the wall socket like I was plugged in or something. It was just like earlier when I'd pulled it from the power lines while kissing Ryan, except not nearly as strong.

I was doing it. I was really doing it. I was controlling the energy. But when Ryan broke the silence and asked how I was doing, I lost my concentration. The moment I lost control, the flow of energy seemed to reverse, and it shot out from me. Not in lightning form, like before, but like when I lose my temper and power surges through the house—which it did right then.

I opened my eyes and realized that the power in the whole house was out. "Oops," I whispered as I met Ryan's worried gaze. "Sorry about that."

"Are you kidding? That was great!"

"Great? I knocked out the electricity."

"But you didn't blow up my room."

This was true and, I admit, highly encouraging. But not really enough to make me feel any better. "Ryan, what am I going to do?"

"What can you do? I mean unless Carter comes back, there's really no way to find him. And we don't know how much he knows or what he has proof of—if anything. We don't even know if he's really working with these science guys. We don't want to go poking around prematurely. The best we can do is keep quiet for a while and wait it out."

Ryan felt it safe enough now to cross the room to me and hold out his hand. I placed mine in it without even thinking. He squeezed my hand gently and then said, "We'll just stop practicing your powers for now and work on our relationship instead. I haven't been in one in so long, I probably need lots of boyfriend practice."

Man, Ryan's smile is hypnotic. I was calm again despite myself. Ryan smirked when he saw me trying not to crack a smile, so I ripped my hand from his. "I am not your girlfriend!"

Ryan, though he clearly thought otherwise, just smiled again as if to say, "suit yourself," and then led me back to the kitchen and his very confused mother.

"Sorry, guys, it's the whole house," she said, referring to power. "I can't figure out what's wrong, but the oven's electric, and the lasagna's not anywhere close to being done. It looks like we'll be dining out tonight."

"Oh, actually, it's probably just the—"

Ryan was going to say circuit breakers, but cut himself off when I crushed his hand.

"Just the what?" his mother asked curiously.

Ryan glanced at me and then shrugged. "Chinese sounds good."

Superpowers—one. Tofu lasagna—zero. Sometimes life's not all bad.

The next day the tension at school was thick. It was the first day that Ryan and Mike were back from their suspensions, and the entire student body, myself included, was anxious to see what would happen.

While I sat in my car, trying to pick out Ryan's voice among the chaotic chatter of the school, his truck slid into the empty parking spot next to me. I was listening so hard that I didn't realize he was there until he tapped on my window. The sound echoed in my ears and sufficiently startled me to stop my heart for a single beat.

"You going to stay in there all day?" Ryan asked through the glass.

I actually *had* been contemplating skipping school, but Ryan would have just followed me and gotten in trouble.

With a sigh, I heaved myself out of the car. "What do you want?" I asked as I began heading toward the school.

Ryan flashed me a killer smile. "I want to walk my girlfriend to class. Is that a crime?"

"Considering I'm not your girlfriend, so what you're doing could be considered stalking? Yes. As a matter of fact, it is a crime."

Ryan smiled, ignoring my jibe completely, and fell into step at my side. We walked in silence for a minute. Then, as we headed up the front steps, I began to hear the whispers of the students on campus. I stopped walking, stunned by what I was hearing. What people were saying. Not just people, but Mike. I stood there unable to do anything but listen in shock until Ryan broke me from my trance. "Jamie? What's wrong?"

"It's Mike." My voice was a faint whisper, and I wasn't able to get the full story out.

"Don't worry about Mike. I'm sure he'll be fine."

"No, you don't understand."

"Jamie, I don't care about Mike," Ryan interrupted firmly, and suddenly slipped his hand into mine, lacing our fingers together. If it didn't feel so good to have it there, I would have zapped him.

I made a pathetic attempt to pull my hand free, but Ryan defiantly tightened his grip. "You're going to have to fry me if you want me to let go."

I looked down at my hand in his, and really, I didn't want to let go any more than I wanted to hurt him, but I didn't have much of a choice. "Ryan, this"—I pulled our interlocked hands up to nearly eye level—"really isn't a good idea. Not today. Not now."

"What do you mean?"

"The gossip since you and Mike were suspended has been out of control."

"Oh yeah?" Ryan tried to keep his tone joking, but it was impossible to hide the strain entirely. "Everyone think I went crazy or something?"

"Don't worry. They aren't blaming you."

"They're blaming Mike?"

I wish. "Oh, no. Most people are siding with Mike. They're just not blaming you."

"That doesn't make sense."

"Sure it does. I mean, it's not *your* fault that the ice queen has brainwashed you."

It made perfect sense to me, but Ryan was stunned by the news. He stopped walking and gazed at me with a tortured expression. "People are blaming *you* for my fight with Mike?"

"Not to my face." I shrugged with a hint of a smile, but Ryan didn't think it was funny. I sighed again. I didn't want him to feel guilty on my behalf. "It's fine. Really. I honestly don't care if people hate me."

"People don't hate you. They're just surprised. They'll come around. Even Mike, you'll see. He's my best friend. I'm sure he got it all out of his system when he punched me."

"You think so?"

"Of course."

I hated to be the bearer of bad news, but he was going to find out soon enough. Better he heard it from me. "Ryan, Mike found out about my accident. He told the whole school about it."

"What?" It came out in a half gasp, half growl. "How did he find out?"

"The whole story is just a Google search away. I guess Carter showing up made him curious. He seems to be going with the leading tabloid theory—that I caused the accident on purpose because Derek dumped me. Paige is practically staging an intervention to get you away from me. She said she was going to petition to have me kicked out of school."

Ryan's face looked a little green, and it took him probably a good thirty seconds before he was even able to speak. "Jamie, I'm so sorry."

"It's not your fault," I said, but that didn't make him feel any better. "Look, it doesn't matter, okay? You don't care about my past, and that's all that matters to me. I don't care about the rest of them. But the problem is you do, and I don't want you losing your friends because of me."

Ryan opened his mouth to say something, but the warning bell went off before he could. I squeezed his hand and then pulled my fingers from his. "Let's just get through today before you go ruffling any more feathers with this whole girlfriend nonsense."

"But—"

"Go to class, Ryan."

"I'll see you at lunch," he promised stubbornly, but then walked away from me.

I hurried to my first class, and even the teacher fell into an awkward hush when I walked in. I kept my eyes on my desk, but I could feel the stares of everyone in the room. I tried to not let them bother me, but I couldn't manage it. Thanks to Ryan, I wasn't the ice queen anymore. I was just Jamie Baker again, and Jamie Baker had feelings. Jamie Baker was vulnerable. She was scared and weak. Broken. And everyone could tell.

That was the worst day I'd had since I came to Rocklin High. It rivaled the days at my old school after Derek died. The comments made were a little harsher, and the glares burned a little hotter. Maybe it was because of my extreme sensitivity to the topic being discussed, or maybe it was due to my guilt because this time they were right. I really was dangerous for Ryan, and I really did kill my last boyfriend. They had a right to be worried about Ryan.

I felt sick by the time lunch rolled around. I sat in my usual spot and picked at my food. I had no intention of eating it, but it gave me something to focus on other than the friction in the room. Everyone seemed a little on edge, but when Ryan found his way into the cafeteria it went silent. You could hear a pin drop even if you didn't have my hearing.

I wasn't surprised to see Becky at his side. She had taken up the habit of eating lunch in her car while Ryan was out on suspension, and I knew Ryan wouldn't let her get away with that any longer, but it seemed to be a little surprising to everyone else.

Everyone watched and waited to see what they were going to do. They stood there a moment meeting all the curious gazes, and while Becky looked terrified, Ryan seemed outraged. Becky gulped, waiting for Ryan to do something first, so he took her hand and began dragging her in the opposite direction of the cool kids' table. You wouldn't think such an action would cause such a reaction from the student body, but when it was clear that Ryan was not going to sit with his friends, the silence was immediately replaced with murmurs of shock.

Paige, still bitter from rejection, watched wordlessly, but Mike suddenly jumped up from his chair, once again causing silence to sweep the cafeteria. "Miller!" he shouted, making his way to Ryan. "Come on, man, where are you going?"

Ryan ignored him so he addressed Becky. "Becky? Where are you going?"

"Drop dead, Mike!" she shouted.

Her outburst was so surprising that even Ryan was startled and stopped walking. He looked at her with the same concern he'd shown me when he learned of my past, and she was every bit as defiant as I was when he looked at me that way. "I'm fine," she said coolly. "Keep going."

Ryan started to walk again, but Mike stepped in his way. "Don't be stupid," Mike warned. "You're still the king of this school. Don't give it all up over a freak like Baker."

I don't know if anyone else saw the way Ryan's face went flush with rage, and how his eyes seemed otherwise lifeless when he looked at his best friend, but I saw it, and I know Mike saw it. Ryan squeezed Becky's hand and then began walking again, smacking his shoulder into Mike's with force as he passed.

Everyone's eyes seemed to follow Mike back to his seat. Even Becky and I were so captivated by the look of betrayal he displayed that neither of us noticed the direction Ryan was walking—my direction. We realized this at almost exactly the same moment and met each other's murderous gaze momentarily.

"What are you doing?" Becky whispered to Ryan as soon as she looked away from me.

"I'm going to go sit by Jamie."

"What?" Becky gasped, pulling Ryan to a halt. "You're going to ditch me after you practically forced me to come in here?"

"Of course not. I'm going to introduce you."

For once, Becky and I seemed to share the same opinion. "Are you crazy?" she said. "I am not going to eat lunch with Jamie Baker."

"Just trust me on this. You don't know her like I do."

"I don't have to know her! Look at what she's done! She's ruining your life. Stealing you away from all your friends, getting you *suspended*! She's trouble, Ryan."

I'd heard these types of things and worse all morning, and even though they'd grated on my nerves I could tolerate it, but it was different coming from Becky. I couldn't chalk her speech up to a love of gossip and trash-talking the school outcast. Becky sincerely cared about Ryan more than any other person in this school, and she honestly believed what she was saying. She knew him better than anyone too. Way better than me. If she said I was ruining his life, who was I to say she was wrong? The look in her eyes was real—her concern for Ryan, her hatred for me. It made it impossible to hate her back.

Ryan had actually started to convince me that I didn't have to be in self-exile. True, I couldn't kiss him, and the practicing had to stop while he was present, but I was starting to think he could still be in my life. That he could still be my friend. Becky was taking that away from me and making it very hard not to see things her way.

The more I listened to the two of them argue, the more my feelings spun out of control. Within seconds, the lights in the cafeteria were flickering, and I didn't even realize it until I heard Ryan whisper my name. He'd said it so quietly that not even Becky heard it.

He started toward me, but Becky tugged his hand. "Please don't do this, Ryan," she pleaded with tears in her eyes. "Please just trust me and stay away from her."

Ryan suddenly went rigid. "Why should I trust you?" he snapped. "You won't trust me! Jamie's not the one ruining my friendships. Mike and Paige are doing that to themselves. I thought you might be different, but I guess not. After all the times you've told me I need a girlfriend, I finally find the perfect one, and you won't even give her a chance. You won't even say hello."

"She's your what?" Becky gasped. Her voice seemed to crack like a whip over the buzz of the lunchroom.

"She's my girlfriend!" Ryan yelled so angrily he could have given my dad, the grizzly, a run for his money.

The cafeteria went silent as the grave again. Forks were dropped, the lunch line stopped moving. Even Paul Warren, who'd been trying unsuccessfully to impress a couple of soph-omores, froze mid-moonwalk. Then, of course, being Paul, he abruptly shattered the stillness by yelling, "Da-amn!" in a *Not Another Teen Movie* kind of way.

Ryan pulled his attention back to Becky, who was still speechless, and lowered his voice. "I'm not giving her up, so either get used to it or go back to Mike and Paige."

Becky glared at me, and I glared right back until she finally turned around and stormed out the door she'd just walked in. Ryan looked at me expectantly, but I just con-tinued to glare. I mean he'd just announced to the whole school that I was his girlfriend! I don't know why that made me so angry, but I'd already been on such an emotional roller coaster that day that I simply didn't have the will to try any-more. I let myself get angry. I let myself radiate. Then I let myself blow up each and every stupid fluorescent light in the room.

As the other kids ducked the raining shards of glass in confusion, Ryan frowned. I kept up my glare and then stomped out of the cafeteria. I didn't look back to see if he was following me or not, but I didn't have to. "Thanks for the support, Jamie," he grumbled, knowing full well that I could still hear him.

I felt awful when I realized that Ryan was angry with me. Ryan doesn't get angry with people unless he has a very good reason. It was very surprising, and it actually hurt. I froze when I heard the cafeteria door slam behind me. "It wouldn't have killed you to come over and say hi to her either," Ryan said when I didn't turn around to face him. "They wouldn't all hate you so much if you would just try."

I heard him close the distance between us, and I took a deep breath before turning to face him. It was harder to look him in the eye than I'd expected, so I stared at his feet.

"You can't be both people," he said. "Either you're the ice queen, or you're Jamie Baker. And they're right, you know— the ice queen isn't worth it. But Jamie is, so you decide what you want, and then come talk to me."

And then Ryan Miller walked away from *me* without looking back.

Nothing in the entire world could make me feel lousier than I felt for letting Ryan down. I went through the rest of my day like a zombie. I guess on the bright side, all the comments from the other students no longer bothered me. I was numb. At least I was until last period, when I had to see Ryan again.

I'd been sort of wandering aimlessly, but my body was on autopilot, so I still found my way to class, unfortunately, but I got there a little late.

"Ms. Baker! Thank you for joining us," Mr. Edwards said as I took my seat. I don't know what kind of look I gave him, but his voice sounded nervous when he said, "Since it's your first offense, I'll let it slide, but let's try not to make a habit of it."

I have no idea what we talked about in class that day, but I know that there were a lot of angry glances being thrown around the room and almost no talking. Not even when Mr. Edwards asked us questions. With only fifteen minutes left in the day, Mr. Edwards couldn't take the suspense any longer.

"What is with you guys today? Huh? It's a little chilly in here."

"I think you mean *icy*," Becky grumbled.

I looked up just in time to see Ryan look at Becky. "What?" she snapped at him.

Mr. Edwards sighed and put down his dry erase marker since none of us was listening to him anyway. He looked around the room and then leaned against his desk with his arms folded across his chest. "All right, who died?"

It was an unfortunate choice of words. If possible, the room got a good ten degrees colder, and then Paige opened her big fat mouth. "Why don't you ask Jamie?" she spat.

Everyone looked my way, and just as Mr. Edwards followed their gazes, big wet tears started streaming down my face. I couldn't help it, I couldn't stop it, and even though I knew I would regret it later, at the time I didn't care.

They were all shocked to see me, cold-as-ice Jamie Baker, crying. Nobody said anything, nobody even breathed, except Paige, of course. "Well, what do you know?" she said. "The ice queen does have feelings."

"Give her a break—her boyfriend died."

I looked up in shock because it wasn't Ryan who'd come to my defense. It was Amy Jones, and she shrugged at me apologetically.

I think everyone in the room was as surprised as I was, but before I had time to react her friend Allysa Madsen followed her lead. "Yeah, Paige, don't be so cruel."

"Yeah!" This time it was Scott Cole, and he was actually smiling. "And you wonder why Ryan dogged you so hard last week. Good show, Miller."

Paige was now beyond angry. Becky was still staring in shock at Allysa and Amy, and Ryan just sat there looking at me expectantly. I'm not sure what he wanted, but I couldn't have done whatever it was he seemed to be waiting for me to do anyway. My head was spinning.

I looked back at Allysa and Amy. I didn't know if they were defending me, or if it was more about putting Paige in her place, but either way it was a bit overwhelming. Everyone was staring at me, and I was still crying. I was scared, confused, and humiliated. My emotions were all over the charts, and I was starting to lose a grip on my power, so it's a good thing Mr. Edwards has a heart. It was obvious I needed a break, so he let class go a full ten minutes early.

"Okay, people, that's enough for today. Everyone except Jamie get out of here. Paige, you work on your manners or we'll practice them in detention."

No one hesitated to escape the awkward situation except Ryan. He was the last to leave the room. When he sort of lingered by the door, waiting for me, Mr. Edwards cleared his throat suggestively and said, "Have a good day, Mr. Miller."

I was relieved when Ryan obeyed Mr. E.'s subtle command and left me alone, but when the door clicked shut behind him the silence in the room became suffocating. Mr. E. finally said something after I was forced to break the quiet with a loud sniffle.

"How are you holding up?"

"How does it look like I'm holding up?"

The lights in the room flickered when I snapped, scaring me calm. Mr. E. looked up curiously for a moment but didn't let himself get distracted from his golden opportunity to give me the lecture he'd been dying to give me since his first day teaching here. He handed me a box of tissues and waited for a minute longer to speak.

"It's okay to cry, you know."

"Not in front of them," I sniffled. "Never in front of them." I surprised us both with my unintentional honesty.

"Afraid they'll figure out that you're a normal girl with real feelings?"

I scoffed bitterly at the word "normal."

"What, you don't think you're a normal girl? At the very least on the inside?"

"Especially not on the inside," I grumbled, more to myself than anything.

Mr. Edwards was intrigued by my comment and studied me for a minute. No doubt he was trying to figure out how to get me to open up to him or agree to seek professional help. He finally went with the question "Why do you say that?"

"You wouldn't understand."

"Try me."

Yeah, right. "It's nothing, Mr. E. Forget about it."

"You lost a loved one, you have survivor's guilt, and you feel responsible for Derek's death. That is not nothing."

I was shocked at the mention of Derek's name, as I always am when I'm not expecting to hear it. Mr. Edwards raised the box of tissues my direction again when I was hit with a new wave of tears.

"All of those feelings," he continued, "are the most normal feelings anyone could have after being involved in an accident like yours."

"How... How do you know about..." I couldn't say Derek's name out loud this time. "About my accident?"

"It only took me ten minutes that first day of class to see that you weren't exactly like my other students. I was concerned, so I read your school file. It's all in there."

"I'll bet. Right along with my old guidance counselor's assessment of my mental stability. Did you enjoy that part too?"

"Jamie."

"You really think you're going to be able to fix me any more than she could?"

Mr. Edwards shrugged sheepishly but managed a sincere smile. "I'm not interested in fixing you, Jamie. I actually think you're doing remarkably well, considering."

No push for counseling? That was surprising. And hard to believe. "Then what's with all the Afterschool Special?"

"I just don't want to see you take any steps backward. Don't let them hurt you."

"Easy for you to say."

"It should be easy for you too. You're special now, Jamie. Powerful. Don't be afraid to use that power."

"Excuse me?" I didn't mean to sound panicked all of a sudden, but come on. You know you'd freak out a little too.

Mr. Edwards studied me again, considering the sudden edge in my voice. He seemed to proceed with caution. "You have the upper hand here, Jamie. You're so much more ahead of the game than Paige or any other kid here at Rocklin High. You know what it's like to be them. Only sophomore to make the varsity cheer squad, dating the prom king, most popular girl in your old school... a beauty queen?"

"All that in my file too?" I grumbled, feeling a little embarrassed.

Mr. Edwards chuckled this time. "Mr. Miller's biography was very enlightening."

I blushed, strangely ready to murder Ryan, while Mr. E. continued with his lecture. "You know what it's like to be them," he repeated, "but they have no idea what it's like to be you. You've endured far too much real pain to let mere words hurt you. You're too strong for that now."

Oh, okay. Metaphorical power. I get it. Oh, the irony. "That was quite the speech, Mr. E." Oddly enough, though, it made me feel a little better.

"Sorry." Mr. Edwards chuckled. "One of the downfalls to studying literature. Everything always has to be dramatic."

It's no wonder I felt comfortable with him then. My mom doesn't call me a drama queen for nothing. "I must be destined to be a lit professor someday," I mumbled under my breath. Mr. Edwards heard me and laughed.

I wiped away the last of my tears and even managed to return his grin with a small smile. The smile seemed to placate him for the time being, and he headed back to his desk with his box of tissues. "Good night, Ms. Baker," he said before I left the room. "And remember, you're the one with all the power."

You have no idea, I thought as I pulled the door shut behind me.

Mr. Edwards's speech had actually given me a lot to think about, so instead of going home, I headed for the hilltop that overlooks the football field. I sat down just about the time the football team started trickling onto the field in their practice clothes.

I couldn't take my eyes off Ryan as he ran out onto the field. There was no spring in his step, no smile on his face. He looked as miserable as I felt. He was having a really bad day too, and not only was it not over for him, I seriously doubted Coach Pelton was as understanding as Mr. Edwards. He was obviously still not happy about two of his star players' suspensions. Barely able to speak without yelling, he just choked out the word, "Laps!" and pointed his finger at the track.

Ryan started running, and as soon as Mike showed up, he was ordered to the same punishment. Mike hit the track and quickly caught up to Ryan, but the minute he tried to speak to him, Ryan picked up his pace. "Miller!" Mike yelled, catching up to Ryan again. "Come on, dude. This is stupid."

Ryan suddenly stopped running and whirled around to get in Mike's face. "Get out of my face, Driscoll, before I pound yours!"

"Fine. If that's how it's gonna be."

For the rest of practice, Mike was stone cold to Ryan and pounded him into the ground every chance he got. More than once, the coach had to pull him off Ryan before they started a brawl.

I hated watching Mike use Ryan as a tackle dummy, but it was even more depressing to see Ryan so upset. It was so unlike him to be yelling and threatening to pound people's faces. I missed that happy-go-lucky guy who made everyone around him smile. I wanted him back, and I realized that there was only one way that was going to happen.

Mr. Edwards was absolutely right about me having all the power. I was the only one who could fix the rift between Ryan and his friends. I had to prove to people that he wasn't being brainwashed by the freak. I had to make an effort. I had to be nice. It was true that I couldn't be both the ice queen and Jamie. I had to choose. Right here. Right now. And thanks to Mr. Edwards, I was sure I was strong enough to make the right decision.

Well, pretty sure.

Okay, I wasn't sure at all, I was terrified. But I had to. For Ryan.

My eyes fell on Mike and I cringed. There was just no possible way I could ever play nice with him, but then I looked across the field at the small group of cheerleaders doing cartwheels and toe touches. I fell into a moment of nostalgia as I watched their routine. I used to love cheering so much. Once upon a time I even wanted to cheer for the Chicago Bulls professionally.

My smile faded when the group stopped and I heard Paige's shrill voice. "I swear, Becky! You're a half second late on the entire routine, your handsprings are sloppy, and you haven't landed your dismount in weeks. If you don't get it together, you're out! The qualifier for the state championships will be here before you know it, and as captain it's my job to not let you ruin it for everyone. Let's do it again! Everyone, from the top!"

Okay, I could never tolerate Paige either, but Becky? I didn't harbor any real resentment toward her. And today in class, with Amy, Allysa, and even Scott? Surely it wouldn't kill me to smile at any of them once in a while. I didn't have to be friends with them necessarily; I just had to be civilized. I could do civilized.

I sat there watching and listening and mostly thinking until practice was over, and I decided that I had to start with Becky. She was still the most popular girl in school, at least for now, and she meant the most to Ryan. Building some kind of relationship with her would make the most difference.

I felt sick to my stomach, but I knew I had no choice, so I took a deep breath and headed back to school. I waited around the corner from the locker room doors, sort of behind the bleachers. I figured it'd be best to catch her alone, but I wasn't the only one with that idea. Becky was the last to drag herself from the field, and right before she reached the girls' locker room, Mike grabbed her by the arm. "What was all that back there with Ryan? What have you been saying to him?" he growled.

"You mean did I tell him what you did to me after the homecoming dance?" she hissed, yanking her arm free from his grip.

"I didn't do anything to you that you didn't ask for."

"Right."

"Is that what you told Ryan? Is that why he won't even talk to me?"

My anger was raging inside of me as I listened to their conversation. I couldn't believe I hadn't seen it before. Ever since the dance, all of Becky's odd behavior, her clear hatred for the guy she'd happily gone to the dance with, it suddenly all made sense. And I wanted to kill Mike for it.

"Leave me alone!" Becky screamed, but Mike stopped her again.

"Did you say anything to Ryan or not?"

"No, all right?" Becky screamed again. "You think I want the entire school to know what you did to me? So everyone can stare at me funny and talk about me behind my back? No thanks."

"They wouldn't believe you anyway."

"Yeah, well, I haven't told anyone, so just forget it! I know that's what I want to do." Becky had tears in her eyes now, and she jerked herself free from Mike again. "Don't ever touch me again!"

"Well, if you didn't say anything, then what the hell is Miller's problem?"

"Are you dense? The guy is head over heels for Jamie, and you told the entire school that she killed her boyfriend. She actually *cried* in English today. Of course Ryan's mad at you!"

This news seemed to amuse Mike. As if I didn't want to kill him enough already? "No way! She cried?" He laughed.

"You are such a jerk," Becky said with utter disgust. "Stay away from me."

Becky took off without bothering to hit the locker room, and since I was a few volts shy of a lightning storm, I had to sit down. It was going to take Buddha himself to calm me down, so I went back to my hill and tried to breathe. I sat there for fifteen minutes until the football players and the cheerleaders began to trickle out of the locker rooms one by one.

When Mike was the first person to come out, I simply couldn't help myself. I knew I'd decided to resurrect my inner Jamielynn for Ryan's sake, but I thought this particular situation called for the ice queen just one last time. I had the emotions under control again, so I flew down to the school and leaned against the end of the bleachers just before Mike got there. "Hey," I said casually as he walked past.

Mike was a little startled to see me, but his curiosity got the better of him and he stopped. "What are you doing here?"

I didn't answer his question. "Why did you help me?" I asked instead. Mike looked confused, so I elaborated. "The day that reporter was harassing me in the parking lot, why did you help me?"

Mike kept an excellent poker face. I couldn't read it at all. "Seemed like the thing to do," he said, shrugging.

"So why did you tell the whole school about my accident?"

He shrugged again. "Seemed like the thing to do."

Mike still seemed completely casual, but I could keep my cool too. I nodded understandingly. "Is your beef with Ryan really about me?" I asked with a friendly smile. "You always seemed fine with the idea of him nailing me before. You encouraged him even."

"That was before you turned him into your little ice king."

"So it has nothing to do with the fact that he got on your case about Becky?"

Mike flinched beneath his perfect expression. "I don't know what you're talking about."

Oh, he knew exactly what I was talking about. I could see it in his eyes. "Man," I said. "The guilt is really eating away at you, isn't it?" His eyes narrowed, but I kept going. "Or is it fear I'm seeing? Are you afraid that your best friend is going to figure out that you raped his best friend?"

I enjoyed watching Mike's face turn white. "Listen, you little—" he started.

"No, you listen!" I knew Mr. Edwards had been speaking metaphorically about using my power and all, but I chose to take him literally right then and grabbed the collar of Mike's shirt, yanking him toward me, lifting him onto the balls of his toes. Gotta love superstrength. Even if it had been guilt in his eyes before, it was definitely fear now. "Killing my boyfriend may have been an accident, but if you ever touch Becky, or any other girl, ever again, killing you won't be. Understand? And while we're at it, stop talking crap about me. It upsets Ryan."

I let go of Mike with just enough of a shove for him to fall backward. I slammed my foot against his chest, flattening him on his back. I may have used a little unnecessary force, but I knew I wasn't really hurting him. Hey, the guy's a linebacker. Sometimes brute force is the only way to get through to them.

"Oh, and if you ever tell anyone about this conversation, you'll regret it." I flashed him a beautiful smile as I removed my foot and added a perky "See you tomorrow."

Would I have ever actually hurt Mike? Of course not. Well, not on purpose. But did I feel bad about making him believe that I would? No. Maybe I should have but I didn't. I walked away feeling better than I had all day.

I got almost to the parking lot when I noticed that Becky hadn't left after her talk with Mike. She was out on the field doing handspring after handspring. After threatening Mike I was feeling pretty good, so I figured I'd better give this whole making-an-effort thing a shot before I chickened out. With a sigh I changed course for the football field.

"Your problem's in your footing. Your toes tend to point out when you land," I said when Becky's tumbling came to a stop.

Becky was speechless, and color me paranoid, but it didn't seem like she was all that grateful for my critique. "I used to have the same problem," I offered. "My coach told me to try to lift my toes inside my shoes when I jumped. I know it sounds a little crazy, but I started sticking my landings after that."

Becky was still frozen in shock, so I just kept talking. "It's been a long time, so I don't know that I'd be much help, but if you ever want someone to practice with who isn't going to constantly bite your head off, I wouldn't mind."

I couldn't believe I'd just told her I wouldn't mind hanging out with her. And the craziest part was, I felt like it was the truth. I really wouldn't mind. Once I'd said it, I realized I wasn't just doing this for Ryan. It would be so nice to have a girl to talk to again.

I tried to smile, but that's kind of hard to do when you're so nervous you feel like you're about to vomit. When Becky finally caught up with the moment, she didn't yell, but her voice was as cold as, well, ice.

"Leave me alone."

She was hostile enough that I wanted to grant her request, but I owed it to Ryan to try a little harder. "I know what you're going through."

"You don't know anything about me," Becky said through clenched teeth.

"I'll bet I know what really happened between you and Mike," I said softly, and Becky's face turned green. "You and I have a lot more in common than Ryan thinks. And trust me, if you keep the secret to yourself long enough, trying to pretend it didn't happen, you'll end up exactly like me. I'm not trying to scare you, and I won't tell anyone. I'm just saying I've been there, and if you ever want to talk about it… Well, I know *I* could really use a friend who understands anyway."

Becky didn't say anything for what felt like a long time. Her eyes filled with tears, and her whole body started to shake until she finally exploded. "You have no idea what you're talking about!" she yelled. "We don't have anything in common! I don't need your friendship, and I don't want it! I *hate* you! You've taken the only decent person in this school and turned him into a jerk! You're so selfish that you're letting him ruin his life for you!"

I didn't know what to say. It hurt when she said she hated me, but I couldn't blame her. And she was right about one thing: Ryan was ruining his life over me. But she was wrong in thinking that I wanted him to. I'd been trying to push him away since day one.

Before I had the chance to defend myself, Paige and Tamika were suddenly there, and they were protectively clamping their arms in Becky's.

"Go away!" Tamika shouted at me.

"Yeah!" Paige said. "Nobody wants you here, freak! Why don't you do us all a favor and just kill yourself like you killed your last boyfriend!"

I started repeating Mr. Edwards's words in my head. *I'm the one with all the power. I'm the one with all the power.* But somehow I think this emotional power must be a lot like my physical power. It was going to take a lot of practice.

It wouldn't have been so bad except I couldn't help thinking how much Paige was right. Everything that was wrong between everyone in this school was because of me. Okay, well maybe not what was wrong between Mike and Becky, but everyone else? These people all used to be one big happy family before I came along. Why would they let me into their lives when I was the one responsible for breaking them all up?

It was the same exact thing as my old school. I'd taken Derek from them and they hated me for it. Why would I expect things to be different here? I wasn't even friends with these people before I took Ryan from them. I know Ryan had faith, but suddenly I was sure that any attempts to be friends with anyone in this school would be useless.

I didn't know what was with me and the waterworks lately, but I started to cry again. "Right," I sniffled eventually. I ignored Paige and Tamika and looked straight at Becky. "Forget I said anything."

I turned around to leave only to nearly run into Ryan. "Don't touch me," I warned when he reached out to pull me into his arms.

"What's wrong?" he asked as he pulled his hands back.

"This isn't going to work, Ryan," I said through my tears. "You and me, friends, a life, any of it. And I am so tired of fighting about it with you. You said I can't be both people, but the truth is, I can't be either. I'm sorry."

I started to leave when I finally broke out into full-on sobs.

"Jamie, wait!"

"No! I tried, okay? I really did. But it's not going to work, and I can't take this anymore, so just stop! Please!"

I walked away, and it was hard to keep myself at a normal human pace because I could still hear Ryan as I headed for my car.

"It's really better this way, Ryan," Paige said with a sympathy that made me nauseous.

"Better for who?" he asked her. "For Jamie? For me? Or maybe just better for you. I can't believe you, Paige! You have no idea what she's been through! Pain like you could never imagine! And you're throwing it in her face over and over again for what? Because I'd rather go out with her than with you? You call her the ice queen, but Jamie would never do something like that to anyone."

"But look at what she's doing to you," Paige said.

"She's done nothing but make me happy, and she's had to turn her entire life around just to do it. You guys are the ones doing all the damage!"

"But, Ryan—"

"Don't start with me, Becky! I told her you were different. I begged her to give you a chance. Do you have any idea how hard that was for her? She tried to be nice. She was terrified of you, but she did it for me because I promised you weren't like everyone else, and you crushed her!"

As I reached my car I heard Ryan sigh. "Maybe she was right when she chose not to be friends with any of us," he said, sounding more resigned than angry now. "I thought I was helping, but all I did was give her hope and then throw her to the wolves. I've probably hurt her more than anyone. Thanks a lot, you guys."

It sounded as though someone was crying, and I realized it was Becky when she gave Ryan a weepy apology. "Ryan, I'm sorry," she said.

His response was "Just forget it."

I don't know if he said anything else because I was in my car now, and I revved the engine and blasted the radio so that I could tune them out. Then I went home and accidentally slammed my brand-new bedroom door through the bathroom wall again.

I guess I shouldn't have been surprised when Ryan showed up at my house not ten minutes after I did. I mean the guy's painfully dedicated *and* convinced that he is my boyfriend. It would make sense that he would come to me after he finished yelling at his friends on my behalf. But for some reason, when he showed up and begged my mom to let him in, I was still shocked. Shocked and angry.

"Hello, Ryan," my mother sighed when she answered the door. I may have been stunned, but she didn't sound all that surprised to see him. "Thank you for stopping by, but I really don't think Jamie is up for any visitors right now."

"Please, Mrs. Baker? Please just let me try to talk to her."

The power in the house was already out, but I was angry enough that the walls shook at the sound of his desperate voice. I didn't mean to be so upset with him because I knew he really cared about me and he'd done nothing but treat me better than I deserved, but a girl can be told that things will be okay only so many times. I'd definitely reached my limit.

My mother sounded scared as she attempted again to shoo him off. "I'm sorry, Ryan, but now is just not a good time."

"It's okay, Mrs. Baker." There was silence for a moment while Ryan hesitated. "I know about Jamie. About her powers, I mean," he finally admitted. "And I know the rules. I won't get too close, but you have to let me see her. Please! It's my fault she's so upset. I owe her an apology."

"You what?" my mother gasped.

I'd like to pretend that my mother was surprised because Ryan claimed he was the reason I was crying, but I knew that's not what caught her off guard. Ryan apparently knew it too because the next thing he said was, "Please don't be mad at Jamie for telling me about herself. I sort of didn't give her a choice. And don't worry—I swear I will never ever tell anyone." There was a pause for a minute, and then Ryan spoke again, in a much smaller voice. "I care about your daughter, Mrs. Baker. A lot. I want to protect her just as much as you do."

I knew Ryan cared about me—that much was obvious—but I'd never heard him say it out loud before. And for him to say it to my mother! It was so bittersweet. It made me feel so much better and so much worse, all at the same time.

My anger subsided, but my despair increased tenfold and I started crying even harder.

I was too exhausted now to keep up the anger inside me, and the house stilled. My mother knew I could hear the conversation and must have figured that what he said had calmed me down, because she didn't say anything, but Ryan let out a huge breath. "Thank you, Mrs. Baker!"

"Ryan?" my mother called with an exasperated sigh. "Keep your distance."

"I will."

Ryan didn't say anything as he came down the hallway and crossed the war zone of my bedroom's threshold. I guess he wasn't all that surprised to see my missing door. Eventually he broke the silence with a simple "I'm sorry."

"Go away!" I shouted, and then my voice broke.

"I'm so sorry. I was wrong about my friends. But just forget them, okay? I did."

His face was sick with worry, and I suddenly felt guilty all over again. "They're your friends," I said, attempting to gain some control of myself. "You can't just forget them."

"If they were really my friends they wouldn't treat you like that."

"But they're right. I'm a jerk, and you've been different. You can't blame them for hating me—they're just worried about you."

"That's bull! They're just jealous, and if they can't get over it, then it's their loss. Jamie, if I have to choose a side, then I choose yours. And for once in my life I don't care if it makes everyone in the entire school hate me, just as long as you don't."

"Don't be stupid. You can't give up everyone you know because of me."

"But that's just it—I shouldn't have to. I don't want to be friends with people that expect me to forget about the best thing that's ever happened to me, just because they don't understand you. They won't even listen to me long enough to let me explain."

"Maybe that's because they're right this time. I'm no good for you. You may not want to listen to them, but I don't have a choice. Becky's right. I've been selfish because I like you, and for your own safety it has to stop. I'm sorry, Ryan, but there's no side to choose. I'm on their side this time." I dried my tears and looked him straight in the eye. I meant it this time, and I had to make him see that. "It's over."

I don't know how long he stood there just staring at me in silence, but it felt like forever and I had to look away. I couldn't keep staring at the tortured expression on his face because I absolutely couldn't give in this time.

"You can't give up," he eventually whispered. "You were doing so great. You can't just quit because of something Paige or Becky said."

"You don't get it!" I screamed. "It's not about what they said!"

"So explain it to me then, Jamie! Because I honestly can't understand why won't you let me get close to you. I know you want to!"

When I didn't answer him, he lowered his voice and kept talking. "I don't just mean physically," he said. "You're scared to be in a relationship at all. You're scared to let me in. Is it because of Derek? Because you can't let one accident keep you from ever living your life again."

"It's not Derek."

"Then what is it? Don't you want me? Don't you trust me?"

"Of course I do."

"Then what?"

"Ryan." I sighed. "You know what."

"What, your powers? I'm so sick of you using that as an excuse."

Ryan's voice sounded so resentful all of a sudden that it startled me, and I became defensive again. "It's not an excuse!"

"It *is* an excuse! Don't tell me you can't control your powers because we both know that you can. Maybe not one hundred percent but enough. We've been fine for weeks. It's just that this is finally turning into a real relationship, and you can't handle it. You're scared!"

I was suddenly enraged, and I jumped to my feet. "Of course I'm scared! Have you forgotten that I nearly killed you yesterday? What if it had been *me* lying there unconscious in front of *you*? Would you be able to live with yourself if you ever hurt me like that?"

This time it was Ryan that couldn't meet my gaze. Tears poured down my angry face, and my body started to shake, but I had to keep talking. I had to make him understand,

and there was only one way I could see to do that. I had to tell him the truth. I had to tell him the one thing I'd sworn I'd never tell another living soul. I figured he would hate me after that, but I didn't see any other choice.

"I killed Derek!" I screamed through my tears. "Me! Not the truck, not the power lines, *me!*" I took a breath and lowered my voice. "The accident wasn't even my fault," I explained. "It was his."

"What are you talking about?"

"That night Derek and I got into a huge fight, and I broke up with him."

"What?"

I ignored the shock in Ryan's voice. "He tried to argue but I took off running. Like I told you before, I beat him back to the car. When I started the car, he figured I was going to drive off and leave him stranded in the middle of nowhere. He dashed onto the road without looking first. The truck driver swerved to miss Derek and ended up hitting me instead. The accident—the toxic waste, the power lines, the explosion—it was Derek's fault, and he watched it all from safely across the street."

I suddenly felt weak and had to sit back down. Ryan looked worried about me, but he kept his promise to my mom and stayed back. Even from across the room, though, I could see the look in his eyes. He was finally starting to get it.

"When I woke up I thought I was dead because nothing hurt the way it should, but then Derek was there, screaming my name. I climbed out of the car, and of course he rushed over and threw his arms around me. But I was so mad at him, and I was so frightened. When I started to electrocute him I didn't even know what was happening. He just started screaming and shaking. He couldn't seem to let go of me, and I couldn't escape him. I was in shock. The way he looked and the smell... And then he just stopped screaming."

I fell silent for a minute as I remembered the single most horrific moment of my life. "I had to pry myself out of his arms," I sobbed when I could speak again. "Derek is dead because of me. *I* killed him. I know it wasn't my fault—I get that—but, Ryan, you have to understand that's exactly why we have to stop this."

For once in his life, Ryan was speechless, but surprisingly, that only made me feel worse. "It's the only way I can be sure that I won't hurt you like that," I whispered.

After that I had to get out of there. I turned to leave and froze when I found my mother standing in the doorway to my room, completely shocked. I took one look at her horrified expression and the tears flowing down her cheeks, and I freaked out. "I'm sorry," I cried. "I just never knew how to tell you."

I didn't stick around for any kind of reaction from either of them. How could I? I didn't want to hear what they would say. I couldn't bear the looks on their faces. I just wanted to be alone.

I was so mentally exhausted that I didn't have the energy to do anything but walk. I had no more fight in me. No Grand Canyon this time. No Miami Beach or Mount Rushmore. Just up my street and down the next.

Eventually I ended up in the park. It was deserted since the sun was starting to set, so I decided it was the perfect place to sulk, and found the nearest bench. I lay down, closed my eyes, and tried to empty my mind. But I couldn't rid my brain of my problems until I felt a faint surge of energy pop up around me. It startled me, but it was only the street lamps turning on as it became dark.

I don't know what happened then, but I just snapped. I couldn't take it anymore. I hated the energy I felt. Hated it! No matter what I did or where I went, I couldn't escape it.

My hands flew up, and with a frustrated scream, I pushed the energy away from me, sending it back to those lights with as much force as I was capable of. It was like pure rage shot out from the palms of my hands in the form of lightning bolts that went whizzing across the park.

I didn't just burst the bulb of the lamppost I was aiming at—I blew the whole freaking pole out of the ground.

For a split second, the whole world came to a stuttering stop, and I blinked down at my hands. I'd not only controlled the lightning, but it somehow felt twice as powerful as it had at Ryan's cabin. And I felt stronger too. I wasn't fatigued like I'd been then. My muscles weren't weak.

I didn't know how I'd managed it, but I was sure I could do it again. Yeah, somewhere deep down I was vaguely aware of what I was doing. But it felt too good to release all that pent-up rage. Way too good. So before I knew it I had blasted two more streetlights.

The power was intoxicating. I mean, there I was in the middle of a public park, where anyone and their mother's dog could have seen me, or even been severely hurt by my actions, but I hadn't stopped to think about it. It was like I wasn't in touch with reality anymore. At least not until I heard my name being called.

"Jamie!" Carter screamed frantically. "Stop it before you kill somebody!"

He startled me so badly that I instinctively whirled around and let go another burst of lightning, which obliterated a small tree just to his left.

"Whoa, Jamie! It's just me! Cut the pyrotechnics before someone sees you!"

I looked in the direction Carter was pointing. A crowd was already gathering around the mess in the street, and now they were all squinting at me through the dark, trying to see what had blown up the tree.

Reality started to catch up to me and I panicked. My instinct to protect myself kicked in and without thinking I grabbed Carter and took off. Seconds later I was dropping him on the front steps of the school.

It took him a few minutes to recover from traveling at superspeed. And it gave me great satisfaction, twisted as it may be, when he hurled all over the bushes. It was enough of a distraction that I could finally think rationally again. Well, as rationally as I was capable of where Dave Carter was concerned.

"You do *not* want to mess with me right now, Carter!"

"I didn't realize you had any control over the lightning stuff," he said after wiping his mouth on his sleeve.

Not that I would have shot a lightning bolt through him any more than I would through Mike Driscoll, but like Driscoll, Carter didn't know that, so I held my palm out in his direction. "You want to find out just how much control I have?"

Carter waved off my threat. "You're not going to hurt me, Jamielynn. You don't have it in you."

Okay, maybe he was a little smarter than Mike, but I wasn't in the mood to play around, and his cockiness wasn't cute like Ryan's. Not even close. I had him pinned to the ground before he could blink, and he grunted beneath the pressure my fists were putting on his chest. "You're so sure about that?"

"If I wasn't," he grunted, "I wouldn't be here."

I guess the man had a point. He obviously knew I could kill him if I wanted to. Just showing up in the first place was a way of calling my bluff. Still, I couldn't just admit to my weakness. "You have thirty seconds to convince me not to prove you wrong."

"I'm not here for a story. I'm trying to protect you."

Now, that was just funny. Except I wasn't laughing. "By selling me down the river in the name of science?"

Carter stopped struggling beneath my weight, and his eyes got huge.

"That's right," I said. "I know all about Visticorp."

"You mean they contacted you?"

I didn't understand the fear in his voice. "How much are they paying you?"

"They aren't paying me, Jamielynn."

"Why? They demanded proof first? If you think I'm going to let you give them anything on me, then you're more delusional than Ryan."

"Will you let me go so that we can talk?"

I debated his request for a minute. I really didn't want to let him go, but I did need answers. Besides, it wasn't like he could run from me.

Carter got to his feet and brushed himself off, scowling at me the whole time. "Nice to see you being rational for once," he grumbled.

He wasn't the only one who could be cranky. "You'd better tell me what is going on right now, or I'll get really irrational really quick."

"I think we're past the threats, Jamielynn," Carter said dryly.

Sadly, I may have been getting better at controlling my power, but my temper? Um, yeah… That still needs some work. I'm embarrassed to say that Carter's annoyed attitude was all it took for me to lose it. I let out a scream of frustration and then pushed him against the wall of the school.

All right, fine. I picked him up and threw him against the wall. But I didn't hurt him. I just startled him. "I am so sick of your attitude! You come to *me,* and you act like *I'm* the one trying to ruin *your* life?"

"Well, you sure aren't making it any better," Carter grumbled, still a little breathless from his short flight. "You think I enjoy babysitting an obnoxious teenager all the time?"

Obnoxious? Okay, maybe I had to give him that one. I wasn't exactly the queen of pleasantries when he was around. But "babysitting"?

"Watching out for you? Covering for you?"

"How is contacting genetic research companies covering for me?"

"Jamielynn, they contacted me!"

"Right!"

"They did! And not for the first time either. Visticorp has been keeping tabs on you since I printed the story of your first accident. They stopped bothering me when I couldn't find any evidence, but the moment you saved that gardener they came back. They're sure of you this time, and they wanted me to get them proof."

I have really got to work on my poker face. It probably wasn't in my best interest to let Carter see how scared I was, but I was so stunned by his revelation that I gasped. My worst nightmare was coming true. There were people out there that knew. They knew and they wanted to study me. And this man was here to bring me in.

I staggered backward, and let the energy inside me boil until I could feel it whipping my hair wildly about my head again. I could feel it radiating off my skin, burning through my eyes, ready to attack at my command.

"Incredible," Carter whispered as he scrambled to his feet.

"You're not turning me in to them," I warned, and this time, I wasn't so sure that I wouldn't hurt him.

Carter remained calm, though, ignoring my hostility. "I don't want to take you to them," he snapped.

"Then what *do* you want?"

"I told you. I want to help."

"You've never been interested in helping anyone but yourself."

"I met these guys, and they aren't the kind of people you want to be involved with. Not even someone like you."

I dropped my hand to my side, willing myself to be reasonable and listen to him. I asked the only thing my brain could come up with. "Why?"

"They're rich, powerful, and like to play God. You wouldn't be able to stop them by yourself."

"But why would you help me? All you've ever wanted to do is expose me. They must have offered you a lot of money. Why not just take it?"

I was surprised by the expression that washed over Carter's face. Guilt, anger, fear, and even remorse. All emotions I was sure the man was incapable of, and yet they were all right there, plain as day in his eyes. "Just trust me on this." His unsteady voice was merely a whisper. "I'm here to help."

Yeah. Like I was going to trust him? He was totally hiding something. But I still couldn't ignore how shaken he was. "And how do you plan to help me exactly?"

Carter swallowed hard and then straightened his posture. "The only way I can think to stop them is for you to out yourself before they get their own proof and come for you."

I started to shudder at the "come for you" part until I realized exactly what he'd said. "Out myself?" I took a deep breath when I felt my rage creeping to the surface again. "Come clean? Tell the world my secret? And just how is that supposed to help me?"

"Jamielynn, I don't think you understand how valuable you are. Even the guys at Visticorp don't know the things you're capable of. If you came forward, you'd be the most famous person in the entire world in a matter of minutes. No one would be able to touch you. The government would have to protect you."

"What makes you think the government wouldn't do everything these Visticorp guys plan on doing?"

"They wouldn't be able to because you'd already be a celebrity. They'd want to claim you as their own. Show you off to the rest of the world."

No way did I ever want that happening. "I think I'd rather take my chances with the mad scientists."

"It wouldn't be all bad. There's definitely perks." Carter slowly reached inside his jacket and pulled out a video tape. "This footage is worth so much more than Visticorp offered to pay me. *You're* worth so much more. If you let me take you public, I could turn you into a star. I could make you rich beyond your wildest dreams. Your parents would never have to work again. Think about the possibilities."

I was beginning to feel overwhelmed by the amount of energy pulsing through my body. The anger created by his lies was starting to push me over the edge. I clapped my hands sarcastically, and my voice shook as I fought to keep control. "You almost had me fooled. You reporters will say anything for a story."

"Jamie, I'm serious. I'm not just—"

"Your thirty seconds are up," I interrupted.

I was so angry that I turned on the juice and gave him just enough of a shock to writhe in pain for a minute. He never expected I would actually hurt him, so even though I didn't do any real damage, the jolt broke his confidence.

When I saw the fear in his eyes, the thought of just finishing him off flashed through my mind. After all, he was evil. He wanted to ruin my life. He wanted to out me to the world for his own fortune and glory. He'd tried once already and in a way succeeded. This time he had the proof that could destroy my family and my entire life forever, instead of just forcing me to relocate. All I had to do was push a tiny bit harder and my problem would be solved. I doubted that anyone would even miss him.

For one tiny second, the thought of killing him consumed me, and I knew he could see it in my eyes because the look on his face instantly turned to fear. "Please!" he coughed with what little breath he had. "You may have killed Derek, but that was an accident! You don't want my blood on your conscience. You're not a murderer, Jamie!"

Derek's name, the image of him dying in my arms, his charred lifeless body resting at my feet, snapped me back to reality and brought reason back to my thoughts. Shocked by my actions, and the feelings of malice I was apparently capable of, I collapsed on the steps right there in front of my school, letting my tears flow freely.

I hated to cry in front of Carter. I hated giving him the satisfaction of seeing me vulnerable, but he was right. I didn't want his blood on my hands. I'd never felt more confused or scared in my entire life. The thing of it was, I wasn't upset that I'd wanted to kill him. I was upset that I couldn't. Here was a man who could destroy me, and as powerful as I was, there was nothing I could do about it. Even with superpowers I wasn't strong enough to protect myself.

Knowing I was angry for not being able to do it made me feel awful. It made me feel like a monster even though Carter was still breathing. It made me wonder about Derek. Made me question whether or not I was glad he was dead.

And if I was glad he was dead, then I may as well have been a murderer, accident or not.

While I sat there having a legitimate mental breakdown, Carter managed to get himself back on his feet and put the tape back inside his jacket. I wanted to swipe the tape and fry it right then and there, but knowing Carter, he'd made a copy. I didn't know what other proof he had. I had to make sure that there was nothing else, so I got myself under control and played his game. I asked, "Can I think about it?"

"You don't have much time, Jamielynn. If I don't bring them something soon, they'll send someone else." I hated that he sounded sympathetic.

"You're asking me to give up my whole life. Just let me sleep on it."

He looked at me for a moment and then released a deep sigh. Nodding reluctantly, he said, "Tomorrow. Or I'll release this tape with or without you."

"How do I find you?"

"I'll find you."

Ha! He didn't know who he was dealing with. I was the ice queen, remember? And if he was going to try to blackmail me, then I was going to put him on ice. "Tomorrow then," I agreed coldly, and flew from his sight in a flash.

I was around the corner before he was done muttering, "Incredible" again, but I didn't go any farther. I was on a mission now.

It wasn't hard to follow him without being caught, and the stupid guy headed straight home. Nice place, by the way. Not. I thought I'd try to exploit me for money too if I were him. On the bright side, I didn't feel too bad about ripping down the front door to get in after he left the house again. Not as though anyone was going to try to break in. Well, besides me, I guess.

It gave me the creeps to go inside. I've never really been one to break the law, but it's a really good thing I followed my instincts this time. Carter had been watching Ryan and me for weeks. There were surveillance photos of me and my parents, me at school, and me and Ryan at the cabin. Pictures of basically everyone I interacted with at all—Paige, Mike, Becky, even Mr. Edwards. There was a whiteboard with what seemed to be a timeline or a schedule. There were all kinds of articles about my accident, and then one about the accident I tried to stop. Next to that one was a copy of the police report with certain parts highlighted.

None of that, though, was as disturbing as the small pile of videotapes and CDs piled on his desk with my name on them. First of all, video tapes? I know Carter is probably pushing fifty, but you'd think a reporter would welcome the digital age. On the bright side, I'm pretty sure there weren't a bazillion copies of whatever was on those tapes hiding safely on the Internet.

I hit play on the video camera that was still connected to the TV, and my face immediately came on the screen. I was sitting on the porch swing with Ryan at the cabin.

You know how creepy it is when you watch a movie about a serial killer or whatever, and there's that scene where he's stalking his next victim? More specifically, when he's watching them through the bushes or a window or something? Well, it's five million times creepier when you're the one being stalked.

I left the video playing, but I knew what that was going to show, so I flipped through the pile of CDs. They all had different dates on them. I popped the one that had today's date on it in the CD player.

"Jamie?" I heard Ryan ask.

And then I shouted, "Go away!" Or a recording of my voice did.

I wasn't sure exactly what I was listening to until Ryan said, "I'm so sorry. I was wrong about my friends. But just forget them, okay? I did."

Sounds familiar, right? "The guy bugged my room! He bugged my freaking room!"

This was going too far, even for a stupid tabloid journalist! Coming into my house, going through my stuff. Leaving bugs in my room so that he could hear my conversations? Didn't Carter know by now that it's unwise to make me angry? Well, one thing was for sure. None of this stuff was ever going to get out, and Dave Carter wasn't going to get a single penny from me.

I'd had some fun messing around with my powers in my day, but this? This I was really going to enjoy. I looked around the room, wondering how I was going to do it, but then I saw myself on the TV and froze at the sight. I was standing at the bottom of the porch steps. My hair was whirling around my head like I was standing in the wake of a jet engine, and there was a hint of a glow radiating off my skin.

It was kind of cool to see actually, until I saw myself open my eyes. They were glowing like a jack-o'-lantern. It was like my yellow eyes had turned into flashlights and were shining through the green filter of my contacts. It was the craziest thing I'd ever seen until I shot bolts of lightning out of my hands. Then *that* was the craziest thing I'd ever seen.

I was stunned. I just stood there watching, with a combination of shock and awe and utter terror, sweeping through me. "How did Ryan not run screaming?" I whispered, still marveling at the sight of what I had become.

"I believe it's because he was unconscious at the time," a voice said behind me.

I was startled badly enough to explode the desk lamp, and the power in the whole house went out.

"You know, Jamielynn," Carter said as he retrieved a flashlight, "for someone with superhearing, you're awfully easy to sneak up on."

I hated that he was so right. "I was a little distracted," I grumbled. "But don't worry—I'll be a lot more paranoid from now on."

"There won't be any need to be paranoid once the secret's out. I'm glad to see that you've come to your senses so soon. You're making the right choice."

"Oh, believe me, I know. And the right choice is not going public with you. I'm not going to let you expose me."

"But, Jamie"—Carter looked like he was starting to get annoyed again—"just think of how good it will feel not to have to hide your secret anymore. You can't tell me you like keeping it—I know you don't. You hate your life."

Carter was just so sure he had me figured out. But as I stood there staring him down, enraged by his accusation, I realized just how wrong he was. I didn't hate my life. Not at all, actually. I have the world's best parents and the world's most understanding boyfriend. Granted, that probably makes him a little crazy, but he's really cute, so, you know. I also have the entire continent at my disposal, and that super-kissing thing? Yeah, so worth it.

"It's not so bad," I said with a sudden burst of confidence. "Sure, I have to keep a secret, but I get to do things like this…"

Carter gulped nervously when I held out my hands. "What are you doing?"

"You'll see."

The power in the house had gone out when he startled me, but there was more than enough juice in the power lines that ran behind his house. I took a deep breath and then pulled so much power to me that the walls of the house started to shake. When my hair started flying and my eyes started glowing, Carter's eyes grew really big. "What are you doing?" he screamed again, only he sounded so nervous that I'm sure he already had it figured out.

"Disposing of evidence," I answered anyway.

"Jamie, wait! We need this!"

Carter started to reach for the stack of tapes on the desk, but I was just too quick for him. Before he even got a single step I was standing in front of him with my hands pointed at him. "I wouldn't make me angry right now," I warned.

"You've spied on me enough to know that I tend to lose control when I'm emotional."

"Okay, Jamie," he said, slowly backing up a few steps. "Quit messing around. You could kill someone."

"Then I suggest you get out of here."

I pointed my hand at the video camera, and when I zapped it, I accidentally got the TV too, blowing them both into a million pieces.

"Jamie!"

"I'm a little busy," I snapped as I aimed at the computer next. "You know, this would be a lot more fun if you had nicer stuff. Haven't you ever heard of The Mac Store? Seriously, digital camcorders? Laptops? MP3 players?" With that, I blew the computer into tiny pieces.

"Jamie, stop! I promise I won't tell anyone. We'll find another way."

"It really won't matter if you tell anyone now. Once I destroy all of this, no one will believe you anyway. Without proof you're just another sleazy tabloid journalist. In fact, I doubt anyone would believe you even *with* proof. But I'd really rather not risk it."

I looked at the wall covered with my photos, and then smiled at the electrical outlet at the bottom. "I hope you have fire insurance."

"Fire insurance?"

I didn't bother to explain myself. I shot a bolt of lightning into the socket and sparks flew everywhere. "The problem with old crappy houses like this isn't the wiring," I said as the house caught fire. "It's the wallpaper."

Within seconds, the room was ablaze, and the photos that had covered it were gone. Carter had finally seen enough, and he tried to make a run for it, but I wasn't quite finished with him yet. I'm not really a violent person by nature, but throwing that jerk felt really good.

I picked him up by the back of his shirt and flung him across the room. He took a pretty good hit when he slammed into the wall, but he'd be fine. I stood over him with the fire burning quickly out of control around us, and I smiled when I saw his fear.

"Please!" he begged.

I let him stew for a minute, and then, when the ceiling started to collapse, I picked him up and flew out the door. "You can't hurt me now," I said confidently, dropping him to the ground. "Your proof is gone."

"It's not me that wants to hurt you. What are you going to do about Visticorp?"

"They have no proof either."

"They'll get it."

"I'll never use my powers again. I can control them now, remember?"

"You'll slip up, and they'll be waiting."

"Then I'll take care of them!"

I was done being threatened. I borrowed a little more energy from the power lines because that whole hair-on-fire, glowing-eyes look is kind of intimidating, and I wanted the dramatic effect. What can I say? I am my mother's child.

Just to prove I was serious, I grabbed Carter's hand and gave him enough juice to drop him to the ground. "If I ever catch you spying on me again, I'll do a lot more than burn your house down."

He looked sufficiently scared, and I could now see the lights of the fire trucks coming up the street. "That's my cue," I said.

And then I was gone.

I didn't come home for two days. I didn't mean to cause my parents a world of worry, but I needed some space. I mean, I did just become an arsonist. That's a lot to wrap your head around for someone my age. Plus, all these events happening in my life lately had dredged up a past I'd spent the last year and a half trying to forget.

I had never really come to terms with what happened to Derek; I simply buried it. Telling Ryan the truth, actually saying it out loud, forced me to deal with the fact that I was responsible for taking a life. I hated to use the term *murderer*, but how else do you describe what I did?

After nearly two days of thinking about it, though, I finally found a little clarity and went home to face the music.

I've never seen my parents quite like they were. I don't exactly know how to describe it, but angry is not the right word. It doesn't seem like nearly enough. I let them yell and cry and hug and kiss me until they had it all out of their systems. Then, once they'd settled down, the only thing I could think to say was "I'm sorry."

"You could have told us about Derek," my mom whimpered.

"I couldn't. You loved him too. Everybody loved him! And I killed him!"

After that my mother and I were bawling in each other's arms again. My father stepped in quickly, though, not wanting to lose focus on the point of this discussion.

"Jamie," he said, pulling me away from my mother, "your mom and I think it's time you see somebody." He hesitated for a moment out of guilt, but then looked at me very sternly. "This is getting out of hand. You need help that your mom and I just can't give you."

"You want to send me away?" I gasped out of sheer horror. "You want to let people experiment on me?"

If I thought Ryan was tying my heart in knots, I was mistaken. I'd never felt pain like I did right then. I knew that my parents might be afraid after learning the truth about Derek, and I knew they would worry, but I never in a million years thought they would betray me.

"Of course not, Jamie! I meant counseling. A psychiatrist. Not a scientist. Honey, how could you think we would ever?"

"Because I'm a murderer? I killed someone! Aren't you scared of me?"

"You are not a murderer," my father argued.

After two straight days' thinking about it, I knew this was true. Ever since my accident, I'd not only blamed myself for Derek's death, but I'd always questioned whether or not I allowed it to happen. I was so mad at him that night. I hated him that night. Of course I didn't fry him on purpose, but could I have stopped myself?

I wasn't sure until the other night, but the answer is no. I couldn't have stopped what I did to Derek. I knew that now. See, I wanted to kill Carter when he told me he was going to expose me to the world, and I could have, so easily, but I didn't. Not because I didn't want to, or even thought it would be wrong, but because I couldn't. I didn't have it in me to kill him. And I wouldn't have had it in me to kill Derek either.

"I know," I said, forcing a sad smile to my mom and dad. "Derek's death really was an accident. I understand that now. I don't need a psychiatrist. Honest. I mean, what am I supposed to tell one anyway? That I'm messed up because I fried my boyfriend with my super-electric-girl powers?"

My parents both opened their mouths to argue, but neither could come up with anything.

"Mom? Dad? No doctor is going to be able to understand what I'm going through. The only people that can do that are you guys. Well, and Ryan now. But don't worry. With you here to help me, I'll be fine. I'm already starting to feel better."

"What do you mean 'and Ryan now'?"

I didn't understand why my dad was so angry all of a sudden until I saw my mother cringe.

"You didn't tell him?" I asked.

"Well, I…" My mother stumbled over her explanation because she knew she was busted. When she couldn't think up a good excuse she shrugged in defeat and snapped at my father in annoyance. "I knew you would overreact."

I love my mom. I love my dad too, but I really, really love my mom. She's always got my back. It would have been nice if she'd told me she'd covered for me before I went and told my father that Ryan knew about my powers, but I've still got to love her for the effort. And at least now we were busted together.

"Okay, Dad, look, don't freak out."

Yeah, my dad didn't take my advice. "How much does he know?" he roared.

I cringed. "Everything."

My dad wanted to yell at me, and he tried to, but when he was finally able to form words they were directed at my mother. "You knew about this?"

"Honey, it's really not that big a deal."

"Not a— But— It's— He—"

My dad could no longer form a complete sentence, and the vein in his forehead was back and popping out farther than ever.

"Dad! Could you calm down a little? I can hear your heart beating, and trust me, that can't be a healthy pace."

"Ryan's a good boy," Mom promised.

"He won't say anything," I added. "He wants me to be safe."

"And actually"—Mom wrapped her arm around my dad in an attempt to keep him from physically exploding— "it's probably better this way."

I was just as surprised as my dad by my mom's statement. I mean, I thought it was better that he knew, but I didn't understand why she thought it was better.

"It will be safer," my mom explained. "He knows he has to be careful."

"And he's helped me so much already! He's the one who said I had to learn to control my powers. He's been teaching me yoga and meditation so that I don't cause as many power outages."

"Yoga?" my mom asked surprised. "Really?"

"Yeah! It's great!" I said excitedly, getting sidetracked. "You should totally try it."

My mom and I got a little carried away for a second about the health benefits of yoga and completely forgot about the topic at hand until my father plopped down in his chair, utterly exasperated. My mother and I couldn't help but giggle at the poor guy. He was always outnumbered in our house.

"Daddy, everything will be okay. I promise."

My dad still wasn't happy, but he seemed to be taking the what-can-I-do-about-it approach, instead of the enter-the-witness-protection-program route I had expected.

"I hope you're right," he finally sighed, his voice resigned.

I hoped I was right too, and for the first time since my accident, I actually believed things would be okay. I was a little nervous about having to see Ryan again, but only a little, because knowing him, the fact that I literally killed my last boyfriend would only motivate him to come up with some hairball scheme involving more 60-watt bulbs to make me feel better.

It turned out that I was right. I had absolutely no reason to be nervous about seeing Ryan. When I got to school the next morning I had stepped only one foot in the quad when he spotted me and nearly tackled me to the ground. "Jamie!" he hollered, rushing across the lawn without caring the least bit about the scene he was creating.

The next thing I knew, my feet were off the ground and I was squished so tightly in Ryan's arms that I could barely breathe.

"Okay, Ryan?" I coughed in a hushed tone. "This is exactly the kind of thing that can get you killed."

"I don't care, I'm not letting go. Don't ever disappear like that again!" he scolded, but his voice was more relieved than angry. "It's been days! You had your mother worried sick!"

"My mother?" I questioned sarcastically.

Ryan laughed as he finally set me back on my feet. "Okay, fine, me too."

He still wouldn't let go of me, though. He was gripping my arms while he looked at me with those eyes, and that smile... You know, being all Ryan-ish. And then, when I got lost in the moment, he totally took advantage of how whipped I was and he kissed me. The jerk. He just pulled my face to his right then and there, in the middle of a crowded quad full of students, where I could have accidentally unleashed an electrical storm at any moment. And okay, maybe I liked it, and maybe I even needed it, but still! You can't just go kissing Jamie Baker whenever you want, even if you *are* Ryan Miller!

"Ryan!" I yelled as soon as I was able to pull away from him—which admittedly took a minute.

"I'm sorry." Ryan laughed with this big dopey grin on his face and then kissed me some more.

I had to push him away from me. "Don't be sorry, just stop!"

I realized I was screaming at him when I felt a hundred different pairs of eyes on me. I tried to ignore the audience that Ryan seemed oblivious to and dropped the audio a few decibels. "I wasn't kidding when I said this has to stop. Look, I will be your friend. I *want* to be your friend. But that's it. We can't be anything more. It'll never work."

Ryan watched me for a minute and then whispered, "Don't do that." I was shocked to hear the sudden emotion in his voice. "Don't give up."

It was hopeless.

"Fine!" I snapped. "I'll be your stupid girlfriend!"

Big shocker, me giving Ryan his way, I know. But let's face it—it's just what I do best. I had to at least act a little tough, though. "But!" I said in the harshest voice I was capable of. "You can't ever touch me unless I say. No more tackling me, and especially no more surprise kissing."

He actually laughed at my request. "No promises."

Stupid, cocky boyfriend.

"You're crazy. You know that, right?"

Ryan got this big cheesy smile on his face and said, "Crazy about you."

"Ugh," I groaned. "Would you be serious for a minute? Why do you insist on putting your life in danger?"

"Because I like you."

His stupid grin was infectious. I wanted to be angry, but how could I with him looking at me like that?

"I'm not worth it, you know," I said stubbornly. "I have issues. I'm unstable."

"You're cute when you're unstable," Ryan said, "and I like your issues."

The stupid boy was straight-up giddy now. But he was so cute that I cracked a smile despite myself. "You really are crazy," I muttered.

Ryan just smiled proudly and then held out his hand. "Come on. I'll walk you to class."

I'm sure people stared that day as Ryan walked me to my first-period class hand in hand. And I'm sure they talked about how he kissed me as he said good-bye, but I didn't notice. Nor did I care if they did. I was on cloud nine that morning. Sure, I still had my doubts, and I was afraid I would cook Ryan one of these days, but at that moment it didn't matter.

I was in such a good mood that day that even when Ryan and I walked into the cafeteria at lunch and the whole place stopped to watch us head through the lunch line, I didn't notice. In fact, I didn't even realize there were other people in the room until the girl in front of us slipped on a blob of spilled potato salad and Ryan caught her fall. When she realized who saved her she had the exact same reaction I would have if I suddenly found myself in Ryan's arms. She sighed, entirely smitten. "Thanks."

"It was my pleasure," Ryan insisted playfully as he put her back on her feet. "I'm a quarterback, you know? I never get to catch."

The girl started to laugh until she saw me standing there, and then her face went white. She mumbled a quick "Sorry" in my direction and then practically took off running.

Ryan and I watched her go and managed to hold back our snickers until we got to our table.

"Poor thing," I said, laughing as we sat down.

"Yeah," Ryan teased. "I remember the first time I had to interact with you. It's pretty scary."

"Oh yeah, I'm sure you were real terrified as you were asking me to make out with you. But that's not what I meant." I laughed when Ryan looked at me puzzled. "That poor girl just slipped on potato salad and fell in love forever."

Ryan rolled his eyes at me, but I saw him smirk a little as he glanced over at the girl he'd just rescued. "She'll be over it by the end of lunch," he said.

"Right. Just like Amy Jones got over it? Or like Paige will *ever* be over it? You do realize you could have your pick of any of them, right?"

Ryan glanced again at the girl and then seemed to do a quick sweep of the cafeteria. "Yeah, I know," he said, failing at his attempt not to grin.

"So why me? If any girl in this school would go out with you, and all of them would have given you less trouble about it than I did, and none of them risk killing you if you get too close, why go through all the trouble?"

Ryan didn't even have to think about it. "That's easy. Because you kissed me that day."

"Because I kissed you? Seriously? You only like me because I'm a good kisser? That's it. We're not doing this. I'm not letting you risk your life just because you can't think with your upstairs brain."

"No, you twit." Ryan laughed. "Because you kissed me that day. I expected the ice queen and got a funny, go-with-the-flow girl that didn't care what anyone thought about her. A girl willing to stir up gossip just so that I could win a date with someone else.

"You didn't have to help me. In fact, you probably should have been insulted, but you weren't. You kissed me, you smiled, and then you wished me good luck. No one's ever surprised me like that. I couldn't figure out why you did it, and I just had to get to know you after that."

I had no idea that stupid kiss had that kind of effect on him. Charged him up like a battery, sure, but do all that? All this time I really thought it was just the superkissing that kept him coming back. I looked down at my lunch, feeling a little ashamed of my lack of faith in him, but Ryan couldn't stop there.

Oh, no, not Ryan Miller.

"After that day, every time I was with you I got brief glimpses of the real Jamie, the one who is dying to break out, and she was this fun, relaxed, smart, funny, caring girl. Finding out the truth about you only made you that much more incredible. You're so strong. You've gone through so much, you're *going* through so much, but you never stop trying. You're amazing."

I was surprised when I felt Ryan's hand lift my chin up. I didn't want to look at him, I knew what would happen to my heart if I did, but I couldn't stop myself. I craved him too much.

When we made eye contact, his face lit up and he whispered, "I love you, Jamie Baker."

It came out of nowhere, and it stole the breath from me, leaving me speechless. Ryan stared at me, just waiting for some kind of reaction, and then I was the one who broke the no-kissing rule.

It wasn't my fault. He totally cheated! Like *anyone* could resist Ryan Miller when he's touching your face and saying he loves you?

I threw myself at him so fast that I startled him for a change, and he was the one who had to pull me off him when his hair started to stick up.

"Sorry," I breathed as he pulled away.

"Don't be sorry," he teased. "Just stop."

"Sorry," I said again when I noticed that his leg was now bouncing under the table.

"Yeah. Looks like I don't get to sleep through economics today."

"On the bright side, Coach could make you run laps all practice long and you'd be fine."

We had a good laugh, and then I was even more clueless as to what was going on around me than before. It was honestly the best day I'd had since I'd come to Rocklin High. I was in my own little world, and for once, it was a happy world.

I went home and my mother knew something was up
the minute I walked in the door. She was so shocked
to see me in such a happy mood that she suckered me into
dishing the dirt over mani-pedis the way we used to before
my accident.

It was the best day ever, and I didn't think anything
could spoil it until Becky Eastman knocked on our door
while my mom and I were making dinner. Since I knew
Ryan had to work after practice, I let Mom get it. When I
heard Becky ask my mom if I was home, I was so stunned
that I accidentally knocked the potatoes off the counter. Of
course I caught them before they hit the ground, but still,
surprised doesn't even begin to cover it. I wasn't the only one
who was shocked either. My mom staggered back into the

kitchen and seemed to have trouble getting the words out that someone was there to see me.

I figured that after today, with Ryan and I officially a couple in the public's eye, Becky had finally had enough and she'd come to kill me. I listened for the angry mob, but it was just her. My mother had invited her in, but Becky said she couldn't stay. When I found her she was still standing on the front porch, looking as if she were afraid my house would come to life and swallow her whole.

"Look," I said, not giving her a chance to say anything, "you hate me, and that's fine. I deserve to be hated. And I know I'm the worst person in the world for Ryan, okay? But you're wrong about me. I don't want him ruining his life over me any more than you do. You have no idea how many times I've tried to tell him to get lost. I even tried to tell him to go out with you instead. I've done everything I can, but he just won't listen, and I'm tired of fighting him, so just lay off me."

I think she was a little surprised by my speech, and she looked absolutely terrified to be confronting me, but after a minute she started to relax. "I know," she said, and shrugged matter-of-factly. "It's not your fault."

I was so shocked I could barely understand the words coming out of Becky's mouth. She cracked a smile and said, "When Ryan decides he wants something, he gets it. You never had a chance."

I still had no idea what to say or do. I didn't think to let her in or tell her to go away, I just sort of stood there until it got awkwardly quiet. Becky was the first to speak. "I'm sorry about the other day. I shouldn't have said all those things."

The apology was even more surprising still, and I wanted to say something nice in return, but I was speechless.

"Ryan's been my best friend for practically my whole life," Becky said when I didn't respond. "I was just worried about him, but I've never seen him as happy as he looked today." She paused for a minute and then said, "Anyway, I just wanted to say I'm sorry. I'm glad he's finally found someone."

All I could do was force a bewildered smile. "Thanks."

"Yeah," she said, and then turned to leave.

"Hey, Becky? For the record, when Mike punched Ryan and got them both suspended, they weren't fighting about me. Ryan's really worried about you."

I was able to smile for real this time when she turned around, and I wasn't all that surprised when her eyes glossed over. She stood there for a minute wiping at her eyes, and then took a deep breath. "How did you know?" she asked. "About Mike, I mean. The other day you said you know what really happened."

"I know the signs." I sighed and sat down on the front steps. "I told you we have more in common than you think."

Becky's eyes got really big as my meaning sank in. It took her a minute to work up the courage, but eventually she smiled. "You want to go to the mall?" she asked. "I could really use a smoothie and some new shoes right about now."

I can't even tell you how excited I was by her offer. I mean, it had been a year and a half since I just *went to the mall* with my friends. It sounded like such a normal teen thing to do that I couldn't believe I was being included. I kid you not, I almost cried. My face lit up and I started to nod, but I could smell the aroma of my mom's stuffed chicken wafting from the kitchen and remembered it was Thursday. "Oh, you know, I'd really love to," I said, "but my parents and I already have plans tonight. How about tomorrow?"

Becky smiled but shrugged. "Friday. Game day."

"Right."

Becky and I were both startled when my mother came to the door. "Jamie, honey, don't be silly. You girls go have a good time. Thursday will be here next week too."

I should have known my mother was hovering within hearing distance. I also should have known she'd be quicker to blow off family night than me. She was as desperate as I was for me to have girlfriends, if not more, so I didn't argue with the woman. "Thanks, Mom."

She actually cried as she hugged and kissed me good-bye, and told us to have fun. It was a little embarrassing, but what can you do?

"Sorry about my mom," I said once Becky and I were browsing the mall, smoothies in hand. "She's a little excited to see me talking to people again. The first time Ryan talked to me outside of school, we saw him at the theater. All he did was say hi to me and she *hugged* him."

"How embarrassing."

"She can't help it." I sighed. "She's just been too worried about me for too long."

"So, you were really…" Becky stopped when she was unable to say the word and changed her sentence. "It happened to you too?"

"Not exactly," I admitted. "It was right after sophomore year ended. There was this festival, and my boyfriend suggested we—"

"Go someplace quiet?" Becky offered dryly, as if Mike had used those exact words.

I nodded. "So we could *talk*."

"Us girls are so gullible, aren't we?" Becky groaned. "What guy ever just wants to *talk*?"

I laughed but then sighed. "Yeah, well, I bought it hook, line, and sinker. Derek and I had been together for about five months, and he had just graduated. He was going away to college in the fall, so I thought that's what we were going to talk about." I shrugged sheepishly and added, "We got lost in a cornfield for a while."

"At least that's kind of romantic." Becky frowned. "Mike just took me back to his house and got into his dad's liquor cabinet. I had a drink, but I was *not* drunk." Becky's voice turned harsh, and she started to cry again. "I told him to stop! I begged him. But he just kept telling me that it was okay and that I was so beautiful and to trust him."

Suddenly there were tears in my eyes too. "I'm sorry."

Becky shrugged, grateful for the sympathy even if it didn't make the pain go away. As she batted away her tears, I decided to share my gory details too. "Derek and I were making out, and when he started getting too aggressive I said I wasn't ready. He told me he loved me and that if I loved him too I'd do this for him. I felt bad so I started kissing him again. He was a lot more forceful the second time, and when he pushed me to the ground I got so scared."

"What happened?" Becky asked after I'd stopped talking. My mind had drifted back to that night.

"I tried to fight him off. I kneed him pretty hard, and he got so mad that he hit me. Gave me my first black eye. It surprised him as much as it did me. He tried to apologize, but I screamed at him that it was over and took off running."

"But at least people knew, right? I mean you were black-and-blue. At least he got in trouble, right? I think that's the worst part about it. Mike just got away with it. Even if I tell people what happened no one will believe me. It's Mike. Everyone loves Mike. Even Paige and Tamika just assumed he played me, and they were supposed to be my best friends. Ryan's the only person who would believe me, but I can't tell him. Mike's his best friend, and he'd probably kill him if he knew what he did."

"I know exactly how you feel."

Becky was surprised to hear this, and I tried to smile, but it didn't quite work. "No one ever knew what happened to me either. We got in a car wreck on the way home from the cornfield that night. Both Derek and the truck driver that hit us were killed, and everyone just assumed my bruises were from the accident."

"I'm sorry."

I shook my head as if to tell her not to worry about it and continued on with the story. "Derek was like a god in our town. Ryan and Mike put together. He was headed to the University of Chicago on a football scholarship."

I took a minute to get my emotions under control and then said, "I was the one behind the wheel. I was the only one who survived. There wasn't a person in town that didn't worship the ground Derek walked on, and everyone blamed me for his death. I walked around with that black eye for weeks and actually had to apologize to people when they talked about it.

"My parents eventually moved me here to get away from it all, but even they don't know what really happened. How could I tell them? How could I tell anyone? What would be the point? He was dead."

Becky had tears in her eyes because she felt bad for me, but I smiled because it felt good to finally tell someone the truth, especially someone who understood how I felt. "As you can see, moving here didn't help all that much. At least not until Ryan came along." I blushed when I said Ryan's name. I wanted to kick myself for doing it, but I'm pathetically hung on that kid. "Ryan's been kind of great, actually."

"He usually is," Becky said with a long sigh. Then after a nice, little laugh we got back to our comfort shopping.

It turns out that Becky's kind of great too. I mean, besides Ryan and being molested by jerks, we actually have a ton of other stuff in common. Maybe we were both just feeling a little relieved after our confessional, but we had a great time. We got a killer deal on some shoes too, and the next day at school, when Ryan and I went through the lunch line, Becky came up to me and smiled as she said, "Nice boots!"

"Thanks," I replied, and pointed to her feet. "Love the shoes! Anthropologie, right?"

Becky and I laughed, and then we noticed the look on Ryan's face and laughed even harder. "Are you feeling all right?" I asked as I slipped my arm around his waist and squeezed him. "You look a little pale."

"Me?" he asked, still fluttering his eyes back and forth between Becky and me. "Are you sure *you're* feeling okay?"

"Actually, I feel…great!" I grinned at Becky. "You?"

"I feel better than I have in weeks," she admitted truthfully. "You guys mind if I sit with you today?"

Becky waited for Ryan to answer, and eventually he stuttered out something that sounded like "Of course not."

As the three of us walked over to the table I used to have all to myself, the only sound in the whole cafeteria was a lovely little string of expletives from Paige. The funny thing is, Paige wasn't even mad at me this time. "I don't think I'm the hot topic of conversation anymore," I said.

Becky and Ryan followed my gaze to Paige. Paige stared us down for a minute until Becky finally got angry. "You know what, I've had enough of this," she said, and then began dragging both Ryan and me over to Paige's table.

Becky was absolutely determined to reclaim her throne as the most popular girl in school, and Ryan seemed equally as happy to be returning to his old seat. He did, however, tighten his grip on my hand like he was afraid I was going to make a break for the exit.

I wasn't sure I was too excited about causing such a ruckus, but it's not like I haven't caused more than enough of those lately. And on the bright side, I knew it was going to aggravate the crap out of Paige. That was reason enough for me.

Everyone sat up straight as we approached, but most of them showed more curiosity than fear in their shocked faces. "Hi, guys," Becky chirped as she plopped her tray of food down in her old seat.

"What are you doing?" Paige asked under her breath.

"Having lunch with my friends," Becky answered simply, and then smiled at the rest of the group. "Is that a problem?"

It was dead silent for a moment as everyone gaped at Becky and then shifted their gazes to Ryan and me. No one really knew what to do, but one thing was for sure—none of them was going to argue with Becky. Mike was the only person at the table who seemed as upset as Paige, but when he started to say something I gave him my best death look, and he bit his tongue. Allysa Madsen, though really nervous, was the first to break the silence. "It's good to have you back, Becky," she said as she nudged the others at the table to scoot over to make room for Ryan and me.

"It's good to *be* back," Becky agreed. She grabbed my arm and pulled me down into the seat next to her. "And I have Jamie to thank for that. You guys all know Jamie, right?"

The tension was still a little high, but then Justin Reader, who was sitting next to Mike and directly across from me, smiled really big and stuck his hand out to me as if he were as friendly as Ryan. "I don't think we've technically been introduced."

I looked down at his hand and hesitated. A few months ago I wouldn't have been able to accept the greeting even if

I'd wanted to. Now, not only did I actually want to, I *could*. It was safe. Unless I was in the middle of some kind of epic breakdown, I wasn't going to hurt him and I knew that, so I reached out and let him take my hand. I was surprisingly shy about it even though I've never been shy a day in my life before, and all I could manage was a very nervous "Hi."

"I'm Justin."

Justin continued to shake my hand until he was elbowed in the side. When he jerked back, Scott Cole took my hand next. "And I'm Scott," he announced, choosing to kiss my hand instead of shake it.

The moment was kind of surreal, and I couldn't stop myself from looking to Ryan for help. "I told you they were curious about you." He chuckled under his breath.

"I'm Jamie," I finally croaked, still surprised by the warm greetings.

Ryan protectively pulled my hand away from Scott and playfully warned, "She's also my girlfriend."

That managed to break the tension, and everyone at the table laughed, but I guess all the warm fuzzy feelings being thrown at me were too much for Paige to handle, and she snapped. "Just like that?" she screamed. "She's been the biggest witch in this school for over a year, and you're just going to be her friends now?"

I didn't see who said it, but it was definitely one of the cheerleaders who grumbled, "She hasn't been the *biggest* witch in school."

As people tried to hide their snickers, Becky met Paige's glare. "People change" was all she said in response to Paige's question.

I wasn't sure if Becky was talking about me or herself, but either way, Paige looked like she was about to explode. She was too angry to say anything, and almost fell on her butt when she stood up because she was shaking with so much anger. She looked around the table one last time and stopped when she got to Ryan's best friend. "Mike?" she questioned as if asking him to come with her in some sort of protest.

I hate to say it felt good to watch Mike struggle, but you know what? It really did. He seemed genuinely confused as to what he should do, but ultimately he was too much of a chicken to leave. He glanced quickly my direction and then shrugged. "Miller's my boy," he mumbled. "If he says she's cool…"

"Thanks a lot!" Paige huffed, and then stalked off. She got about four steps and then turned around and glared at Tamika. Tamika hesitated but then rolled her eyes and followed her best friend out of the cafeteria.

After Paige left, things were a lot better. Everyone was still a little awkward and nervous, but they were curious, like Ryan said, and they were actually trying to be nice. And I knew they were probably only doing it for Ryan and Becky, but after lunch, in government, when I didn't have either Becky or Ryan around, Allysa still asked me to sit by her. I was touched by the offer, and talking to people other than Ryan and Becky went a lot smoother than I expected.

I actually walked to English with Scott. When we got there he insisted I take his seat so that I could sit next to my boyfriend, and he took Paige's seat since she refused to sit anywhere near Ryan, Becky, or me. People were still adjusting to the change, but after everything at lunch, nobody was very surprised to see the new seating chart. Well, mostly no one. The look on Mr. Edwards's face as he watched Scott's gallant gesture was rather amusing.

Mr. E. was so surprised that he was actually a bit distracted during class, and when it was over, he looked almost perplexed as Ryan and Becky dragged me from the room. I couldn't leave the man in such a state, so I told Ryan and Becky I'd catch up to them. I tried to wipe the smile from my face when I approached Mr. Edwards's desk. "You all right, Mr. E.? You're looking a little pale."

"Oh, no, I'm just... Well, I'm shocked! What happened?"

"You said I was the one with the power to change things. I just followed your advice."

Mr. E. seemed genuinely confounded but quickly composed himself and began to tease me. "What did you do, use some kind of brain warp on them all?"

"Sorry, mind control isn't one of my superpowers," I joked back. I wasn't joking, but he thought it was funny.

"Could have fooled me." He laughed.

"Actually, I did something a lot crazier than brainwash everyone."

Mr. E. perked up. "Really?" His eyes sparkled with curiosity.

I glanced around the room and leaned in like I was going to give away a big secret and then whispered, "I was *nice*."

I laughed when Mr. E. looked disappointed in my confession. "I know, it was a little anticlimactic for me too," I teased. Then I thought for a second and shrugged. "It was mostly Ryan's doing. He sort of killed the ice queen a while ago."

"Ah, yes. Mr. Miller." Mr. Edwards rolled his eyes as if to say, *of course he was involved.* Apparently I'm not the only one who gets a little annoyed with Ryan's perfection.

Speaking of Ryan, he was probably wondering where I was by now, so I stepped back from the desk. "Anyway, thanks, Mr. E. I really think things are going to be a lot better for me now. You can chalk up your first teaching success and take me off your troubled students list."

I was just giving him a hard time as I said that, but instead of laughing, he sat there deliberating. Finally he nodded and said, "Good for you, Jamie. I'm glad to see things are working out for you."

"You're all right, Mr. E.," I admitted as I headed for the door.

"See you later, Ms. Baker."

Ryan and Becky were waiting right outside the classroom for me. Ryan pulled my fingers into his as if the five minutes we'd been apart had nearly killed him, then he glanced back in the room at our teacher and asked, "Everything okay, Mr. E.?"

The poor man was trying his best to look like he wasn't watching us, but he was still in too much shock to pull it off.

I gave him a quick smile and then turned my full attention back to Ryan. My grin tripled in size. "Everything's great," I answered, bemused by the truth in my words.

Ryan pulled me into his arms, squeezing me like he'd never been more proud of anyone in his whole life. "I think this calls for a celebration. Let's go do something before the game."

"Actually," I said, "Becky asked me if I would practice her routine with her for a while, but you can come watch us do backflips if you want."

"Are you going to put on your old cheer uniform?"

Ryan was a little too excited by the thought of me in a costume, so I squashed that idea, and fast. "In your dreams."

"Not exactly." Ryan grinned wickedly. "In my dreams you're usually dressed like Wonder Woman."

Ugh. I wondered how long it would take for him to start in on the superhero crap. Obviously, not long. I was not amused, but Ryan seemed to think himself hilarious. I could also tell by the look on his face that he was quite confident he'd have me in costume one day. "Never gonna happen," I assured him. "Ever."

And of course he responded with that classic, cocky smile. "Just like you were never gonna be my girlfriend, right?"

All I could do was groan. I started to drag Becky off, but Ryan called out to us, saying, "Are you really going to ditch me?" and Becky stopped walking.

He pouted with this face that was just so pathetically adorable I wanted to both smack and kiss it, but Becky was the one who gave in first. "Ryan, if you really want to go out, I'll grab Scott, and we can double or something."

"Becky!" I had to laugh. "You're worse than me! It's no wonder he's such an egomaniac."

"What? You're telling me you can say no to that face?"

I wanted to say yes, but it would have been a lie and we all knew it. "Fine." I sighed. "Why not? A double date could be fun." I looked at Ryan in defeat. "So, where are we going?"

"Nowhere," Ryan said as he pulled me into his arms again. "I'm not going to interrupt your girl time now that you're finally having it. I just wanted to see how long it would take for you to give in." Ryan's smile was back and bigger than ever. "You get easier every time."

Ryan Miller. Honestly. What can you do? Of course I laughed. I didn't want to, but I couldn't help it, so I don't think my accompanying eye-roll was all that convincing. In fact, I know it wasn't because Ryan pulled me against him so that my face was just an inch from his, and said, "Permission to kiss my girlfriend?"

Not that I wanted him to get his way again, but as if I could say no? He gave me a quick kiss good-bye and then handed me off to Becky and told her to take good care of me.

"You sure you don't want to come?" Becky asked.

"No, no. You girls go do your thing. We can get a group together after the game instead." Ryan stopped suddenly and gave me a puzzled look. "You are going to come, aren't you?"

I was actually startled by the question. I'd been watching the games for a while now, but I guess I hadn't told him that, and I'd never thought about sitting in the stands. "What? Um, well, I was just going to…"

"Oh, come!" Becky cried. "It'll be fun. I promise."

Suddenly, I now had two people I couldn't say no to. When I shrugged, Ryan's whole face lit up. "Come find me before the game starts."

"We will," Becky answered for me, and then carted me off to the practice field.

It felt so good to be out on the field, messing around with Becky. It was a little weird at first because I hadn't done any gymnastics since my accident, and I had to be careful not to let my power escape while doing all those flips. Becky seemed a little self-conscious at first, but once we got going she was perfectly fine in all her tumbling—kicked my rusty butt out of the water. I think she'd only been screwing up lately because she was so stressed out over the whole Mike thing.

We stayed at it for so long that we were barely going to have time to go home, hit the showers, and be back before kickoff. I was mentally searching for the perfect outfit as I drove home, but all thoughts of getting cute or even going to the game flew out the window the minute I pulled up to my house and heard Carter's voice coming from the living room, filling my parents' head with stories of mad scientists.

That man was *so* dead.

I thought for sure he'd get the hint after I torched his house, but apparently it was going to take more than that to get rid of him. Maybe I'd throw him off the edge of the Grand Canyon. Or better yet, just leave him in the middle of northern Canada somewhere and let him find his own way back. That wouldn't be murder, right? Not technically.

I barged through the door ready to throttle someone, but surprisingly, my dad looked twice as angry as I did. Angrier than I'd ever seen him, and trust me, that's saying something. Funny thing was, he seemed angry with the wrong person.

"Jamielynn Baker!" When he shouted, the walls of the house shook, and for once I didn't have anything to do with it. "You are grounded until you're DEAD!"

My teenage instinct to rebel won out over my shock, and I screamed right back. "What did *I* do?"

"You should have told us he was here!"

"I had it under control!"

"Control?"

Oops. That was the wrong thing to say. My father was choking on his words he was so irate. "You burned down a *house!*"

"I burned creepy surveillance photos and videos that prove I have powers. The rest of the house was an accident."

"And what about the physical assault?"

Carter told my parents I physically assaulted him? What a baby. I barely even threw the guy. "He was trying to destroy my life again. I was a little angry. And besides, you know where I get my temper. You'd have hit him too, and you know it."

"He *did* hit me," Carter grumbled under his breath.

I glanced at Carter for the first time and noticed that he was holding a bag of frozen peas over his left eye. It was easy to picture my father answering the door and punching Carter before he could get a single word in. "Nice." I showed no sympathy when I finally addressed Carter. "Let's see it."

Carter grudgingly removed the vegetables, and half his face was black-and-blue. I'll admit the sight of him gave me an overwhelming dose of sick satisfaction and also made me quite proud of my dad. I raised an eyebrow at my father and laughed when I noticed his lips twitching as he fought back a smile. "You're still in trouble, young lady," he said stubbornly.

I was good and ready to argue my punishment and defend my actions. I mean, yeah, maybe I burned the guy's house down, but it was a crappy one anyway, and he really didn't leave me any other choice. But then something else occurred to me. "Wait! Why is he even still here?"

My mother finally spoke up. "He came to warn us."

Warn us? *Puh-lease.* I rolled my eyes. I know my mom hates that, but I couldn't help myself. "Don't tell me you're buying—"

"What choice do we have, Jamie?" My mother cut me off with unusual harshness. "If there's even the tiniest bit of truth to this, and people are really looking for you, then he's done us a great favor."

"A favor?" I asked, too incredulous to actually scream. "Even if what he says is true, that means he's the reason we're in this mess in the first place! All those stupid articles he wrote back in Illinois! Can't you guys see that he's just trying to scare you into coming forward? He's still just looking for his story!"

Carter's patience finally wore thin, and he joined in the argument. "Is *this* just a story?"

Carter threw a large manila envelope across the coffee table at me, and despite all the control I'd gained recently, when I saw it, I blew the circuit breaker again. "If this is more blackmail pictures, Carter, I swear I am going to launch you off the Golden Gate Bridge!"

"Jamie, easy on the death threats, honey," my dad warned. But I could tell he liked the idea.

"But, Dad!"

"Just look at the picture, Jamielynn!" Carter snapped.

I wanted to be stubborn, but my curiosity got the better of me, and I slid the photo out of the envelope. "Big deal," I said. I'd seen this picture before. It was the same picture of guys in lab coats from the Visticorp website, only this one was ripped from a magazine. "This is an article on stem cell research. It doesn't prove that they know about me."

"Look closer," Carter said. "Recognize anyone?"

I looked closer.

Shocked does not even begin to cover it.

"After you destroyed everything," Carter explained as I stared at the picture in front of me in disbelief, "I didn't know what to do. So I did some digging and figured out who exactly had been contacting me. It wasn't easy because I was looking at Visticorp employees, but he doesn't work for them anymore. He quit just months after Derek died."

I was still too overwhelmed to process everything he was telling me. "B-But," I stammered. "This isn't right… This can't be right!"

It just couldn't be. I mean, I trusted him. But there he was, sporting a white lab coat, standing proudly with his research team in an article ripped from the pages of *Time* magazine. "He cared about me. He *helped* me."

"He suckered you." Carter used a softer voice than I thought him capable of, but his words were still harsh.

I felt so stupid, so young and naive, like Carter once told me I was. His comment wounded my pride as well as filled me with fear. I mean, if he could have me that fooled, any-one could. I would never really be safe. My eyes filled with tears, and I was grateful when both my parents scooped me tightly into a Jamie sandwich.

I think the closeness of my family made Carter a little uncomfortable. Or maybe it was my falling apart in front of him.

"It's not too late, Jamie," he said, clearing his throat to break up our group hug. "The good news is, Visticorp doesn't know about you. Without them, he's just one man. And his plan isn't to expose you."

"How do you know what his plan is?" I snapped.

"Because I know why he left. He was convinced you were special. Obsessive about it. But Visticorp never believed him, so he quit. He was probably trying to get close to you in hopes that he'd eventually be able to convince you to go back with him. He wants to prove Visticorp wrong. He wants to study you. He wants to be the one to figure out what happened. He's looking for a Nobel Prize. If you were exposed, he could never keep you to himself. No, he doesn't want your secret getting out at all. But, Jamie, he's still dangerous. If you don't give him what he wants, he'll expose you to Visticorp just to prove he's not crazy. And if they find out the truth…"

My mom shuddered.

"That's exactly why Jamie needs to come forward," Carter told her.

And that's where he lost me. "Un-be-freaking-lievable! You just never quit, do you!"

"Jamie, it's the only way."

"No! You're not taking away my life! You're not putting my family in danger!"

"You don't think they're in danger now? Jamielynn, he knows everything. He's obsessed with you. You don't think that when he realizes you're not going to cooperate, he'll use the people you care about as means to persuade you to go with him?"

I heard a gasp, but I wasn't sure if it had come from my mother or me. I looked at the picture again. He'd never seemed dangerous until now. "He… He couldn't." I glanced frantically at my parents. "I can protect them." I didn't sound anywhere near confident enough in my declaration. Probably because I wasn't.

We all stood there locked in a staring match until my cell phone rang, startling us all. I glanced at Becky's number on the display, but now was not the time to answer it. My mom chose the distraction as a way to break the deafening silence.

"Jamie, sweetheart, maybe Mr. Carter's right. Maybe it's time."

I couldn't believe what I'd just heard. My heart gave out inside my chest, and I had to sit down before I fell down. I tried to protest, but my words caught in my throat, so I just cried.

"Don't worry, Jamie," Carter said. "I'll make sure you're safe. We'll be smart about it."

Carter's voice was *so* not what I wanted to hear right then. I don't know what kind of look I gave him, but it was enough to make my father step in front of him protectively. He put a hand on my shoulder and said, "Mr. Carter has a point. If the whole world knows about you, then the government or anyone else won't be able to take you away."

"And you're such a sweet girl, Jamie. The world will just fall in love with you," my mother added. I guess she didn't know my nickname was the Ice Queen. "They'll want to help us. Maybe we can finally get some answers."

My phone blared again, and I nearly crushed it in my hand. This time the display read "Scott Cole." As much as I was curious as to why on earth he could possibly be calling me, I threw my phone down on the coffee table and ignored the sounds that rang from it.

Letting my hurt turn to anger again was the only way to get my sobs under control. "I don't want to be a worldwide freak!" I shouted through my tears. "People will never leave us alone—the paparazzi, the government! Even if they can't actually take me away, they'll camp out front of our house, watching us. They'll follow us everywhere. Doctors will show up wanting to study me, just like after my accident, only worse. It'll ruin our lives. And in the meantime, the guy"—I pointed at Carter—"who discovered Electric Girl—or whatever stupid name you invent for me—gets rich and lives happily ever after. Can't you guys see what he's doing?"

I think my parents were starting to listen to me. I could see it in their eyes, hesitation and even fear. I opened my mouth again, but then Carter blurted out, "I'm only trying to help you, Jamie!" At the same time, my phone roared to life a third time and I just snapped.

"WHAT?" I screamed into the receiver.

"Uh, Jamie?" It was Mike Driscoll of all people, and he sounded terrified to be calling me.

It would have been fun to rip his head off, but I was too surprised by his call. "Yeah?"

"Is Miller with you?"

"No. The game's about to start. I'm sure he's at the school."

"He's not. The game should have started five minutes ago. They're not going to let us wait any longer. We're gonna have to put Warren in as QB, and he totally sucks!"

"Well, where's Ryan?"

Mike didn't sound scared anymore. "You tell me! You're the one who's had him on a freaking leash lately."

That did it.

You know, it's kind of funny—but not ha-ha funny—that even with Carter standing right in front of me, trying to turn my parents to the dark side, the person who made me lose total control of my temper was Mike. I pulled the phone away from my ear and held it in front of my mouth so that I could scream a deafening scream more directly into Mike's ear. Then I hung up on him and dropped the phone, unaware that I was stirring up an electrical storm until my parents and Carter jumped back for safety and started screaming at me.

I could see them all just fine through the greenish haze in my eyes, and I knew they were all shouting at me to calm down, but I couldn't really hear anything except the whirlwind of electricity swirling around me. And then suddenly the significance of Mike's call dawned on me.

"Ryan didn't show up to the game," I said, not bothering to calm down. I didn't want to calm down. I had a feeling that Super Jamie was about to come in very handy. "Ryan would never just blow off a game."

Carter's eyes drifted to the picture he'd given me, and I nodded, my thoughts already there.

"He wouldn't," I decided confidently. "Even if Mr. E. does want to study me, he's not evil. He wouldn't hurt Ryan."

He just wouldn't.

But then, Ryan Miller would never leave his team in the hands of Paul Warren either.

I looked questioningly at Carter, but he didn't seem to have any ideas. And why should he? It's not like Ryan was worth anything to him.

In the silence, my phone rang again. I scooped it up off the floor and when I saw Ryan's name I was filled with relief. "Ryan! Where—"

"Ryan can't talk at the moment, Jamie," the voice on the other end replied.

"Mr. E.?"

My heart sank. I was sure it had only been a paranoid fear that Ryan's no-show could have anything to do with Mr. Edwards. I didn't expect that fear to be legit. My stomach turned over and over again as I tried to decide if I was more angry or scared. The two emotions were pretty equal at the moment, but knowing what happens when I am feeling either, it wasn't looking so good for Mr. E.

"Yes, Jamie, it's me," Mr. E. said, interrupting my thoughts. "I'm afraid I have some bad news."

"Actually," I said, trying my hardest not to crush the phone in my hand, "I'm the one with the bad news. I know who you are."

Mr. E. stayed silent for a minute. He was surprised by my confession. "It's not what you think, Jamie."

"Oh, right. Like I've never heard that before."

"I promise you, Jamie. I mean you no harm."

"Yeah, tell that to Ryan!"

"I don't want to hurt Mr. Miller either. He's just here because I know you too well. We need to talk, Jamie."

"Oh, we're going to do more than talk."

"Relax, Ms. Baker. It's not going to do anyone any good if you lose control."

Well, he was right about that. But I *was* in control. Sure, I was a little glow-in-the-dark at the moment, but it was by choice. I hadn't even fried my phone. I had no idea how I was doing it, but for the time being, I was controlling my powers. It was like I was in some kind of super survival mode. Something needed to get done, and I was going to do it. End of story.

"Where are you?" I asked, only it didn't really sound like I was asking all that much.

"The school," he answered. "But please, Jamie, there's no need to get upset. I think you'll like my proposal."

Fat chance. "You really shouldn't have done this."

I heard Carter and my parents call out to me as I disappeared in front of their eyes. I knew they were worried about me—well, my parents anyway. Carter was only worried about his paycheck—but honestly, did the Flash ever stop to explain things before he took off running? There'd be plenty of time to explain everything when it was all over, and I was sure this was not going to take very long.

I didn't hesitate for even a second as I flew to the school and blew through the door to my English classroom. Maybe I should have come up with a plan first because I was *not* prepared for what I found waiting for me on the other side of that door. I knew Ryan would be there. I even expected to see him tied to a chair or something, which he was, but I never dreamed that he'd be wired to a car battery. It was such a disturbing sight that the moment I saw him I freaked the mother of all freak-outs.

"Amazing," Mr. Edwards whispered to himself as the lights in the room burst, raining down in a shower of glass and sparks.

"Amazing" is definitely not how I saw it. What I saw was every muscle in Ryan's body tensed and shaking violently from the electricity being pumped into him. The wattage was so high that he couldn't even scream. It was the most horrifying thing I've ever seen. "Mr. E., what are you doing to him!" I shrieked.

"It's not me, Jamie. If you don't want him to die I suggest you turn off the power right now."

When his words sank in, I was so horrified that my eyes drifted back to Ryan in what felt like slow motion. "I can't just flip a switch!"

I took a step toward Ryan, wanting to rip him free from the torture. But as I moved closer, the energy got stronger. I couldn't free him, so I did the only thing I could think of. I left. And it just about killed me. I left Ryan there, stranded with a psychopath, wired to a car battery, and now, thanks to me, probably half dead. But what else could I do? I was killing him, and unlike Mr. Edwards seemed to think, I couldn't just turn it off. Not when I was so upset.

I ran from that room as fast as my legs could take me. I was too distraught to think up a plan, but it didn't really matter because my phone was ringing just a few short seconds after I took off. I didn't say anything when I answered it—I couldn't get words out between my sobs—but Mr. Edwards didn't wait for a greeting.

"I'm sorry, Jamie." Mr. Edwards sighed, and he had the nerve to actually sound remorseful. "I didn't realize… I was under the impression that you had learned how to control yourself. Honestly, I never wanted anyone to get hurt."

You know what they say: anger does a body good. Or maybe that was milk, but whatever. It certainly did me some good right then to get really mad, because I quit crying like a baby and found my inner ice queen.

"Then why take Ryan? Why strap him to a battery? You're sick!"

"It was self-defense. I knew that if you couldn't use your power around him, then you wouldn't be able to use it on me."

I hated to admit it, but, "Actually, Mr. E., that wasn't a bad idea on your part."

"Thanks."

"Too bad it was all a wasted effort."

"How do you figure?"

"Because I may not be able to stop you right now, but the cops surely can. Don't think I'm not going to call them."

Mr. E. ignored my threats and changed the subject. "I've been to Tahoe, Jamie. I've seen your little practice sessions with Ryan."

I was about to hang up on him and call the police as promised, but something occurred to me then. "It was you I saw that day, videotaping me." I was talking more to myself than him. "I should have known Carter would never be stupid enough to get caught."

"Jamie, the things you can do... You're incredible! Don't you want to understand how it's possible?"

"No. What I want is for you to let my boyfriend go."

"I'm afraid I can't do that. Not until you hear me out."

"You," I growled, "will never get what you want. I would let Carter take me to CNN before I'd let you come anywhere near me!"

"You don't understand what I want," Mr. E. said in a strange voice. I realized a moment later it was desperation. He was pleading with me. "I want to help you master this gift you have. I want to see you happy, Jamie, and safe. We could work together. Just you and me. No hospitals, no doctors, no labs. Kind of like what you and Ryan have been trying to do, except that with the things I know, we could actually get some answers. You wouldn't have to leave your life, and we don't have to do any tests that you don't want to do. I would take care of you."

It was right then that I realized Mr. E. had some serious issues. "Carter wasn't kidding about you being obsessed with me, was he?" I said. "News flash, Mr. E. You're a psycho!"

I don't think Mr. E. appreciated me calling him crazy, because he got mad. Supermad. Super*villain* mad.

"You don't know what's best for you," he said, his voice trembling in the creepiest way possible. "But I'm going to make you see."

"Cuckoo!" I sung. "I'm calling the cops now."

"If you do, Ryan will be dead before they get here."

The guy sounded crazy enough that he might actually be capable of what he was threatening. Something came up my throat then, and no matter how hard I tried, I wasn't able to say anything.

"You leave me no choice, Jamie," Mr. Edwards said.

There was a moment of silence, then a click, and short buzz of static in the reception on my phone. Then Ryan began to scream a pained, muffled scream. "Hello?" I screamed. "Mr. E.? What are you doing?"

Mr. Edwards was way too calm when he finally spoke up again. "The interesting thing about a car battery, Jamie, is that it's really not enough power to kill you by electrocution. That's why people like to use it as a form of torture. You see, what it does is, the electricity makes all of your muscles tighten up so hard that you can't breathe. Eventually you die of suffocation. It's a very slow, painful death."

"This isn't funny, Mr. E.! You'll kill him! Stop! Turn it off!"

"I want to, Jamie, I do. But you're a very stubborn girl. This may be the only way to get through to you."

"But I can't control it!"

"Well, I suggest you learn pretty quick."

Why did this keep happening to me? Why did I continue to hurt people? Derek was dead because of me. And now Ryan was dying. Again, because of me.

I was so frantic that energy raged inside me at an extreme I'd never felt before, and it caused that yellow-green haze to cloud not only my sight, but my mind as well. It was impossible to think rationally. One thought took up all the space in my head: Save Ryan. Do whatever it takes.

As I took off running again something in the back of my head told me that saving my boyfriend might require taking the life of my favorite teacher, well, ex-favorite teacher, but whatever conscience I used to possess had flown the coop. I knew I wouldn't be able to control my temper when I saw him, but I didn't care anymore. Quite frankly, Mr. E. deserved whatever he got.

I was back at school within seconds and stopped in the parking lot. I could still hear Ryan, but his scream was already weak. Too weak. I needed to get in there, but I knew that if I went barging in like before, I would most likely kill Ryan instantly. As worked up as I was, I was probably radiating enough energy to make his body explode or something. That was a nightmare I could live without, but I had to do something.

Slowly, and more focused than I'd ever been in my life, I stretched my hands out in front of me and closed my eyes. Just like that time in Ryan's bedroom, and in the park with the street lamps, I could feel all of the electricity in the world around me. Ironically, it didn't feel like the nightmare that it was. It felt more like a nice warm security blanket. Almost as if it were part of me, just an extension of my arms. I could feel it. I could grab it. I could push it away from me, pull it to me.

It was strongest near the football field, where the lights were now on and the scoreboard was blazing. But this was not the energy I was interested in. I turned one hand away from the field and swept it toward the school. When I found the tiny pocket of energy coming from the direction of Mr. Edwards's classroom, I sucked it out of there as quickly as I could.

When I started to pull the energy into me I heard Ryan's cries of pain stop. He gasped for breath once and then went silent, most likely succumbing to unconsciousness. This actually comforted me more than it horrified me. It meant that my plan was working and the torture had momentarily stopped. But it wasn't over because I still couldn't get myself under control, and as long as Ryan was attached to that battery, every ounce of energy I released in his presence would be pumped directly into his body. So as I walked slowly toward my boyfriend, I continued to swallow up every last drop of electricity in the entire school so that there would be nothing left to hurt Ryan.

By the time I reached the classroom door, the energy I was still pulling in was nearly too much to keep contained. I had to stop. I couldn't take in one more ounce of electricity or I would burst with an explosion that would wipe all of Rocklin High from existence. This was it, the moment of truth, but I was determined. "You will *not* let it go," I ordered myself. "You will *not* hurt Ryan again!"

I looked at the closed door in front of me and took a deep breath as I clenched my burning hands into tight fists. My insides felt like an atom bomb, with particles of energy bouncing around in absolute chaos. "Don't let go," I chanted to myself. "Don't let go. Don't let go!"

I was concentrating so hard on not letting my power escape me that when Mr. Edwards called my name, it startled the living daylights out of me. He must have heard me mumbling to myself. I was reaching for the door when he yelled out, "Jamie? Is that you?"

All I did was flinch because he'd startled me. But there was so much power inside me that when I did, I maybe sort of... blew up the door. Okay, so there was no maybe about it. I exploded that door into a thousand tiny pieces sending

Mr. Edwards ducking for cover beneath his desk. "I guess so," he said with a chuckle when the dust settled.

I don't know if it was the amusement in his voice or the streaks of blood running down Ryan's nose as his body slumped forward in his chair, but I totally snapped. "How could you?" I screeched, and then, without warning, took aim at the desk Mr. E. was hiding behind and blew it to smithereens.

Mr. Edwards was knocked back a few feet by the blast and looked a little scraped up, but ultimately, he was fine. Pity. But on the bright side, he looked pretty scared. "Careful now, Jamie," he stammered nervously. "You don't want to hurt Ryan, do you?"

"Do you hear him screaming?"

Mr. Edwards glanced quickly at Ryan and frowned. "I thought you said you can't control it."

And that's when it dawned on me. I had just walked into this room more charged up than a nuclear power plant, and I hadn't once set off the battery attached to my boyfriend. I'd even done that whole lightning thing twice, and still nothing had hurt Ryan. I was controlling my power. I was controlling it, and I hadn't even realized it.

I was so angry just now that I wanted Mr. E. dead, and it was all I could think about. My power was just naturally following my lead. As I stared at my hands in astonishment, I realized that that's the way it had always been. Whenever I was angry, my power shot out from me with fury. Whenever I was scared, it acted as some sort of defense mechanism. That's even why it never hurt Ryan when he hugged me or kissed me. Every time Ryan touched me the power drew us together, pulling him to me like a magnet, because that's what I'd wanted.

The power inside of me was a part of me. It worked with me, not against me. It really was at my command, and now that I understood that, I had no more cause to fear it. It was the being afraid of the power in the first place that was hurting me.

I thought of Ryan again, and there was nothing I've ever wanted more in my life than I wanted to have him safe in my arms, kissing me until I couldn't think straight. I'd told myself not to hurt him, willed the energy inside me to stay there, and it had obeyed.

I understood now, and I knew that it would obey me again, so I embraced my power. I let it flow through me with force as if it were an ally instead of a curse, and once I'd finally stopped fighting it, it felt different somehow. *I* felt different. I felt stronger, more confident, unstoppable even.

I felt *super*.

First things first. I walked up to Ryan without a moment's hesitation and ripped that battery away from him so fast that I accidentally sent it flying across the room and through the wall. Ryan was completely unconscious, but he *was* breathing, and I could hear his heart beating faintly in his chest.

I wiped the sweaty hair from his forehead and gave him a gentle kiss, whispering, "Hang in there. I'll be right back." Then I whirled around and looked at my English teacher with more confidence than even Ryan could muster on his best day.

"You," I said with enough ferocity to make the blood drain from his face, "are a dead man."

I didn't give Mr. E. a chance to plead his case. Before he could even blink, he was flying across the room. Yeah, I know that revenge is generally frowned upon and that my parents got a little mad when I roughed up Carter, but, hey, I can't be expected to master my power *and* my temper all in one day. Mr. E. went soaring and crashed into a bunch of desks. He groaned a nice painful-sounding groan for a second, but not nearly long enough if you ask me.

"Jamie, wait," he immediately began. "Let's be reasonable. You don't—"

"Reasonable!" I shrieked. "Reasonable?" I picked him up again and threw him into the blackboard. "You almost killed my boyfriend! You *tortured* him! Don't you dare tell me to be reasonable!"

Mr. E. opened his mouth to say something, but I didn't want to hear it. I grabbed his hand and sent a current into him that forced him to scream out in pain. "Is this what it was like for Ryan?" I kicked up the power a notch, making Mr. E.'s body go so stiff that he could no longer scream. "Tell me, what's worse, the electrocution or the suffocation?"

I let go of his hand and let him fall limp to the ground. As soon as he could, he croaked, "Please, Jamie. I'm sorry. I didn't want it to be like this."

His pathetic apology set me off again. The anger inside me only grew worse from the violence. "You're *sorry*? Sorry for what you did to Ryan? Or just sorry that your stupid plan didn't work?"

With that, my rage clouded out the world around me, and I grabbed him again. This time electrocuting him didn't seem like enough. It didn't seem deadly enough, so I slipped my fingers around his neck and began to squeeze. His face was a dark shade of blue when a voice yelled, "Jamie, stop!"

I was so blinded by my emotion that I never heard Carter enter the room. He'd surprised me, but not enough to make me let go of Mr. E. "He was going to *kill* him!"

"Jamie," Carter said again, his voice calm and commanding. "Let him go."

I looked into the face that was starting to lose consciousness, and I was filled with a hate that I'd never dreamed to be capable of. Derek, Carter, Mike… None of them even came close to making me feel the way I felt right now. That hate made it impossible for me to stop. "I'm not going to let him hurt anyone I love ever again!"

I felt a hand come down on my shoulder. "You're not a murderer, Jamielynn," Carter said.

Those words had been said to me a hundred times before. My parents had said them. Ryan had said them. Even Carter had let the phrase slip before. I looked at Mr. E. again, and this time I saw the terror in his eyes. The same terror I saw in Derek's face as he died. Then, suddenly, Mr. Edwards was gone. I could only see Derek lying there beneath my grip, barely able to struggle anymore, and I realized exactly what I was doing.

Carter was right. I wasn't a murderer. The conflict in me finally surfaced, and I collapsed to the floor, breaking into violent sobs as I released Mr. Edwards. Carter let me cry for a moment and then said, "You'll thank me for that someday, Jamielynn."

Again, Carter was right. I was already grateful he'd pulled me from whatever temporary insanity I was suffering from. But I couldn't let Carter see how relieved I suddenly was, and I definitely couldn't let him see that I was in any way thankful for what he'd just done. Dave Carter is just not the kind of guy I need thinking I owe him one, even if maybe I do.

Carter is dangerous, and he's still a scumbag. I wouldn't trust him any further than I could throw him. Actually, I could probably chuck him a lot farther than I trust him. In fact, it really unsettled me that he'd just helped me. It scared me even. It was just so… un-Carter-like. What could he possibly have to gain from Edwards staying alive? Edwards was as much a threat to his precious story as he was to the safety of my family.

When I couldn't take the mystery anymore, I dried my tears. Or maybe they just froze in place when I flipped into ice queen mode. "What are you doing here?"

Carter didn't seem surprised by my question. In fact, much to my chagrin, he was prepared with an answer. A good one.

"I've got a plan to have Edwards locked up for life without raising any suspicion about you or your powers."

"Impossible." It was too good to be true. And even if there were a way, knowing Carter, it was definitely going to cost me.

"Not impossible," Carter disagreed. He was confident in his answer, but he seemed very wary about something, and his reluctance made me extremely uneasy. "But you're going to have to trust me. I'm going to have to write a story."

I may have overreacted to this news just a tiny bit, since Carter's hands flew up. "Hang on just a minute now, Jamielynn. I'm not talking about exposing you. I'm talking about exposing him."

So surprised by his answer, I couldn't help looking down at the man he was pointing to. The man who was trying to sit up and was still coughing. The man I almost killed in cold blood.

"What do you mean?"

"It'll be so easy, Jamielynn." Carter swiped his fingers across the air as if spreading out the headline for me.

" 'Obsessed teacher stalks student. Tries to kill boyfriend in jealous rage.' "

It sounded like nonsense. "What are you talking about?"

"Think about it. He's always paid special attention to you, hasn't he? Always been extra friendly to you? Kept you after class to talk to you? No doubt he was trying to gain your trust. Get you to let him in so you'd slip up about your powers. But think about what it could look like to everyone else with just a little help from yours truly. He's already done all the work by kidnapping your boyfriend. And when the cops go to his apartment and find all the surveillance photos, well, no jury in the world would let him off."

"But he has evidence of my powers! It'll expose me!"

"Don't sweat it. I've already got that covered."

I wanted to smack that smug smile clean off his face, but I was too busy being swayed by his plan. It was tempting. It could work. But... I shook my head in denial. I couldn't give in. This was Carter. I couldn't trust him. "What do you get out of it?"

His smile grew even wider. "The satisfaction of knowing I helped someone in need?"

"Don't mess with me, Carter!" I screamed. "I'm not exactly in the mood for your crap!"

It felt good to see him cringe away from me when I held out my hand in his direction. Sometimes being a scary superfreak has its perks.

"Look, it's a win-win situation. You get to keep your secret, and I still get my story. And this is an even better story because people will believe it a lot easier than they'd swallow the 'Supergirl is real' thing, even with video footage. This story screams hard-hitting journalist. By uncovering the truth I just saved your life and your boyfriend's. We could be talking *Pulitzer*."

Again, he had me stumped. Not that I necessarily wanted Carter to benefit from this mess, but his plan would take care of Edwards. And if Carter got his stupid Pulitzer maybe he'd stay off my case and get out of my life once and for all. Jeez, that thought alone was worth it.

I was subconsciously nodding my head before I made my decision. "We'll have to get our stories straight," I mumbled, realizing that I'd already given in.

"It'll never work," Mr. Edwards croaked out of the blue. "Even if the world doesn't believe my story, Visticorp will know the truth. They'll come after you. You'll never be safe. Not unless you let me help you."

"You stay out of this!" I spat, kicking him in the stomach out of irritation.

Hey, I said I won a beauty pageant. I never breathed a word about being voted Miss Congeniality.

Mr. E. shut up—because I'd just knocked the wind out of him—but his threats had done their damage. I'd forgotten about the group of rich evil scientists that Mr. Edwards used to work for. I looked up at Carter, somewhat frantic, but he just smiled again. "No one's coming for you, Jamielynn," he assured me. He then turned his grin on Mr. Edwards. "Are they?"

Mr. Edwards's face flashed a deep red, proving the truth in Carter's accusation. I looked to Carter for further explanation, and he happily obliged.

"Your Mr. Edwards here is completely on his own. No one will come for you, Jamielynn, because the truth is, they never believed in you in the first place. It was Edwards who heard about your accident in Illinois. Edwards who tried so desperately to get proof, but he never did. He tried for months and months to convince Visticorp you were different, but they never saw the value in his claims. He quit the company and set off on his own to find you."

"That's not true, Jamie! Visticorp sent me to Illinois after your accident to watch you—to see if you were worth the risk. But the more I learned about you, the more I couldn't stand the thought of handing you over to them. I told them you were a regular girl, and then I followed you to California just to make sure no one else came for you."

"He's lying, Jamie," Carter said. "If he was only here to make sure you stayed safe, then why come after you now?"

"That was all *his* fault!" Mr. E. screamed, pointing an accusing finger at Ryan's unconscious body. He was so irate all of a sudden that he had to take a deep breath. Then he looked back at me and said, "If you listen to this man, Visticorp will see the story. They will figure out I lied to them. Even if they don't believe it, they'll send someone to double-check."

"Trust me, Jamie. He can rattle off all the tales of your abilities that he wants, but Visticorp will only see the same crazy obsessed man that the rest of us see."

My head was starting to spin from the two conflicting arguments. The problem was, I didn't trust either Carter or Edwards. Even though it was probable that they were both lying, it was still possible that either of them could be telling the truth. I didn't know what to do.

I was so angry and just so tired of being chased and stalked and threatened that I grabbed Carter and pinned him to the wall. "If you are lying to me, Carter, so help me I will commit my first murder!"

The startled cries of my parents forced me to drop him.

My father screamed my name, while my mother gasped, "What are you doing?"

Carter relaxed a little, and my father helped him to his feet. "Did you do it?" Carter asked him.

My dad nodded and suddenly I was completely lost. "We found everything, just like you said. We destroyed everything necessary and left the rest."

I stared at my father, dumbfounded by how he was already in cahoots with Carter. He looked more serious than I'd ever seen him, like he was reporting to a general or living *Mission: Impossible* or something. But my mom, who was obviously in on the plan too, glowed as if she was thrilled by all the cloak-and-dagger. "I even left some of Jamie's things there," she said proudly.

I couldn't believe it. I couldn't trust Carter, but it was clear that my parents did. Maybe I was a little biased because Carter destroyed my life so thoroughly in Illinois. I mean, my parents are not stupid, and *no one* is more paranoid than my dad. I guessed I had to go along with the plan. Really, what other choice did I have anyway? Go with my obsessed English teacher? Um, no thank you.

"What things did you leave there?" I demanded, trying to make myself calm down.

"Oh, just your old pompons, your crown, and a pair of your panties," my mom said. She shrugged as if it were no big deal and then smiled wickedly. "I stuck those under his pillow."

"Mom!" I gasped.

"Linda!" my dad yelled, every bit as horrified. The blood had drained from his face at the word "panties."

"What?" Mom snapped. "That's exactly the kind of thing a creepy stalker would take!"

"Ugh! At least tell me they weren't any of my nice silk Victoria's Secret ones."

"The little black ones with the lace," Mom admitted guiltily.

"Mom!"

"Ladies!" My dad cringed again, covering his ears. "Please!"

Carter interrupted our little family moment, much to my father's relief. "Uh," he said glancing around the room. "Where's Edwards?"

I wanted to say a really bad word. Mr. E., whom I hadn't even seen get to his feet, was gone. My parents took an inventory of the room as well, and when my Mom's eyes fell on Ryan for the first time her breath caught in her lungs. My dad followed her gaze, and then he *did* say a bad word.

"He needs to get to the hospital," I explained, "but his heart is beating pretty steadily." I knew because part of me had been focused on nothing but that sound since the moment I first stepped in the room.

My mom rushed over to him and untied him from his chair. I felt bad for not having done it sooner, just like I was going to feel bad about having to leave him right now. But there was just so much going on all at once, and I absolutely *had* to deal with it. Sometimes it sucks to be the only person in the world with superpowers.

"You guys call an ambulance, and I'll go find Mr. E. He can't have gotten very far. He isn't exactly in prime physical condition right now."

"Be careful, Jamie," my mom whispered as I left the classroom.

"Don't worry, Mom. I'm not going to hurt anybody." I couldn't help thinking about the control I'd just gained, and a smile broke out on my face.

It had been only a minute or two, and Mr. E. really couldn't have gone far, so I closed my eyes and concentrated on just listening. When I found him, he was running through the quad, nearing the front steps of the school. Conveniently for me, the quad is full of nice little throwable objects like trash cans and vending machines.

Now, I knew I promised I wouldn't hurt him, but he didn't know that, and I was still pretty ticked off about him torturing my boyfriend, so I didn't see any harm in scaring the pants off the guy. I mean, come on, would Johnny Storm—who happens to be my favorite superhero, by the way—do things the boring way? Or would Wolverine—who I also love because of Hugh Jackman in the X-Men movies? Delicious!—let him get off as easy as just being tied up or whatever? I don't think so. So when I caught up with Mr. E., instead of just grabbing him and hauling him back to wait for the cops with everyone else, I picked up the nearest thing I could find and chucked it at him. When the concrete bench I'd thrown came crashing down on the steps in front of him I'd never seen anyone look more frightened.

"Aw, come on, Mr. E. Don't leave yet," I taunted coldly. "I thought you wanted to experiment with my powers."

Mr. E.'s eyes widened, and then he tried to make a break for it around the rubble I'd placed in his path, but there was a trash can just to the side of the steps. I happen to know from personal experience that if you shoot lightning at something it tends to explode from its spot, so I zapped that trash can the minute Mr. E. headed to the left. When it blew up in front of him, he tried to reason with me again.

"I abandoned my whole life for you, Jamie! Don't you see how much I care?"

Oh, I saw all right. I also saw a recycling can sitting on the other side of the steps. Mr. E. saw me take aim and started running again.

I cringed a little when the recycle can I blew up went flying through the window of the administration office. Oops. My bad. My accidental destruction of school property distracted me enough that Mr. E. was able to get down the steps and dash into the parking lot.

I couldn't very well start blowing things up in a big open parking lot next to a crowded stadium full of witnesses, so whatever I did to stop Mr. E. had to look natural from here on out. Well, lightning is natural, right? As long as it's coming from the sky and not the palms of my hands, of course.

There was always plenty of electricity in the atmosphere around me, whether it was coming from buildings or power lines or even the clouds, and now that I knew what it felt like and how to move it, it was almost too easy to make it rain down from the sky like a freak lightning storm.

I ducked behind a large tree and held my hands up to the sky. I started pulling lightning bolts down from the clouds, being very cautious not to hit any poor sucker who might be arriving late to the game or any of my classmates' cars. Mostly, I let it crash down around Mr. Edwards's car as he tried to escape the parking lot, hoping he would run it into some large, stationary object.

Okay, okay, so maybe I accidentally let one slip and blew Mike Driscoll's big, shiny 4Runner to kingdom come. Oops. My bad again. But other than that, I swear I was being very careful!

Unfortunately, all the lightning had gained the attention of the sports-goers, and they were all fleeing the metal bleachers, looking for safe cover. They would be headed my direction any second, not to mention Mr. Edwards was almost free of the parking lot. I looked up at the shiny new marquee standing proudly at the exit and smirked to myself. "Sorry, Mr. Huang."

With one final lightning bolt, that stupid sign came crashing down right on the hood of Mr. Edwards's car. He was going nowhere now, and the cops were already screeching around the corner. Problem solved.

Ryan was conscious when I returned. He looked like death, but just seeing him alive and awake was enough to make me burst into tears. I threw my arms around him, but was soon dragged away when police, firefighters, paramedics, and who knows who else, swarmed the scene.

Ryan was taken to the hospital, while my parents, Carter, and I were all hauled down to the police station. We were there for so long that I actually fell asleep in the lobby on three hard plastic chairs that I'd pushed together. I didn't wake again until I heard Carter shuffle past me.

"Where do you think you're going?" I asked, startling him.

"The police are done with me," he said with a yawn.

"And?"

"And it's one in the morning and I've still got a story to write."

I got up and quickly blocked the exit. I glanced around. No one was paying attention to us. "You and I still have to talk," I said in a low voice.

Carter sighed like he was just so over my threats. "Don't worry. The cops bought the story. Everything's going to be just fine."

"Except we still have one problem."

"Which is?"

"You still know my secret."

"And I'll never breathe a word about it."

"Oh!" I barked with as much sarcasm as I was capable of. "Well, okay then. I guess we're all good."

Carter was as good with the sarcasm as I was. "Thanks for the trust, Jamielynn."

"What have you ever done to earn it?"

"Today wasn't enough?"

I just folded my arms tightly across my chest, and he sighed again. "All those articles I wrote in Illinois?"

I suppressed the anger starting to boil in my stomach. "About how I murdered Derek because he broke up with me?"

"Yes," Carter said. "Did you ever notice how I wrote about anything and everything I could come up with that had nothing to do with what my real theory was—that the accident gave you superhuman abilities?"

I opened my mouth to argue, but it was true. None of his stupid rumors ever came close to the truth about me. I suddenly didn't like where this conversation was headed.

"Jamielynn, back then you were a wreck. You didn't even know what was happening to you, much less have any idea how to control it or hide it. Remember that day you handed your dad a wrench and nearly put him in the hospital?"

I didn't have the heart to answer him, and not just because I was so shocked that he knew about that. Carter seemed to know how upset I was because he softened his voice. "I've always had the evidence I needed."

"B-But…" I stammered, swiping at a couple of rogue tears. "Why?"

I didn't have to be more specific with my question. He knew what I meant. "Visticorp paid me to spy on you after your accident. But when I found out all that you could do? Well, I'm not stupid. I knew how much that kind of power would be worth to people, and I knew what they might try to do in order to get their hands on it.

"I did some digging into Visticorp before handing over my evidence, and it turned out my hunch was right. I was able to hack into some of their files. There was a young girl about fifteen years ago who was in an accident and ended up with special abilities, much the same way you did."

I couldn't stop myself from gasping. I couldn't believe it. "There's someone else like me?"

"Was," Carter corrected solemnly. "Visticorp ran all kinds of tests on her and experiments. They were trying to figure out a way to duplicate what happened to her. There was an explosion in one of their secret labs, and four people were killed, including the little girl."

I gasped again, and more tears sprang from my eyes. For a brief moment I almost wished Visticorp were really coming for me. I dared them to try it.

"Despite what you think, Jamie, I'm not a monster. I couldn't turn you over to them when I knew what they would try to do, so I churned out story after story about you with a million wild speculations about anything as far from the truth as I could think of. I'm sorry for the trouble it caused you, but it was the only way I could think of to keep you safe.

"When you stopped that accident a couple months ago and Edwards approached me again, I panicked. I figured Visticorp finally knew the truth. I really did think that you coming forward was the only way. But after what happened today, with Ryan? If the world finds out about you, there will always be some psycho coming after you. Eventually, someone will die, whether it's someone you love or someone you kill. And no offense, Jamielynn, but I don't think I like the idea of anyone's fate being in the hands of someone with your temper."

I didn't want to smile. I tried not to. But I failed, and we both chuckled while I dried my eyes.

"The way I see it," Carter said, "I have to keep your secret because if I don't call a truce with you, that someone who's going to get killed someday will probably be me."

I shrugged. He was right about that. But I smiled again and held out my hand. "Fine. Truce."

"Truce," Carter agreed, and shook my hand. "So how about a statement for my article?"

"Sure. 'No comment.' "

Carter chuckled and shook his head as he headed out the door. "See you around, Jamielynn," he called over his shoulder.

"I certainly hope not."

I was still watching him go when my parents came up behind me. "What was all that about, sweetheart?"

"Just calling a truce, that's all."

"Well, thank heavens for that."

I turned around to face my parents. I couldn't help throwing my arms around them both, and I started crying again. It's just that I couldn't imagine having to go through all of this without them. Not to mention, they didn't even get mad at me for all the destruction of property back at the school. Granted, they didn't know about Mike's 4Runner.

But a girl's gotta have *some* secrets, right?

We hugged wordlessly for a minute. I mean, really, what was there to say? But eventually I thought of something to break the silence. "I love you guys."

This made my parents hug me again, and of course my mom started blubbering. "We love you too, honey," she sobbed, "and we're so proud of you."

"Yes we are," my dad agreed. "And someday after everything settles down again, we'll have to go do some target practice. I want to see how all this lightning stuff works."

We all had a good laugh, I wiped my tears, and then my mom said the words I'd been dying to hear all night. "They said we're all finished here. You want to go to the hospital to see Ryan?"

I didn't wait to ride in the car with them. I disappeared the moment I stepped out the front door.

It was one in the morning, so visiting hours had ended like a bazillion years ago, but sneaking past the hospital staff was easy thanks to a little thing called superspeed. Unfortunately, I hadn't thought of anyone else being inside Ryan's room. When I opened the door Ryan's stepdad was passed out in a chair in the corner, and his mom was sitting at his bedside, holding one of his hands, running her free hand through his hair and even humming quietly to him. The sight explained so much about Ryan.

I smiled at how adorable they all looked together and then tried to back out of the room as quietly as possible, but the door squeaked and Ryan's mother looked up. "I'm sorry," I whispered, still backing out of the room. "I didn't mean to interrupt. I know it's not visiting hours."

When Mrs. Rosenthal saw me, a flood of tears began pouring down her face, and she practically tackled me to the ground. "Oh, Jamie!" she cried, giving my father a run for his money in the bear hug department. It took her a minute to get her sobs under control enough to speak again. "I can't thank you enough for saving my son's life! If you guys hadn't found him when you did…"

Her voice trailed off again as another round of sobs hit, and it was impossible for me not to get caught up in the emotional onslaught. I hugged her right back, every bit as grateful that Ryan was safe now as she was, but at the same time feeling utterly responsible for the entire situation. "I'm so sorry," I choked out, but was unable to say anything else.

When we finally pulled apart and tried to wipe our tears, I barely even noticed Ryan's stepdad, who had come over to us, because Ryan was watching me with bright eyes and giving me the most Ryan-y Ryan smile that I've ever seen. He held out his hand to me, and when I felt his firm squeeze around my fingers, so much relief washed over me that my tears started all over again.

Ryan's parents not so subtly decided that they needed to get some air. Once Ryan and I were alone, things got almost awkwardly quiet. I was feeling so much but had no idea where to start. The only words that wanted to form in my mouth were "I'm sorry! Ryan, I'm so sorry!"

Ryan waited patiently, patronizing me with a smile, while I apologized over and over again. He must have known this was coming. He must have known I'd blame myself for everything. But I was surprised he let me get it out of my system. He didn't even protest and tell me to stop being ridiculous. Not that he believed it was my fault, he just knows me well enough to know it wouldn't make a difference. Instead he waited until I'd cried just about all I could cry and didn't have any more sorrys in me. Then he smiled and said, "Is it my turn to say I'm sorry yet?"

That confused me. "What do you have to be sorry for?"

Ryan grinned. And not at all apologetically. "I'm sorry for making you fall in love with me."

Well, naturally, this came so out of the blue that it completely voided the thought I was about to vocalize. I sat there gaping at him like a moron. Ryan chuckled every time I tried to speak and couldn't seem to find words. Eventually I gave up and gave him a dry look.

"According to Mr. E., all of this was my fault," Ryan explained. With a little too much amusement if you ask me. "For making you fall in love with me and ruining everything."

"Why did that ruin everything?"

Ryan was quiet for a moment, and I couldn't believe it when his grin changed into that infamous cocky smirk. "You just said you love me!" he accused with excitement.

Again, I gaped at him, temporarily speechless. Of course I denied it. I had to; it was my natural reaction to his ego. "I did not!"

"Did too." He grinned. "You said, 'why did that ruin everything.' Meaning you agree that it happened. You said it. Can't take it back. You love me."

Learning to control my powers was child's play compared to keeping a straight face right then, but I couldn't give in to his smugness. He was just so sure of himself. "Do not."

"Do too."

"Do not."

"So do too."

I rolled my eyes. "Whatever. Even if it was true, which it *so* is not, how would it make everything your fault?"

"Well, apparently, when Mr. E. agreed to let us partner for that assignment, we were supposed to hate each other and end up like you and Mike. I was supposed to make you feel even more miserable so that he could sweep in and be your hero when you fell apart. But then I made you fall in love with me, and suddenly I was your hero and you didn't need to be rescued anymore."

I couldn't hide my skepticism. "The guy jumped you with chloroform. He could have been talking about pink elephants for all you know. "

"Scout's honor." Ryan lifted up three fingers with a grave expression. "He was apologizing for kidnapping me at the time. He said he never would have done it, but after I'd made you so happy, I left him no choice. So you see, it really is all my fault. It's my fault for being so irresistible."

Yeah, he was being serious.

"So, *anyway…*" I said, obviously changing the subject just to annoy him. "I have some good news."

"Better news than you being in love with me?"

"Do they have you on a morphine drip or something?"

"Denial is very unhealthy for a person, Jamie."

"Do you want to know my good news or not?"

Ryan raised one of his eyebrows into a perfect arch.

"I'm not showing you my eyes, Ryan."

"Oh, come on, I totally earned it! I almost *died* for you today."

"No, you almost died *because* of me today."

"Yeah! Which means you so owe me!"

"Ha! You just admitted it was all my fault!"

Ryan took in a deep breath. "Are you going to tell me your good news or what?"

"Hang on a sec," I said, then disappeared and returned before he could even reply.

Ryan eyed my hands behind my back. "Another trip to Monterey?"

I revealed the light bulb I had in my hand. "Go ahead." I offered my free hand to him. "Do your worst."

Ryan stared up at me for a moment and comprehension slowly crept into his face. He tried to hide his excitement and looked at me skeptically before taking my hand in his. He laced his fingers in mine and then pulled me as close to his bed as he could. With one more suspicious glance to me, he began trailing his free hand up my arm, leaving goose bumps wherever he touched my skin.

Let me tell you, it felt so good that I shuddered, and it had absolutely nothing to do with any electricity that might or might not have been jumping around inside my body. Ryan noticed me tremble and glanced up at the lightbulb in my fist. It was still completely dark. "You're going to have to do a lot better than that, Miller," I teased.

Ryan looked up at me, completely dumbfounded that I was not just giving him the go-ahead to touch me, but actually egging him on—like it was all too good to be true. "Maybe I am high on morphine," he whispered, "because I'm pretty sure I'm hallucinating right now."

When Ryan didn't kiss me, my lack of patience got the better of me. I dropped the lightbulb and eagerly pressed my lips to his.

There weren't actual physical sparks, and this time there wasn't any pulsing energy, but that magnet effect? The one that always pulls me to Ryan whenever I get too close? Yeah, apparently that had less to do with my powers and more to do with my hormones because just like the first time we kissed, it started out just my lips against his, and then quickly spun out of control.

I could feel the moment Ryan realized that this was a one hundred percent normal kiss, because the hesitancy disappeared and he kissed me back in a way that he'd never even come close to kissing me before. A way that not even my dreams had been able to do. I felt that kiss all the way to the tips of my toes and then some.

Then the next thing I knew, I had climbed onto his bed and wrapped my arms around his neck. I was probably detaching all kinds of wires, but I simply couldn't help myself. When I finally managed to pull my face away from his, Ryan looked at the way I was straddling his lap and laughed. "Déjà vu."

We laughed for a moment, and I was overwhelmed by the amount of happiness I felt. I'd planned to make him sweat it out for a good few days at least, but in the heat of the moment, the words just slipped from my mouth. "I love you."

Ryan grinned like a fool for a moment but quickly recovered and plastered that perfect Ryan smile on his face. "Told you so."